THE GUY
NEXT DOOR

THE GUY
NEXT DOOR

A NOVEL

KATE PALMER

Covenant Communications, Inc.

To Nate,
who believed in me enough to teach me *excuses are for losers.*

ACKNOWLEDGMENTS

I AM SUPPORTED BY AMAZING family and friends. Thanks, Jenni, for reading my earliest versions when I was too scared to even tell Nate I was writing a book. Your critiques were always insightful. Thank you to my mom and sister Shandrae who read, critiqued, and dared to ask questions and make suggestions about plot and character holes. Thank you to my in-laws, who upon learning that I was writing a romance didn't disown me, but offered encouragement. I appreciate so much the trust Covenant has placed in me throughout this entire process. Finally, thank you to David G. Woolley for providing an incredibly thorough critique of a scene. I learn something every time I reread those comments. They are invaluable to me.

My six amazing children inspire me to keep this writing thing in balance. They are my life. This book wouldn't be possible without my husband, Nate. He's unfailing support made me believe that maybe I wasn't crazy. I love you.

CHAPTER 1

"You bought china without me?" I stared up at my fiancé as I wrestled to comprehend how he could possibly view this as acceptable.

"You're always scrambling to find nice dishes whenever I'm hosting clients." Sean slid two large china boxes farther to the left.

Did all single, thirty-year-old men harbor Martha Stewart tendencies? Images of perfectly coordinated pots, stoneware, and towels from Sean's apartment flashed through my mind, not to mention the granite countertops with an undermount sink. "I kind of thought I would get to pick it out."

"It's perfect, Eva. You'll see." He hung my recently purchased outfit—the one he chose for our engagement pictures—next to the window. Sean was always taking care of these little details for me since Ephraim had no clothing stores. The tailgate of his black cherry Escalade slammed shut. "You know we'll use it."

A heavy feeling settled into my chest. I wasn't willing to let it go at that. What about my opinion . . . my style? "You should have waited for me."

"The pattern's really versatile." Sean brushed a lock of wavy black hair from his eyes before guiding me to the passenger door.

I stopped next to the car door, tilted my head back, and gazed into his deep blue eyes. Could he really not understand my disappointment and hurt? "This is the kind of thing we should have done together."

He looked slightly wounded. "You always say I have good taste."

"I'm not questioning your taste." But picking out china was something I was supposed to do! I wanted to scream it at him, but as usual, I couldn't make my voice cooperate. A queasy feeling stirred in the pit of my stomach; conflict always brought nausea along with it. The queasiness only came when I confronted Sean about something. Talking with upset parents or staff at school never brought it on. Just Sean. I raked through my shoulder-length hair. A few blonde strands clung to my fingers, and I flicked them away. I took a deep breath in an effort to calm my unsettled stomach. "It's a little unconventional for the groom to select tableware . . . alone. You should have at least called me."

"What's the big deal?" Neil's voice slithered through the barely cracked passenger window of Sean's Escalade. The headrest must have concealed him from my view. "So he bought some really expensive dishes without you."

"Neil drove with you?" Neil and Sean had been in the same PhD program at Boise State.

"We met here then picked up some supplies." Sean motioned to Neil's truck parked a few spaces down.

Neil exited Sean's car. He had a trim muscular build but wasn't on the tall side for a man. He wore his dark, straight hair closely cropped atop his broad tan face. Although Neil had graduated and now lived in Las Cruces, New Mexico, he was in town to help Sean with a hot springs search this summer. "Yeah, real sorry I can't stay and listen to you complain about Sean. I left another box of Spanish/English picture books behind Sean's seat for you."

"Thanks." I often felt that Neil was a confusing mix of coarseness sprinkled liberally with compassion. I never knew what to expect from him, but he always made me feel a little uneasy. At least he wouldn't be driving home with us. That was a relief. I had enough variables to deal with already without Neil's unpredictable behavior.

"Do the books help?" Neil asked.

"You know they do."

"How's your parent English as a Second Language class going?"

I shook my head. "Not so good. Manual's father, Felix, stopped coming— and he was making such good progress. I thought losing his job at the turkey plant would give him more incentive to learn English, but he's got some job away from home now."

"It's hard work to support a family when you're from Mexico." Neil turned toward his truck, apparently finished with the conversation. Although my discomfort around Neil was persistent, I appreciated the materials he donated for my adult ESL class.

"See you at dinner later this week." I called after him.

"Our own Miss Black is catering the retreat?" Neil turned.

"That's why she's here. We've got to pick up all the food," Sean explained. Grocery shopping was one errand I didn't trust Sean to do for me, and he respected that.

"First a dress, then dishes, and now grocery shopping. Glad I drove my own car. Time for me to rock and roll."

I watched Neil walk to his truck and climb in as my stomach folded in on itself. I turned back to Sean. "You took Neil shopping for china, but not me?"

He waved my comment aside. "Eva, it wasn't premeditated. It just happened. I saw it while I waited for you and knew it'd be ideal . . . so I bought it." He opened my door.

I swallowed back my frustration. Sean was only trying to help. He knew we were on a tight schedule tonight, and I'd had to sit through a faculty meeting after school today before catching a ride up here to Provo with another teacher going north. Maybe if I steered the conversation in a different direction my stomach would settle itself. "How much did it cost?"

He sighed. "There you go worrying when you don't need to."

Even after a year of dating and four months into our engagement, Sean's free-spending ways hadn't rubbed off on me yet. "China is an extravagance— something to be purchased after the necessities."

"I've got it covered. We're not struggling college students."

Sean seemed so confident. The nausea in my stomach began to recede. "We are until you finish your doctorate."

"Okay, so maybe we're students, but we're not struggling. Besides, after we're married, I don't want you to have to borrow someone else's nice dishes every time we entertain clients." He gestured toward the car's seat.

Resigned, I climbed inside; he knew I couldn't keep up an argument with him. He already held a law degree and was currently on the payroll as part-time legal counsel for his dad's company while he pursued a doctorate degree (courtesy of his father) in geophysics at Boise State University.

"Are you hauling it all the way back to Idaho or giving it to your dad to take to Montana?"

"I thought you could store it." He closed my door.

That's just what I needed to stumble over in my tiny studio apartment. Perhaps Sean was remembering the sprawling two-bedroom apartment I'd had all to myself in Boise, not the two-room (three, if you counted the bathroom) apartment in Ephraim I considered myself fortunate to secure last August.

Sean opened the back of the car, and I twisted around to see what he was doing. Using his pocketknife, he opened a box of china and unwrapped a dish. A moment later he slid into the driver's seat and offered me a square white salad plate with a box of Junior Mints—my favorite. "I'm sorry about the china, Eva."

I knew I should forgive him, but a nagging little part of me felt like I'd missed out on a rite of passage. I looked at him without speaking.

He leaned in and whispered, "I promise there's no blue in it."

I was somewhat impressed that he remembered me telling him I hated blue-patterned china, but I wouldn't be the puppy distracted by a treat, even if it would pacify my skittish insides. Couldn't he see my disappointment at not getting to pick out our china? I stared back at him without reaching for the plate.

"Just look at the plate, Eva. I know you'll love it."

I looked deep into his sea-blue eyes. I should have known better than to look there if I'd wanted to stay mad. Those eyes with their hypnotic spell never failed to draw me in, soften my frustration. Sean could be a bit overbearing, but not because he didn't care. I took the box, opened it, and briefly inhaled the candies' minty scent as I gazed at the plate pattern. Sean's impeccable taste once again triumphed. A solid silver band rimmed a square white plate where long-stemmed, muted black and silver flowers danced. "It's beautiful."

He grinned. "Told you I have good taste."

"I know. It's just . . ."

He leaned over and kissed my forehead. "I promise not to shop for your wedding dress."

"You know you're not even tagging along, right?"

"Are you sure that's the way you want it?"

"Sean!" I sent him a playful glare.

"Right. I know. Maybe you should go when I'm not in town."

"That shouldn't be too hard." I'd be glad when the long distance part of our relationship was over. When I'd moved to Ephraim last August, I'd assumed that would be the end of our relationship. We'd dated on and off for a year, but Sean seemed more focused on his doctorate studies than marriage. I enjoyed teaching in Boise, but I missed my sister, especially since she's all the family I had. So I'd accepted a position teaching kindergarten in Ephraim where my sister Rebecca and her new husband lived. Rebecca had offered to let me live with them, but since I was twenty-seven and had given up the idea of getting married, moving in with newlyweds felt too awkward. Sean surprised me by continuing to call and even meet me in Provo or Salt Lake for dates a couple of times a month. By Christmas, we were engaged. Oftentimes it seemed surreal that this six-foot-two, stunningly handsome man had chosen me. Unlike most guys I'd dated, ambition propelled Sean to be the best. He wasn't looking for a little school-teacher wife to support him. Without my parents to lean on, I enjoyed the security Sean's lifestyle offered me.

Sean checked his mirrors and backed out as the final rays of a golden spring sunset in Provo glistened off rows of windshields. Leaning back into the seat, I concentrated on breathing evenly, trying to let go of the last bit of hurt. After all, Sean was only trying to please me. Not having to borrow formal place settings would be one less thing for me to worry about when we entertained. And I liked the pattern. It was unfortunate that the dinners I would be preparing this week called for more casual tableware. It would have been fun to set out the new plates.

I closed my eyes and mentally calculated timelines for the dinners I would be cooking this week. My future father-in-law's company was sponsoring a geophysics study in the mountains above Ephraim, Utah, this summer. About ten researchers were converging there this weekend for a spring retreat, and since Sean was heading up the events, I'd be running point on a number of them. Sean's work demanded many social get-togethers running the gamut from cozy and informal to professional and polished. I enjoyed planning and preparing the details for these numerous occasions. Cooking's methodical yet creative nature provided a type of escape from reality for me. Best of all, it made other people feel good. I liked giving that kind of a gift to others.

"You're quiet tonight." Sean reached over and took my hand.

"Just mentally going over everything for the retreat dinners. Didn't you say there were two ovens at that Bock-Bock place?"

"It's pronounced *Guh-Beek*."

"I knew it had something to do with chickens."

"It has nothing to do with chickens." He chuckled and shook his head.

"I meant the 'beak' part. I know it's up Ephraim Canyon, but I'd never heard of it."

He glanced at me. "Bock-Bock place doesn't even sound like GBEEC."

"I like Bock-Bock better than *Guh-Beek*, and so do my kindergartners."

"You told your class there's an environmental education center named Bock-Bock?" he asked incredulously.

"Not exactly. I said I couldn't remember the name, but it reminded me of the sound chickens make—bock-bock."

In the shadowy light of the car, I watched him shake his head again.

After a moment, I asked, "So what's the schedule for the Hot Springs Team retreat you're holding at . . . GBEEC?" I pronounced it correctly this time.

"Clearing the snow and cleaning a couple of cabins."

I remembered the warm spring sun from today. "Snow?"

"GBEEC's at such a high elevation it's shut down and snowed in for the winter and spring," he replied matter-of-factly.

"All that work doesn't sound like much of a retreat."

"We've hired some hungry college students to help out with the snow removal and cleaning part. They'll get some pizza and a paycheck. So the rest of us will have quite an appetite by the time you arrive." He flashed a smile.

"Provided all you researchers don't eat pizza before dinner."

"Not a chance. Have you ever been around ten hungry college guys? It's more like inhalation than chewing and swallowing."

"What's on the agenda the first night?"

"We'll be discussing the mountain man myths surrounding a hidden hot springs as well as likely search parameters for the smaller team of researchers— the one returning to take up residence at GBEEC for the summer and conduct the hunt for the springs."

I squeezed his hand. "You'll be part of that group." I said it out loud to remind myself he would soon be closer—only thirty minutes away instead of nearly a day's drive like he had been since I'd moved to Ephraim last August.

He lifted our hands to his lips, kissed my fingertips, and smiled at me. Then his cell phone rang, effectively halting any further conversation.

Over the phone, Sean and his father (a Montana state senator) debated legal issues regarding a patent for the more efficient geothermal pump Sean was collaborating on as part of his doctoral studies. He and his father held high expectations for bringing this technology to Montana's heating districts. Already, they heated their Montana home and all guest accommodations on their adjoining hunting preserve exclusively from an on-site hot springs.

When we arrived at the store, I consulted my list, negotiated store aisles, placed items on the conveyor belt, and used Sean's company credit card while he continued his phone discussion.

Outside the grocery store, I pushed the cart into the parking lot and instinctively turned left as I double-checked my list. Several strides later I was alone, surrounded by unfamiliar vehicles. Hurriedly looking around, I spied Sean—cell phone at his ear—standing near his SUV on the other side of the parking lot. I cursed my lack of an internal compass and hastened toward him.

I wasn't the only one watching Sean. A few cars down from him a group of whispering girls cast furtive glances in his direction followed by more giggles and quiet conversation. His striking good looks never went unnoticed by girls, young and old alike.

Sean opened the back of the Escalade and snapped his phone shut just as I arrived. It appeared that Sean hadn't yet noticed my absence.

We deposited the groceries next to the china. Two huge boxes of china. How many place settings had he purchased? I climbed into my seat and waited for Sean.

When he reappeared, I said, "So about storing this china at my place . . . I'm moving in with my sister when school gets out, remember?"

The ignition caught. "I remember. You're storing your stuff in her basement while we're honeymooning in Iceland, right?"

Immediately following our August wedding, we would fly to Iceland for Sean to finish his dissertation research and shore up relations with Icelandic business partners investing in the new geothermal heat pump. "You want to drop the china off at her place . . . tonight?" I asked.

"Now you're coming up to speed." Sean pulled onto the highway and headed for home in Ephraim. First Provo, then Springville, and then Spanish Fork city lights faded in succession behind us. Finally the last housing development gave way to mountains rising on both sides of the road.

I reached for Sean's hand and settled back into the seat. He gave me a gentle squeeze, and my heart fluttered. There were few things I loved more than holding his hand in mine. It reminded me that this was all real—Sean wanted me for his wife. He could have let us drift apart, but he had pursued our relationship even after I moved from Boise to Ephraim, much to the chagrin of a few ladies in his Boise singles ward—one dark-eyed beauty in particular.

An hour later we pulled into the dirt-rutted driveway of the old two-story farmhouse my sister Rebecca and her husband lived in. No lights greeted us; Rebecca and Ryan must have already left for Snow Canyon since Snow College (where Ryan taught biology) started spring break tomorrow. I pulled out the house key Rebecca insisted I have and stepped off the driveway down the incline toward Rebecca's front door.

I gasped suddenly as arctic-cold water filled my ballet flats. I looked down in shock. Where had all this water come from? Only then did I register the roaring sound of an open water faucet more powerful than the kind attached to homes for a garden hose. I'd heard that sound as a teenager working with my dad to clean out the irrigation system each spring.

At the back of the Escalade Sean called, "You okay?"

"The city turned the irrigation water on today!" I shrieked then sprinted into the pitch-black yard, the rumbling water directing my strides. Neighbor children playing in the backyard must have opened the valve.

Cold mist sprayed my legs as I reached through the torrent of icy water pouring from the three-inch opening and at last grasped the metal wheel. I cranked it down as fast as my frozen fingers could turn it. Finally, silence.

I stepped back, soggy clumps of hair matting against my dripping face. Water trickled from my pal- pink hoodie and capris. The cool night breeze rustled through the trees.

My shoulders involuntarily jerked upward and hunched forward as a bitter chill shuddered through me, causing my teeth to chatter.

Sean appeared behind me, wrapping his warm hands around my chilled arms and rubbing heat back into them. "Are you okay? I'm sorry you had to do that—I wasn't sure what to do to help . . ." he faltered.

Moonlight reflected off standing water here and there where tree branches parted enough for a few moonbeams to reach the now submerged lawn. Ryan and Rebecca wouldn't need their water turn to flood irrigate the lawn this week. The water was far deeper than when Ryan let it flood for his two hour turn. How long had the water been running? I couldn't imagine the water master turning down the season's first water after sunset. It was now ten o'clock. Had it been running for twelve hours? Longer? More importantly, *where* had it been running? The house sat in a low spot between neighbors. The closest neighbor, Ryan's bachelor cousin, sat uphill on the south. He was seldom home since his consulting business kept him traveling. Uphill on the north was a neighbor who had just moved into an assisted living center and the home remained vacant at present. That left only one place for all that water to go—and no one to notice.

My head jerked around toward the dark outline of the farmhouse against the midnight sky. "The basement!" I breathed. Like most homes of its era, the basement windows only sat inches above the ground. If the water had covered my shoes near the driveway, how deep was it at the lowest point of the yard where the house sat? Deep enough to be seeping into the house.

Sean followed my gaze. "We have to divert the water; create a path for it to flow away from the house."

I started back the way I had come. "The tools are in the garage."

Sean followed me, and we waded through ankle-deep water up to the freestanding garage at the end of the driveway. It was pitch-dark inside the garage. I patted the wall as if deciphering a Braille message as I tried to identify the tools. I handed a shovel to Sean and found a hoe for myself.

"Start on the far side of the house," I said as I pointed, "and angle your trenches to the garden." He nodded and set out, and I found myself relieved that he was here with me.

I struck my hoe into the sod and dragged it toward myself. I repeated the action a few more times, widening and deepening the scar before shuffling back a couple of steps to begin again. Water poured into the newly carved ditch and drained away from the house. I had completed my second trench when Sean came to help.

"Why don't you check the damage to the basement while I finish?" he suggested.

Numb and shivering, I climbed the four steps to the front porch and shoved my hands into my capris pockets; they came up empty. I remembered pulling the key out of my purse before stepping off the driveway, but where had I put it? I patted my back pockets hoping to feel the outline of a house key. No luck.

Realization dawned. "Oh no!" I moaned. I must have dropped it when I rushed to turn off the water.

I ran to the porch railing overlooking the yard between the house and Sean's car. Moonlight scarcely lit the lawn sodden with irrigation water and scarred with muddy trenches. Worse yet, fifty-year-old trees shaded most of the side and back yards from the silvery light.

I leaned heavily into the railing, staring at the reflection of a few stars on the water's surface. Finding the key was hopeless.

Perhaps Ryan had left the patio door open when he and Rebecca left yesterday morning. With a sigh, I sloshed my way to the back of the house, carefully avoiding the trenches.

My foot froze in midair above the first step on the back porch. I stared at the plywood boarding up the hole where the sliding glass door should have been. "Oh, right!" I said in dismay. Ryan had replaced the old farmhouse windows last fall, but the weather had turned before the special-order sliding glass door arrived. He had removed the existing door, planning to install the new one as soon as it arrived. But the custom door hadn't arrived until February and Ryan had yet to install it. Plywood and insulation now covered the entry.

I returned to the front porch where two large windows framed the front door. One of those would be my door tonight. I pried the screens off one and then the other but found both slider latches locked. Since when did Rebecca lock her windows? She probably hadn't even opened them after they were installed late last fall. But surely she'd opened at least one window.

I remembered the small window in the combination bathroom/laundry room on the north end of the back porch. If any window had been opened during the cold weather, it would be that one. Only why did it have to be the smallest window in the house? I returned to the back porch, carefully maneuvering over the trenches. Unfortunately, it looked as though my luck, or lack of it, was holding tonight. The window's latch was securely locked down as well.

Determined to find an unlatched window, I launched myself off the porch and crossed around to the north side of the house.

My second step found the trench, and my forward momentum pitched me face first into the mud and water. I struggled to pull my right foot out of the mud-blackened furrow. Sludge gripped my ballet flat, and with a sucking sound my shoe disappeared into the quagmire.

Mud and more mud. It squished between my fingers, clung to my clothing, and gushed between my toes and into my one remaining shoe.

"Need a hand?" Sean asked, clearly trying to stifle a chuckle.

"How d-dirty do you want to g-g-get?" I countered. My teeth were chattering uncontrollably by this point.

"What are you doing? I thought you were checking the basement." He reached out a hand.

I grasped Sean's extended hand for balance and pulled my feet free of the trench. "I dropped my key somewhere between the car and the turn-off valve. Searching the water-covered lawn seemed hopeless, so I'm trying to find an unlatched window to crawl through."

"Is that why the screens are out on the front porch?"

"Yep."

"I have a flashlight in the car. We can use it to see if the locks are down before you take off anymore screens," he suggested.

While he retrieved the flashlight, I fished through the mud until I found my shoe.

The flashlight beam showed that all but the kitchen window was locked, so a moment later I was balanced atop an overturned garbage can that Sean steadied. Headlights swept by us and into the neighbor's driveway on the south; I prayed the driver didn't see us or that we didn't look as suspicious as I felt. "Here, take this." I handed down the screen. Now for the tricky part. I crouched slightly and sprang at the opening. But I only succeeded in propelling my upper torso halfway through the window. My legs and lower torso dangled down the outside of the house.

"Sean, do you hear—" Something smacked into Sean. I heard him grunt and fall into the mud.

It was then that I heard a rich tenor voice ask, "Did you try the doorbell?"

I pushed myself out from the wall and back down onto the garbage can.

Sean was facedown in the mud with a vaguely familiar man kneeling on top of him holding his arms back. Now I remembered who belonged to that voice. Peter—Ryan's cousin who rented the house next door. I'd met him at a couple of family gatherings. Along with Ryan and Rebecca, he'd helped me move into my apartment here in Ephraim. Although Peter had a rock-hard athletic build, he wasn't exactly tall. I never would have guessed he could take down Sean in a matter of seconds.

"Peter, it's all right."

"Eva?" Peter looked confused. "Don't you have a key?"

"I dropped it," I said as Peter released Sean. "Do you have a key?"

"No. Rebecca—"

Without warning, Sean shoved Peter up against the house. "What's with tackling me?"

"Sean!"

"Eva, stay—"

"I thought you were breaking into my cousin's home," Peter whispered as Sean's arm cut off his airway.

I pulled at Sean's arm. Slowly he released Peter. "Yeah, we're that new kind of criminal that ruins a perfectly good pair of shoes making ditches to divert the water from the basement of the house we're trying to rob." Sean began wiping mud from his shirt and jeans. "You've ruined my clothes." Sean spat the words at Peter.

"Sorry, man. If I'd known it was Eva . . ." Peter trailed off as he turned to survey the yard. "Irrigation problem?"

I nodded while Sean sized up Peter, clearly unimpressed. He clenched and unclenched his fists, fighting to stay calm.

"Sean, I could really use a lift please." I tried to distract him from Peter.

Sean glared at Peter before reluctantly turning to help me.

I climbed on the garbage can and jumped toward the window. Then Sean climbed onto the garbage can and placed his hands under my foot.

He hoisted my leg up so quickly I catapulted through the kitchen window. I had to grab the first thing my hand found—the freezer door handle. My weight pulled the door right off of the refrigerator and I crashed with it to the floor.

Three juice cans, a couple packages of hamburger, and an opened bag of popcorn skated across the linoleum as I lay facedown across the freezer door.

CHAPTER 2

"Eva!"

A stab of pain shot through my wrist. My shins burned where they had slid down the counter's edge, leaving a muddy trail.

"Eva, I'm so sorry." Sean squeezed through the gap and jumped off the counter to land next to me. "Are you hurt?"

I rolled my throbbing wrist. It hurt, but I had full range of motion. Slowly I pulled myself onto my knees, careful not to put any weight on my hand. "No, I think I'm fine. Just a few bruises."

Sean reached down for my hands, hesitated when he saw me cradling my wrist, and then placed his hands around my waist, pulling me up. I leaned into him for a moment enjoying the comfort I felt in his arms. He kissed my forehead and asked, "Where's the light switch?"

"On the wall above the table."

Peter's lean frame emerged though the window as well and slid off the dirt-streaked counter just as the kitchen flooded with light. His light caramel hair hung long and loose just above his shoulders, and his face showed the beginnings of a beard. I'd asked him about his long hair once; he'd explained it was a vanity he picked up from the people he dealt with in business. "Eva, what happened to you?" Peter asked. His bushy eyebrows furrowed together as he processed my mud-covered clothing.

"Eva's taken up mud wrestling." Sean gently took my wrist and turned it over, moving it ever so slightly.

I rotated it, reassuring him. "See, nothing major." Turning to Peter I caught a whiff of his cologne, something musty, but couldn't place the scent. "I should have let you or Sean go through the window first." I began picking up frozen food. "Why don't you and Sean reattach the freezer door? I think there are a few tools in that drawer by the wall if you need them. I want to check the basement." Then, turning to Sean, I whispered, "Be nice."

I flipped the basement light switch and headed down the stairs. On the last step I paused before plunging my feet back into the frigid water. Yes, the basement had flooded. Framing for a large family room, storage room, two bedrooms, and a bathroom divided the space while piles of sheetrock and bathroom fixtures along with boxes of tile and paint cans lay scattered like islands in four-inch deep water.

Overwhelming fatigue gripped me. I sank down on the nearest pile of sheetrock, fingertips rubbing my temples. "What now?"

"I have one of those reversible wet/dry vacs in my garage. Does Ryan have one too?" It was Peter.

"I-I th-think s-s-so," I said, my chills returning. My eyes scanned the waterlogged masses strewn across the cement floor searching for a wet/dry vac. "It must b-be in the g-g-garage."

"Aren't there people who get paid to take care of stuff like this?" Sean asked.

I felt the heat warming my face as Peter stared openmouthed at Sean.

Peter started to say something, but I interrupted, "It's," I rubbed some mud from my watch face, "eleven thirty on the outskirts of Ephraim. Who did you have in mind?"

"Forgot where we were," Sean muttered.

"Think of it as your gym workout this week." I hoped my voice sounded upbeat enough not to belie my embarrassment at his suggestion.

"I'll get the wet/dry vac. Be back in a minute." Peter withdrew upstairs, and Sean followed.

I forced one foot in front of the other, clutched the handrail, and climbed the stairs behind Sean and Peter. The aching cold stiffened my ankles and feet. I made slow progress.

"Eva, I'll search the garage. Why don't you wash up a bit?" Sean said eyeing me.

"I'm th-that hideous, eh?"

"Your hair color gives dirty blonde a whole new meaning." Sean grinned and turned me toward the bathroom. "And the warm water will help your shivering."

"Hey, would you grab the g-groceries from the c-car?" I asked as he turned around. "That meat has got to g-go in the f-fridge."

"Sure thing."

Peter poked his head back around the corner. "You should put on some dry clothes too. Sean and I can get things set up," he said then disappeared again, followed by Sean. I heard the front door close.

I opened the door to the combination laundry and bathroom and immediately shut it again. No! This was a dream—a nightmare. Reality TV, but not real. I inched the door open, staring at linoleum, shiny with a layer of water. The quiet, insistent sound of a toilet running greeted my ears. This was not happening. This couldn't be happening. Oh, but it was happening.

After covering the floor with towels and adjusting the running toilet, I examined my reflection in the mirror mounted on the back of the bathroom door. My hair hung twisted and clumped with dirt blending into my mud-caked shoulders. Normally, only my hazel eyes held smudges of brown over the green, but now mud was streaked across my right cheekbone with splatters here and there covering my face. Dirty brown circles highlighted my temples. Mud clung to the front of my cap-sleeve T-shirt and down the length of my sweater. My tan capris were nothing but muddy brown now. Dirty handprints and footprints spotted the towels spread across the floor as well as the toilet tank and lid. I stared at the shower and made my decision.

Before I could convince myself otherwise, I locked the door, peeled off my mud-caked clothes and jumped in the shower. I stood, letting the heat of the water pound into my frozen limbs as long as I dared. Then I quickly washed my hair and scrubbed away the dirt. Mississippi-river-colored water swirled down the drain.

Unwillingly, I shut the water off after a few minutes, pulled on a floor-length terry robe Rebecca kept behind the door, and darted upstairs to her bedroom in the loft. When we were growing up, Rebecca kept a stash of worn project clothes under her bed. I reached blindly through the bedspread and felt denim and flannel. Marriage hadn't changed her habits, but eight and half months of pregnancy had significantly changed her size. I rummaged through her dresser for something more my size—a faded pair of blue jeans and a paint splattered sweatshirt. A worn pair of Nikes from her closet completed the outfit and I joined Sean and Peter, who were already back in the basement.

It was nearing midnight when we hauled the last of the water upstairs. "Sean, you need to go," I said tiredly. "You still have a half hour of driving before reaching your bed at GBEEC." I rubbed my chin, stifling a yawn. "I'll finish up and crash here." I opened the pantry, pulled out a bag of sunflower seeds, and stuffed the package in a paper cup. Tossing them to Sean, I said, "These will keep you awake."

He gave me a quick kiss. "Thanks. Good night, Eva." And he was gone.

"Peter, you may as well go too." I picked up a five gallon bucket of water, straddling my legs on either side of it and waddled to the front door still propped open by Ryan's biology textbook.

"Here, I can help." Peter's hand joined mine on the bucket handle.

I shifted the bucket between us, freeing my burning wrist. Then I noticed that his other hand also gripped a bucket of water. I swallowed the protest bubbling up my throat. I knew my wrist and arms couldn't carry another bucket load of water alone. I was too tired. "Thank you."

We returned the empty buckets to the garage. I faced Peter, "Well, that's about it except for your wet/dry vac." We walked toward the house. "Then you can go home and get some well-deserved rest too."

"Yeah, I always sleep better after I've done my good deed for the day."

Surprised that I could still smile, I laid my hand on his arm. "Really, thank you, Peter. We'd still be hauling water if it weren't for you."

Inside the house Peter collected his wet/dry vac while I poured soap into the washing machine, pulled on the water, and shoved in as many towels from the floor as would fit.

"Do you always do laundry at one o'clock in the morning?"

My head jerked up and hit the corner of the open cabinet door. Rubbing the back of my head, I turned to see Peter stepping through the doorway.

"Sorry, I didn't mean to startle you." Peter stopped at the pile of wet towels. "What happened in here?"

I sighed. "While you and Sean went to get the wet/dry vacs, I discovered the running toilet." I closed the cabinet door and washing machine lid. "Now the linoleum is lifting off all around the edges. Well, worse than it was before."

Peter turned around, eyes scanning the edges of the room. "Nice."

"Yeah. Rebecca really doesn't need this." I squeezed past him. "The floor was already peeling, and now . . . it's really going to bug her. My sister, the interior decorator, is a bit of a perfectionist." I yawned. I doubted I would be able to drag myself out of bed early enough to marinate the chicken before school, which meant I needed to do it now. I took a few steps over to the kitchen and pulled out the chicken and some other grocery bags as Peter trailed behind. "Rebecca tiled the kitchen this winter when she remodeled it, but was planning on tiling the bathroom a few months after the baby comes. She's too awkward crawling around on all fours now."

"Is that the brown tile I saw in the basement?"

"I think so," I said as I rummaged around for a Tupperware container.

"Hmm. I have an idea." A smile touched the corners of his mouth.

"Yes?" I asked as I turned to find the soy sauce.

"Well, my brother is a contractor—"

"Nope, won't work." I mixed the marinade ingredients in the Tupperware.

"You haven't even heard my idea," he said, sounding surprised.

"Rebecca won't pay a contractor for work she can technically do herself." I slid the chicken into the Tupperware and washed my hands. "*I* won't pay a contractor for work I can do."

Peter raised his hands, palms flat. "Whoa, there. Let me finish. I was thinking of borrowing one of his tile saws and helping *you* tile the bathroom floor. We can surprise Rebecca and Ryan when they get back from spring break. Of course, you're going to need cement backer board, a power driver, cement mix, grout, sponges, and a few other tools."

I stopped, not daring to believe my ears. "You've tiled a floor before?"

"Of course." He made it sound like everyone did such things. He clearly hadn't talked to Sean's type; he'd prefer to work sixty hours at the office before considering laying tile himself. But money had always come easier to Sean than to most people. He reasoned that hiring a job done was his way of supporting the economy. And I had to agree; if everyone were like Rebecca and me, there would be a lot of people out of work. I pulled the spinach out of the fridge and began rinsing it.

"So I'll bring the saw over around . . . uh . . . say, ten? I think I saw most everything else in the basement. Good thing the bags of cement mix and grout were on top of the tile and sheetrock."

"The cement backer board is there on one of the piles too," I added. Finished with the spinach, I assembled the lemon dressing ingredients.

"So ten o'clock tomorrow . . . er, this morning?"

"Sure . . . I mean no."

"No?"

"I have to teach tomorrow . . . today . . . Wednesday. Spring break officially begins at three thirty for me." With the lemon dressing mixed, I hunted for a jar lid.

"Three thirty it is, then."

"It might take me a few more minutes to get here."

"Sure." He hesitated once more then asked curiously, "Do you usually stay up all night? I mean first the laundry and now you're cooking? You do know it's past midnight, right?"

I shrugged. "This is just prep work for a dinner tomorrow night at seven thirty. So we can only work until six."

He nodded hesitantly. "That's not much time. If the backer board were already in, maybe we could get the tile done by then . . ."

"It's the best I can do."

Peter's bushy eyebrows arched and a mischievous light danced in his eyes. "Do you trust me?"

I gave him a look. "Trust you?"

"I can come early and lay the backer board if you'll leave the door open when you go in the morning. Or at least one window unlatched." He winked.

Was he always such a tease? "Deal."

"I wonder how wet the floorboards got. Do you have a fan we can put on that floor tonight to dry it out a bit? I think I can pull the old vinyl off where it's starting to peel."

"There's probably one in the basement on the storage shelves."

Peter fetched a box fan from the basement while I put the food away. I met Peter at the bathroom and watched as he peeled back the vinyl flooring, noticing that his square jawline gave him a ruggedly handsome quality. He wouldn't be the type to sport an Italian suit, but he could make some cargos and a fitted T-shirt look dressed up. "Not too bad," Peter assessed the water damage. The floorboards aren't wet past a few inches of the worn vinyl."

"That's good news." I set up the fan.

"Got your faculty dinner ready to go?"

"Faculty dinner?" I asked walking Peter to the front door.

"You know, chicken, lettuce, some yellow stuff you were shaking in a jar."

"Oh, that's for the kick-off barbeque with Sean's Hot Springs Team retreat."

"Hot springs team?" Peter opened the door.

"Sean and his father are in the middle of setting up geothermal heat in their Montana hometown. They're using some natural hot springs up there. Anyway, long story short, an old friend of his father who manages GBEEC, some other connections along the way, and legends of a hot springs up Ephraim Canyon all combined for a research team at GBEEC this summer and a possible partnering in the future if hot springs rumors are confirmed."

"Legends, huh? I've lived here my whole life and never heard any stories about a hot springs." Peter yawned. "Time for me to go. Remember to leave the window unlatched." He winked then melted into the darkness.

* * *

Sleep should have enveloped me the minute I curled up in Rebecca's guest bedroom. Instead, I felt strangely awake with Peter's voice echoing, "Do you trust me?" What did I know about him to trust or distrust? He rented the house next door, and he owned some type of behavioral consulting business that kept him out of town most of the time. He did make it home for the Finch family Christmas party I'd attended with Ryan and Rebecca. He and Ryan had helped me move in. And tonight he'd stayed to the end hauling water from the basement. I knew Ryan and Rebecca trusted him, and that was enough for me. But I decided it couldn't hurt to find out more about him, and I planned to do just that tomorrow while we tiled the bathroom.

* * *

Beep! Beep! Beep! I fanned the smoke alarm but it just wouldn't shut up. I had already yanked its batteries. I couldn't understand why it was still beeping. In desperation I pushed every button my fingers found. Now it played music and beeped. I turned the volume down.

My hazy mind conveyed the message that smoke alarms don't have volume—but alarm clocks do. My eyes jerked open.

I studied my surroundings without moving. The pale yellow walls seemed off somehow. Where was the white? Pieces of last night filtered into my memory. Now I remembered; I was in Rebecca's guest bedroom.

What a night. I heaved my legs over the side of the bed and sat up.

I grimaced. How many leg and arm muscles had I pulled? I groaned as I thought of the long day ahead, bending and crouching on sore muscles to reach eye level with my kindergartners. Maybe I could sit at my desk and call students back for individual reading assessments instead. The thought of struggling to stay awake as students plowed through sight words quickly changed my mind. I needed to finish cutting up the letter tiles I'd left in my bag behind the seat of my car yesterday afternoon.

My car! I fell back onto the bed with another groan. When I'd caught a ride with another teacher going north yesterday, I hadn't planned on spending the night at Rebecca's—my car was still in the faculty parking lot. The hike to school this morning would certainly help limber up my muscles. I sat up then and gingerly stood beside the bed, testing my aching arms and legs. A warm shower and brisk walk ought to loosen things up some.

To my great relief, the last day of school before spring break passed uneventfully, and at three thirty-seven, I was walking up Rebecca's sidewalk. Bright yellow daffodils nodded in a breeze carrying a tractor's hum and the smell of freshly worked earth. The once healthy, green lawn now sported deep brown scars along each side of the house. I cringed when I thought of Ryan returning from spring break to find his yard mangled. He took such pride in keeping it tidy.

Peter was outside on the porch stooped over the saw, guiding a tile through the blade. His shoulder-length hair was secured back in a low ponytail today. He looked up as I mounted the porch stairs. Last night's beard was now a goatee that accentuated his square jawline and enhanced his rustic features.

"Hey, I thought you were just going to lay the backer board," I said, surprised.

"Gotta keep busy." He held up the cut piece. "Let's go see if this fits."

I followed Peter into the house. Tiles lay evenly spaced across half the bathroom. I stared in shock. "You've tiled half the room without me!"

"Not really, I just began in the center and laid out the tiles to the back wall and started making the cuts. Nothing is cemented down yet." He aligned the tile he had just cut as if it were a piece in a floor-sized puzzle.

"I just usually cement and cut as I go." I rubbed my wrist. "My sore muscles thank you for all the prep work. At least I won't have to get up and down as much this way."

"Breaking and entering will do that to you." He winked and grabbed another tile from the stack.

"And you speak from experience?"

"I'll never tell." Peter pulled the pencil from behind his ear and made a mark on the new tile.

I stepped into the room to get a better look. "The backer board looks great. How did you make the circular cut around the toilet?"

"I told you my brother is a contractor. He has *all* the right tools."

"Impressive," I said sincerely. "Guess I'll mix a bag of cement. I think I saw it on the porch?"

"Right."

At first, we worked in silence, spreading cement on the backs of tiles, setting them in place, and laying spacers. Peter's assembly line method proved fast and efficient. Once I got the rhythm, my curiosity about Peter got the better of me. "What kind of companies do you do behavioral consulting for?"

"It varies."

"Obviously. I'd worry if you kept coming back to the same company."

"Guess that would mean I wasn't very good at my job." He grinned.

"That's not what I meant. I just—"

"So where'd you learn to lay tile?" Peter interrupted.

"It's a family tradition." I smiled. "We were always remodeling or adding on. Some families take vacations to be together—we painted rooms, replaced windows, shingled the roof, took out walls, tiled floors; you get the picture." I picked up the next tile.

"No family vacations, really?" He bit his lower lip in contemplation as he worked.

I began spreading cement on the tile's back side and chuckled. "No, not really, but the most memorable times we had together were fixing up the house, not on a vacation somewhere."

"Do your parents still remodel?"

My breath caught. *Breathe,* I reminded myself and concentrated on setting the tile just right and placing the spacers before I answered. "Actually, they passed away four years ago."

His eyes widened. "At the same time?"

"It was a freak accident. A tornado touched down on their first empty-nesters vacation." I'd been home from my mission for a year, had just graduated from college, and accepted a teaching position in Boise. Rebecca had finished two years of college and decided to move out on her own. Then, unexpectedly, we were both on our own. *Breathe.* In. Out. In. Out.

Peter's expression fell. "I'm sorry . . . now I remember Rebecca talking about it. That must be hard for you, especially with an upcoming wedding."

I nodded and swallowed back a lump in my throat, touched by how sincere he sounded. "Yeah, it was the same for Rebecca. It's really hard for her now to know her baby will never meet them." Unexpected tears threatened, and I quickly looked down and spread cement on the next tile. How I longed to talk to my mom! I think she would have liked Peter. *What would she have thought about the china incident with Sean?* I wondered suddenly. Probably that Sean was a thirty-year-old man accustomed to making purchases without consulting anyone, I concluded after a moment.

My cell phone rang. "Hi, Sean."

"I thought you were coming up right after school." His business tone greeted my ears.

"I'm just tiling Rebecca's bathroom."

"You *do* remember the dinner tonight?"

"Yes." I glanced at my watch. "Make sure you get the potatoes in the oven in an hour."

"Dinner is at seven," he said uneasily.

"Don't worry; I'll make it there on time or early."

"We need to synchronize colors," he said without missing a beat.

"Pants or skirt?"

"I always like you in skirts."

"How about my light-blue knee-length circle skirt and . . ." I remembered he'd been clearing snow today. "Blue sweater?"

"All one color? You need to break it up."

"The skirt has a pattern."

"That'll work. If you're tiling, how's dinner coming?"

"It's marinating. I just have to toss the salad and dressing while the chicken grills."

"Okay, then. I'll see you no later than six forty?"

"I promise. Bye." I snapped the phone shut and put it back in my pocket. I glanced at Peter's raised eyebrows.

"Sean wants to borrow your skirt?" A teasing glint danced in his cocoa-colored eyes.

"What?" I mentally retraced my conversation with Sean. "Oh, he was just color coordinating our outfits. He's done this since our first date."

"First date, really?"

"Yeah, he was taking me to a play and the night before he called to arrange the color scheme for the evening. It really bothers him if his clothes clash with his date's." His request had baffled me until later when I discovered the public life Sean's family led. His father started into politics early and now served as a Montana state senator. That, coupled with his extremely successful, very prominent business dealings, kept the spotlight trained on his family. In that environment, looking put together became second nature and Sean's ambitions mimicked his father's.

"Hmm, I wonder how many times my clothes have clashed with my date's." Peter picked up a tile and headed for the saw.

I wondered what type of girl Peter dated. "You should double with Sean and me sometime."

"I'm not sure he'd approve of my wardrobe."

Peter had observed Sean's expensive taste in clothes. It was probably something any behavioral analyst would notice. "I'm sure you wouldn't have to coordinate with him."

"Yes, but would I have to synchronize with my date?" He winked at me.

"Only if you want to impress Sean," I teased.

Peter stopped spreading cement on his tile and looked right into my eyes. "That could never happen if you were there."

Heat rushed to my cheeks. I dipped my head to hide the color from him and bent low to fit a tile into place. "That's the last tile on my side," I said, changing the subject.

"I've got two more and I'm done. The floor needs to sit for twenty-four hours before we can grout it. So let's say I meet you back here at three thirty tomorrow?"

"Grouting's pretty easy. I can probably handle it myself."

"Nope, that's not how it works. If I do the work, I want to see the finished product. Since I have to leave town again tomorrow night, it would be torture for me to wait until I got back. So I'll meet you here tomorrow afternoon."

"Do you have problems with impulse control?"

"Impulse control?" Peter spread cement on the last tile.

"When students react before thinking—like impulsively shouting out, standing up, or striking others—it's an impulse control problem," I explained though I wondered why he didn't know this.

"That's so textbook sounding."

"Didn't you study impulse control in your behavior classes?"

"Yeah, sure, but I call it something different with my clients." Peter set the last tile in place.

"Like what?" I began gathering tools.

"Socially deviant, stupid, a few other things." Peter slowly scratched his goatee. "Anger management issues—that's a big one." He picked up the bucket of cement.

"How do your clients react when you tell them that?"

"I don't tell them that's what I'm thinking. See, I have impulse control." I glanced at my watch.

"Time to go make your eyes blue. I'll clean up," Peter said as we walked down the hall.

I turned toward him. "I don't wear blue eye shadow."

"No, you don't. But your eyes change color with your clothes, and I believe you and Sean chose a blue sweater and blue skirt with a pattern."

I stopped in the kitchen, surprised.

"Don't worry, I've got this covered." He set the bucket down, put his hands on my shoulders, and turned me toward the fridge. "Get your things and go."

I gathered the salad, marinated chicken, and walked to my car in a fog of confusion. I had tried to learn more about Peter, but I'd ended up sharing about myself instead. But why was I even trying? He would fly off to consult with another company soon anyway. I would marry Sean this summer and move away. Still, I was curious. He was Sean's opposite in almost every way. The first pulsings of a headache began in my temples. I pulled into my apartment and checked the clock. I had just enough time to run inside, change, and swallow some Ibuprofen along with a glass of milk for what promised to be a pounding headache—a painful reminder of last night's lack of sleep. Hopefully Sean and I could find some time to just relax tonight.

CHAPTER 3

THE RETREAT'S PRE-DINNER BRIEFING DETAILED each of the known accounts of a hot springs in the area and pinpointed three areas of focus in which to begin the search. Dinner had, thankfully, gone smoothly and now the ten Hot Springs Team members chatted comfortably with each other at the banquet table. A fire crackled in the massive stone fireplace rising from the cabin's center, giving the room a warm glow. The main topic of discussion drifted between the various myths surrounding an elusive hot springs somewhere in these mountains. I gleaned snippets of information while I tidied the adjoining kitchen.

Sean deftly maneuvered between the numerous conversation clusters, pausing at each for a personal welcome and infusing a spirit of enthusiasm for the upcoming challenge. People's faces brightened then relaxed as he spoke with them. His quick wit won many smiles. Sean, at ease and in his element, positively beamed.

When he had greeted and spoken with all the others, Sean and Neil stood in front of the fireplace and discussed mapping patterns as, one by one, the other researchers left for their cabins.

"Did you see my Facebook post, Eva?" Neil asked as I moved past him and Sean to begin wiping the table. "You haven't commented lately."

I hoped he didn't suspect that I'd blocked his status updates, which were too often crude. "I haven't checked Facebook for a couple of days," I answered truthfully.

"It might even make *you* laugh."

Not if it was your normal, tasteless variety of humor, I thought. Like the time he brought skimpy women's underwear as a white elephant gift to a Christmas party.

"Leave a comment and let me know what you think."

I looked up at him and back at the table. Maybe he would interpret that as a nod and I wouldn't have to hear what he thought was so funny. Like always, he made me feel uncomfortable.

"Have you heard of the California Distance Learning Project?" Neil asked me.

"I don't think so," I answered.

"It's a website with news articles. It's English reading practice but with current events."

My smile wasn't very encouraging. "Sometimes I bring the *Sanpete Messenger*—it's the local newspaper—to our night class."

"It's not a newspaper—it's more interactive than that. When you click on an article, it shows a basic article. You can click on it and the computer will it read to you. Each article has a vocabulary section where you can hear the words spoken. If you want to go all-out teacher, it even has a spelling test where you actually type the word in after the computer says it."

I reluctantly considered what this would mean for my parent ESL night class. "So if we could meet in the computer lab—"

"Your students' parents would have a lot more interesting stuff to read." Then Neil smirked. "Leave it to California to figure out a useful way to teach English to adults. Progressive thinkers. Just like with Proposition 215."

Not that again. Weary of discussing Proposition 215 with Neil, I kept moving down the table. "I'll have to check it out."

Behind Neil, Sean mouthed, "I've got this." Sean knew how I hated discussing Proposition 215 with Neil. He, thankfully, came to my rescue by setting out a map and markers on the table in front of Neil. "How do you want to divide up the search?"

Neil picked up a marker and focused on the map. "I'll take charge of this section," Neil said as he circled a large area.

Sean looked thoughtful. "That's the area last year's deer hunters were chased out of . . . something about an overprotective sheep rancher trying to keep hunters away from his grazing area. It didn't make much sense because sheep come off the mountain October first—a month before deer hunting begins."

"Maybe it was during the bow hunt," Neil offered.

"Maybe." Sean didn't sound convinced. "You'll need to be careful. It's all Forest Service land, but this rancher doesn't want anyone near where he grazes his sheep. He forgets that he only has a permit for grazing sheep on the land—he doesn't own it."

Neil finished and rolled up the map. "I'll work it out," his overconfident voice assured.

I moved back to the kitchen area to finish cleaning up as their conversation continued. As I stacked the dry dishes into a box to take home, I heard the cabin door creak open and slam shut. Neil had finally left. Now Sean and I could have some time to unwind.

Smoke from the fire mingled with the lingering aroma of grilled lemon chicken. Sean crossed the room, and put his arms around me. I turned within his gentle embrace, wrapped my arms around him, and laid my head on his chest.

"The evening went well." Sean rested his chin on my head while he stroked my hair. "They're a good group. Intelligent yet willing to listen and share." His voice sounded deeper through my ear that lay against him. "And even-tempered. I'm hopeful we'll accomplish our goals here this summer." He moved us toward the fire.

"I'm glad." I pulled my arm away to cover a yawn as we maneuvered around scattered chairs. Sean scooted a bench in front of the fire and pulled me down beside him. I curled up and snuggled into his side.

"Your chicken was superb."

"Mmm."

"Tired?"

"So tired." I closed my eyes and inhaled his aftershave. Sean's fingers traced a pattern from my shoulder to my wrist and back, again leaving a tingling sensation up and down my arm. I felt so secure and loved in his embrace. I relaxed into him.

He kissed the top of my head then tilted my face up and kissed the tip of my nose before gently placing his warm lips on mine.

My heart gave a loud thud and I returned his kiss, twining my arms around his neck. It was a soft lingering kiss that immediately led into another. Sean's hand on my lower back pulled me closer.

His lips touched my ear and he whispered, "Why don't you stay here tonight?"

"There are people in every cabin. No room." I brought his lips back to mine for another kiss. I nestled deeper into his embrace.

He kissed my eyelids. "There's room in here." Sean was the only one sleeping in this cabin even though six bunkhouse-style beds lined the walls of the single room occupying the second floor.

I stiffened. "That's not a good idea."

He kissed me again. I tried not to reciprocate. Reluctantly, I turned my head to the side.

"Come on, Eva. You're tired." Sean coaxed.

I pulled back, looked up into his sea-blue eyes and studied his olive complexion and strong jawline. I ached to lay my head against him, close my eyes, and feel the contentment of being in his arms. It had been such a nice evening; I didn't want it to be ruined. But Sean never comprehended how hard it was for me to stop kissing him. Invariably, I offended him. I hoped tonight could be different. "That makes staying here with you a really bad idea."

"Eva, nothing will happen."

I turned away from him, squeezing my eyes shut. I swallowed. "You're right, because I'm leaving." I stood and picked up my box of dishes.

"You're being impossible."

A wave of nausea started in the pit of my stomach—an inconvenient reaction to the moment's stress. "Sean, it's not a good situation."

His eyes narrowed. "Do you really think so little of me? You should know I would never let things get out of control!"

I kept my head down and walked past him to the door. "Avoid the appearance of evil."

"Eva, you are completely overreacting here. I'm not evil!"

"I didn't say *you* were evil." I clamped my teeth together against the rising queasiness.

"But that's what you meant!"

My vision blurred, making it impossible to find the door handle. I spun to face him and wiped my eyes. "Stop twisting my words."

"You're crying?" he said in exasperation.

"Yes, Sean, I'm crying. I'm also tired and would like nothing better than to curl up with you in front of the fire." His eyes softened. "I want to be in your arms. I like the warmth of your lips on mine." I dabbed at more tears. "I want to marry you in the temple. Staying in the same cabin alone with you is not a risk I'm willing to take because I love you."

"It's not a risk."

I opened the door and picked up the box. "Yes . . . it is a very real risk. Good night, Sean."

I had to pull over just outside the entrance gates. The tree-lined road was too blurry. I pressed my forehead to the steering wheel and let my sobs echo into the stillness of the night. He said he wouldn't let things get out of hand, but why was it always me who had to pull back? Just once I wanted to be able to count on him to draw the line.

* * *

I slept until my eyes peeked open at eight o'clock the next morning. The sun streamed across the bed, gently waking me. I stretched, testing my sore muscles. They were worse today, but I knew they would be better tomorrow.

My apartment's bathroom mirror reflected my tear-stained cheeks and make-up–smudged eyes. Should I call Sean? What more could I say than I had last night? No, I wouldn't call him. I'd see him at dinner tonight anyway.

Dinner, I remembered. I scattered borrowed Crock-Pots around my apartment wherever I found an available outlet. Within a few minutes I had added beef roasts and au jus ingredients to each one, put the lids on, and turned the dials. All set.

It's not a risk. Sean's words repeated inside my head.

I sighed, weary of the same argument. I knew he didn't mean any harm, but every time a situation like last night happened, I found myself feeling hurt. He insisted I was too careful, that I was being prudish. But I couldn't give in like I had with the china. Prudish or not, my standards were not negotiable. I didn't want to even get close to crossing any lines.

I set two large pots of water on to boil, washed and chopped the green salad ingredients, scrubbed the potatoes, and called Kent's bakery to confirm the roll order while I slid the potatoes into boiling water. Once the salads sat chilling in the fridge, I ate a quick bowl of cereal while scenes from the night before persistently invaded my thoughts.

I took a deep breath and walked to my desk. Some new music ought to keep my mind off the twisted knot that still sat in my stomach. I brought up iTunes and quickly located an alternative rock group another teacher had recommended. I imported their newest album for my iPod shuffle and began catching up on some long overdue housework. Rebecca liked to tell me I used cleaning as an avoidance technique. Maybe she was right, but at least my apartment would get cleaned and, hopefully, the nausea would fade.

I loaded the dishwasher, and then my cleaning began in earnest. I scrubbed the kitchen sink, swept and mopped, then moved to the bathroom. The new band had a nice instrumental style that made learning the lyrics easy. I sang along while dusting and vacuuming.

The tantalizing aroma of roast beef grew heavy in the air as I moved the last load of laundry to the dryer and glanced at the clock. Eleven thirty.

My stomach rumbled and more of Sean's words echoed in my mind. *Do you really think so little of me?*

I needed something else to distract me. School. I threw some string cheese, a roll, and an apple into a lunch sack, and filled a water bottle. As I packed my laptop, my eyes drifted to the cell phone lying next to it. I wondered if Sean was still angry with me. Staring at the phone, I slung the bag over my shoulder. I reached out, hesitated, then pulled back and escaped out the door without my phone.

At school I cleaned off my desk. Sorting and filing the papers occupied my thoughts. I even packed two boxes in preparation for my move this summer. Then I started washing the plastic Unifix cubes I used for math lessons.

You're being impossible. Sean's exasperated voice filtered into my mind.

I crammed the unwashed blocks and plastic teddy bears back into their respective canisters along with the washed ones. This mindless chore left a gaping hole in the roadblock I'd carefully constructed against last night's memories. I scanned the room for something to keep my mind busy and saw my lesson planner lying neatly in the center of my desk.

After outlining five days of lesson plans, I searched the library for supporting books, then prepared and printed next week's newsletter, gathered the needed masters, and made all the copies for the next week.

I checked my watch. Three o'clock. I wondered yet again if Sean had tried to call—and then if I should call him. No, I preferred to save the confrontation for after dinner. Maybe he would be in a better mood after he'd eaten. That hadn't helped last night, I remembered, but I resolved to take my chances later. For now I had just enough time to drive to Rebecca's and get the grout mixed before Peter arrived.

At Rebecca's I methodically folded the grainy mixture into the water. The rhythmic action, however, only served to give my mind time to dwell on what I had been trying to avoid all day. *Had* I been unreasonable last night? Had I hurt Sean's feelings? I didn't understand his anger. I thought we were working toward the same goal: a temple marriage.

Peter jogged up the steps. Grateful for a diversion, I looked up. "Back for more are you?"

"Hey, I have to see a project through to the end." He smoothed his hair back and pulled it through a black ponytail holder.

"Glad to hear it." If I could keep him talking, I knew I wouldn't have time to obsess. "So, I've been meaning to ask you—tell me more about your consulting business."

"That grout will blend perfectly with the tiles." He squatted down across from me. "Who picked it out?"

Had he deliberately change the subject or had he not heard my question? "Rebecca the designer, remember? She's really good with colors and patterns."

"Did she learn that in school?" He filled a small bucket half full of water and carried it into the house.

I followed with the grout. "Some, but she's always had a knack for it."

"How's that?"

"Growing up we'd decide to redecorate our room, so we'd pick out colors and visit the fabric store to find material for quilts and curtains. I'd do okay picking out colors, but she'd always pick out patterns I never would have put together, and, you know, they just worked. Her rooms have depth and texture. She's good at what she does." Evidence of her flawless sense of style touched each room we walked through. Warm paint tones on the walls were highlighted by family photographs hung in eclectic groupings of frames scavenged from the D. I. and garage sales then refinished to bring out their beauty. The whole effect was quite striking—antique with a modern flair.

We set our buckets down. "What about you?" Peter asked.

I used the trowel to push a mound of grout into the gaps between tiles. "What do you mean?"

"Are you good at teaching?"

I thought for a second "I hope so. I truly enjoy it."

"So what part do you enjoy about it most?" Peter washed the tiles and smoothed grooves into the finished grout.

"Lots of things. I especially like to see the light go on when a child really grasps a concept they've been struggling with."

"What else?"

I smiled. "I like to make learning fun, make it an experience, something real, not just paper and pencil. Although that's necessary too."

"Give me an example."

He sure was inquisitive, but I didn't mind sharing. "Okay, before I moved here I taught fourth grade and we were learning about rivers carving the landscape. So I got a cookie sheet and filled it with dirt and a few rocks. I propped it up at an angle. Then I poured a pitcher of water down it and let the students observe the erosion."

"Cool."

We worked, lost in our own contemplations for a time. Despite my best efforts, thoughts of Sean still occupied my mind. He was so much better than I was at quick responses. It was only after the fact in a conversation that I knew what I should have said to get my point across. As usual, I felt a bit better only after reimagining the scene a few dozen times. Too bad it never changed what had actually happened.

I took a deep breath and picked the conversation back up. "When did your family move here, Peter?" Maybe a different topic would get him talking and distract me.

He glanced up from his work. "My family relocated to Ephraim when I was eight. At that time, Ryan's parents, my aunt Suzette and uncle Cal, lived in this house. We moved in around the corner and up two blocks. My parents are still there. You came there for a Christmas party last year, remember?"

I nodded. Rebecca and I never spent Christmas apart, so I had attended the party he was talking about with her and Ryan. I had handed Peter a cup of wassail when he walked into the kitchen. With a stroke of clarity, a memory flashed to the surface.

Peter's gaze had locked on my hand then tracked it to the tray of cookies. I asked him what kind he liked. Only then did he lift his eyes to meet mine.

"You're engaged?"

Warmth had spread across my cheeks. I'd told Sean the ring was too much, that I didn't need a diamond you could see across the room.

I shook my head to clear the memory. "Ryan talks like your families did everything together."

"Suzette and my mom are sisters. Suzette's the oldest, then five boys, and my mom is the youngest. Our families were always close, but Ryan's birth really intensified the bond. My youngest brother and Ryan are just two months apart. Suzette was fifty when Ryan was born."

"Fifty? I knew she was older, but fifty?"

"It was a shock for sure. Suzette said she felt almost like Abraham's wife Sarah."

I smiled. "I can see that."

"Since she'd never been able to have children before then, she was kind of like our second mom."

"Yeah, Ryan calls you his big brother."

He nodded. "Suzette treats us like her own children. We always knew we could stop by day or night for a visit and a cookie or two. I think we ate more of her cookies than either Ryan or his dad ever did." He grinned showing a dimple in his left cheek.

"I don't think she minded." I leveled off the grout.

"Why'd you move here?" he asked.

"To be close to Rebecca. She's the only family I have now. I'd been teaching in Boise for two years when Rebecca and Ryan got married. Then Ryan got on as faculty at Snow College, and with his family here I knew they wouldn't be moving. At the time, Sean and I were only dating off and on. I'd convinced myself he wasn't serious. I could be single and alone in Boise or I could be single and near my sister. It was a pretty easy decision when I looked at it that way."

He nodded slowly. "So are you and Sean planning to settle near here?"

"Not likely. I'm pretty sure Sean will take over his father's business in Montana in the near future."

"So how do you feel about being so far away from Rebecca?"

I hesitated. Just like yesterday, his perceptiveness startled me. "That's just part of life if I want to be Sean's wife."

"What is?" a familiar voice demanded.

My stomach flip-flopped. The trowel fell to the tile, splattering me with grout. I picked it up with unsteady hands and raised my eyes to see Sean filling the doorframe. "What are you doing here?" I stammered.

"You haven't answered your phone all day." His voice sounded flat. He was still angry.

My heart pounded faster. "It never rang this morning."

"I've been calling you every half hour since noon."

I quickly scooped more grout onto the tile in front of me. "I left my phone home."

"You've been here all day?" He clearly didn't believe me.

I took a deep breath. "No, I was at the school for a few hours." Why did I feel like I was about to be grounded?

"During spring break?" Sean's insistent attorney voice made it clear he wasn't convinced.

I pushed the grout into the crevices. "I had to get caught up on a few things and get ready for next week."

Peter dipped his sponge in the water bucket and wrung it out. "I think we need fresh water." He edged past Sean and out the door—probably grateful to escape the tension.

"So what's 'just part of being my wife'?" his courtroom tone pressed.

I put down the trowel and sat back on my heels. I took a deep breath and let it out. "Peter asked how I felt about moving so far away from Rebecca."

"Do you *want* to be my wife?" A shadow of pain flickered across his sea-blue eyes, but his authoritative tone continued. "Last night you couldn't get away from me fast enough." He clenched his jaw shut.

My chest tightened. "Did you come here to argue?"

"No." His voice softened.

"Then why are you here?"

He stepped through the doorway, running a hand through thick black waves of hair. His voice was barely more than a whisper, "Eva, do you want to be with me?" His self-assured mask slipped. A look of vulnerability crept into his features.

I stood and looked into his eyes. "That's why I'm marrying you."

He grasped my hand. "I need you by my side," he whispered.

My heart melted. "I'll always be there." He tucked a stray lock of hair behind my ear and bent to kiss me. I threw my arms around his neck, pulled his face to mine and kissed him back.

He drew back and wiped my cheek. "More tears?"

"Happy tears. I missed you."

He cleared his throat. "About dinner . . ."

My stomach folded in on itself as heat crept up my neck. "I might have been a little hurt last night, but I'm not irresponsible. I would never do that to you." I dropped to my knees and vigorously scraped more grout across the tiles. "Roast beef is simmering in the slow cookers at my apartment, the salads are in my fridge, and I confirmed the roll order this morning."

Relief evident in his features, Sean said, "That's my Eva. You know I couldn't get along without you."

CHAPTER 4

The first Sunday afternoon in May, I sat next to Sean in Rebecca's backyard while holding my new niece Melody Anne Winters. They'd blessed her earlier in the day, and we had all gathered here for dinner after church. I'd brought Sean over yesterday to meet his new little niece. However, a business call required that he spend most of the time in the other room discussing something I'm sure was important. At least he could be here with me while he was working, I had reasoned, but I had still felt a little hurt nonetheless. I'd be glad when the first week of June came and Sean could move into GBEEC. We'd have more time together then, and the phone calls wouldn't feel so intrusive.

But today was Sunday—we could relax and enjoy being with family. I slipped my free hand into Sean's and gave his hand a squeeze. Sean stopped his conversation with Ryan's mom, Suzette, long enough to give me a quick smile.

I gazed down at Melody Anne again. Anne had been my mother's name. Melody even looked like Rebecca and my mom with her dark eyes and wisps of dark curly hair framing a perfect pale face. I resembled my dad's coloring, with blonde hair and hazel eyes. My parents would have enjoyed this day—the day their first grandchild was blessed. I swallowed the lump forming in my throat, took a deep breath, and surveyed the yard.

It was a clear spring day with only a hint of winter chill. The crisp air carried a fresh, washed-clean scent. The ditches Sean and I had dug were filled in and reseeded but not yet growing. Ryan and Rebecca had been so thankful we had stopped by that night and diverted the water. And since Melody was born two days after they'd returned, Rebecca was doubly grateful Peter and I had retiled her bathroom. The back door was no longer boarded up. Ryan had installed the special-order sliding glass door, and the freshly tilled garden spot awaited planting.

Rebecca sat down next to me and brushed a section of her dark ringlets back over her shoulder.

"You've got quite a crowd here today." I motioned to all the little cousins running around the yard.

"It's always like this when all five Finch boys are in town. Peter's the only one not married." Rebecca said.

"All the little cousins get along so well."

"It's a party, for sure." Rebecca leaned over and whispered, "Speaking of parties, have you told Sean I'm doing the decorating for your wedding yet?"

I checked to make sure Sean was still in conversation with Suzette before lowering my voice and saying, "I told him I'd hire someone with impeccable taste, and I have. Well, technically, I haven't hired you, but I'll cover your costs."

"Aren't you worried Sean will want to choose something?" Rebecca arched her eyebrows. "You know he always has an opinion."

I smoothed the blanket over Melody. "Oh, I let him pick the caterer, and he's handling the menu with very little input from me." I looked at Rebecca. "I know what you can do, and you know my tastes. So don't worry, it'll all work out."

Rebecca leaned toward me, eyes sparkling. "Good. Because I picked up a few more things while we were on spring break."

"That was over a month ago! I can't believe you haven't shown me yet. Let's go see what you bought."

"Not a chance. I still need a couple of items before you'll get the full effect." Melody fussed, and Rebecca reached out to take her from me. "She's getting hungry. I'd better take her inside to nurse."

"You have to show me soon, or you know I'll come snooping around your house."

"Good luck finding my stash. I know you far too well to get caught," Rebecca said over her shoulder then turned and continued toward the house.

I listened to the various conversations around me at the table. With her white hair secured in her usual twist, Suzette reminisced with redheaded, wiry Jayne about their boys growing up together more like brothers than cousins. Suzette's face possessed a serene quality, and she laughed easily, while Jayne's mischievous green eyes darted here and there, observing her grandchildren's antics. Sitting nearby, two sisters-in-law traded silly toddler stories. Farther down the table, Peter questioned Sean about the supposed hot springs location and its possible research purposes.

"A flowing hot spring at that elevation can be piped underground next to plants, warming the soil and greatly extending the growing season. Utah State University Extension is very interested in that possibility," Sean said.

"They do that in New Mexico. I worked there a couple of years ago and heard about it," Peter said.

"I visited there last fall and saw it firsthand. The method's quite ingenious. In Oregon, they pipe the water under sidewalks and roads to keep them from freezing over."

"Didn't I hear something about the Boise, Idaho, heating district using—"

My eyes meandered over the lawn as I lost interest in the talk about hot springs. Peter's nieces and nephews wandered aimlessly through the yard. They were growing restless while the adults enjoyed catching up. A girl with short, light-brown hair framing a pixie face strolled near me. I smiled at her. "Hey, round up your cousins and tell them to meet me by the big tree in the middle of the yard. We'll play some games," I said. She nodded eagerly, and I excused myself from the table just as Rebecca reappeared and handed Melody to a waiting Suzette.

I played a couple of circle games with the children, and then we decided to play Red Rover. Each team was strung out, holding hands, when four-year-old Jeffrey yelled, "Be on my team, Uncle Pete. My team, my team!"

I turned to see Peter walking toward us, a grin across his face. "Sure, Jeffrey. The teams look a little lopsided to me."

Jeffrey smiled widely and let go of his cousin's hand to make room for Uncle Pete.

I looked around to see if Sean wanted to join in the fun. I spotted him pacing near the house while talking on his cell phone. He smiled and waved. Children tugged at my hands, and I reluctantly turned to play.

Three rounds of red rover ended when, at some unseen cue, all the children rushed Peter. "Come on, Eva! Help us get Pete!" The pixie-faced girl tugged at my elbow.

I crouched down beside her. "Oh, I don't think I'd better get in that mix." Then, in a more conspiratorial whisper, I suggested, "But if you sneak around behind Jeffrey, I bet you can grab Uncle Pete's ankle and topple him."

Quick as a hummingbird, she flitted off toward the flailing group. Seconds later, Peter fell to his knees, taking one of the older boys with him. He looked up at me just then, clearly convinced I'd had something to do with his demise.

I shrugged my shoulders but couldn't keep a grin from spreading across my face.

Then, with much screaming and giggling, the children tackled Peter to the ground and piled on top of him.

Jayne touched my arm.

I jumped slightly; I hadn't heard her approach. She nodded toward the mountain of children. "This happens at nearly every family get-together. Peter just can't resist."

"He likes it?" I didn't have any brothers, and Sean only had one younger sister. I couldn't even imagine Sean submitting to the mound of squealing arms and legs before me.

"You hear his laughter mixed with theirs?"

She was right. A deeper, lower laugh mingled with the children's higher-pitched giggles. I looked up and glimpsed Sean apart from the family banter, still standing at the corner of the house with the cell phone to his ear. A nagging worry nested inside me. I'd never seen Sean interact with children—even on the two occasions he'd visited my classroom. I quickly reassured myself that it would be different if they were his children. He was a guy, after all. When it was our baby, he'd be interested.

CHAPTER 5

MELODY HAD BEEN SCREAMING INTERMITTENTLY for the past twenty minutes. I sat next to her in the backseat of Ryan and Rebecca's car trying to somehow entertain and distract her. The three-and-a-half-hour drive from Logan was half an hour longer than my tiny six-week-old niece liked to wait between meals.

We had spent today, Memorial Day, visiting our parents' graves in Logan, reminiscing and crying together. Melody's recent birth and my upcoming wedding delineated two more events marked with their absence. Four years.

I heard the click of a seat belt release and watched my sister turn around in her seat. Rebecca's head appeared between the headrests. "Just hand her to me," she said wearily, "I'll hold her the rest of the way home."

"Wait." I held up my hand. Melody's wails subsided and she finally latched on to the pacifier. "See, she's calmed down a bit. I think she can make it the last ten minutes to Ephraim if I hold her binky in."

Rebecca relaxed. Then came Ryan's guttural scream, "NO!"

The car turned sharply. My body was hurled forward, the seat belt cutting into me. A thunderous crashing and screams reverberated through the car. Then blackness.

* * *

Crickets chirped their night song on the gentle breeze that carried the rhythmic *chtt—chtt—chtt—chtt* of sprinklers delivering water to a pasture and the low bleating of lambs so very like a newborn's cry. The sound of a running motor and bright light bathing the interior of the car combined with the smell of gasoline and antifreeze dispelled the idyllic country scene. Another cry. This one was closer than the lambs.

Melody. I found her pacifier and put it back in her mouth. That helped to calm her. Melody looked to be in the same securely strapped in position as before . . . before what? I rubbed my neck where the seat belt had cut into my skin. What had happened? I remembered Ryan's shout.

"Rebecca?"

No answer. I saw Ryan slumped over the steering wheel.

My heartbeat quickened. "Ryan?"

Nothing. A knot dropped into the pit of my stomach.

"Rebecca . . . Ryan . . . please answer me!" My voice shook. I fumbled with the seat belt. My trembling fingers couldn't undo the latch. At last I heard the familiar click and my seat belt slid back over my right shoulder. I peered more closely at Ryan. There was no movement, not even the rise and fall of his shoulders.

My throat grew thick and every muscle tensed. *No! Please no!* "Ryan! Ryan! Wake up!" I shouted and climbed into the empty front passenger seat.

My body froze. I couldn't even lift a hand to see if Ryan's body had a pulse. No, not empty. The seat couldn't be empty. Where was Rebecca?

"Rebecca!" I shrieked. "Where are you? Rebecca?" Only then did I see the gaping hole in the windshield and the mangled hood of Ryan's car, which I now realized was smashed against an SUV.

My heart pounded faster. I tried to open the door but it wouldn't give. Gripping the handle, I threw my shoulder against the window. Nothing. The SUV's one functioning headlight illuminated the jagged edges of the shattered windshield.

I squinted my eyes against the brightness and picked my way through the glass shards and out the windshield, trying not to cut myself. Melody whimpered as the sounds of crunching glass broke the stillness of the night. Everything was so blurry. I rubbed my eyes to clear my vision and felt hot tears.

Where was my sister? "Rebecca . . . Rebecca?" I called as I picked my way around the crumpled car and SUV.

"Eva." A whisper of a voice floated up to me. "I'm here."

I looked down and to my right. There lay my crumpled sister. Her lower body and arms lay at odd angles with her torso. Blood seemed to stream from everywhere.

My stomach twisted and heaved. Forcing the bile back, I sank to my knees and stroked her face. I didn't dare do more. "Oh, Rebecca." I sobbed and pulled my cell phone out of my jacket.

"Melody?" She asked. Her voice wasn't more than a whisper.

The phone quivered in my hands as I punched numbers. "She looks fine." My voice broke. "I think she's going to be just fine." Two nines showed on the display. I gripped the phone tighter, deleted a nine, hit the one twice, then the send button.

"911. What's your emergency?"

"Umm. We're—there's an accident—a car accident." I stared at Rebecca's twisted body. "We need an ambulance." My voice broke.

"What's your location?"

I forced my mind to think. "We're between Mt. Pleasant and Ephraim." What did the locals call this intersection? "Please hurry. It's . . . it's . . . by that turnoff."

"Turnoff?"

"Yeah." Junction was in the name. Something about a line . . . "Straits Junction," I said louder than necessary.

"Got it. We've alerted the emergency responders. I need to get some information from you, so please stay on the line."

After answering too many trivial questions, I tucked my phone away and focused on Rebecca. "Help is on the way, Becca." I used her childhood nickname.

"Where's Ryan?"

I swallowed hard. More tears flowed down my cheeks. "I don't know," I whispered. "He's . . . he's unconscious."

"Eva?"

"Yeah?"

"It hurts so much."

"I know, Becca."

She turned her head and coughed, and blood trickled out the side of her mouth.

The black pavement and Rebecca's broken body all began to spin. I squeezed my eyes shut as my mind repeated a desperate prayer. *Please help her, Heavenly Father!* I forced my eyes open. "Becca, just hang on." I laid my hand against her cheek. Blood warmed my palm. "The ambulance will be here soon, and . . ." I swallowed hard, "we'll get you something for the pain."

"Take care of Melody."

"She's safe in her car seat now. I'm not leaving you until help gets here." My thumb traced her cheekbone.

"I mean, raise her as your daughter." Her voice sounded weak, far away.

My breath caught. An intense ache rose in my throat. "Rebecca, you're just hurting . . . I know. It's painful even to look at you . . . but you're going to pull through this." I pulled my fingers through her long dark ringlets, now blood-soaked, as tears spilled over. "Stay with me, Becca," I choked.

"Ryan's gone, isn't he?" Her voice was too calm. Her wide dark eyes waited for my response.

I bit my lip, not knowing how to answer her.

"That's what I thought." Her eyes closed, and tears squeezed out the corners.

"Becca, I don't know for sure. I came to look for you before I really checked." Hot tears stung my eyes and flowed into Rebecca's hair.

"Eva." She coughed; more blood escaped her mouth. "I'm dying. Please—"

"No! No, you're not." It came out harsher than I had intended.

Her eyes fluttered open. "Please . . . just promise me you'll raise Melody for me."

"I'm not giving up on you, Rebecca," I said as I stroked her forehead.

She struggled to keep her eyes open. "Please, Eva. You're the only family I have . . . that she'll have." Her eyelids fell closed, but her ragged breathing continued.

"You know I love her like a daughter," I rasped. "But, Becca . . . don't leave me. You're all I have left. Don't leave me alone." I rubbed her cheek where my tears traced paths in her blood. "Please, please just hold on." I pleaded. "Help is nearly here. Listen . . . hear the sirens?"

Rebecca took a deep breath and let it out slowly. A look of peace settled over her features. "Thank you, Eva . . . I'm ready, Ryan."

"Becca, don't. Oh, Becca, please don't leave me!" My eyes raced over her, searching for something I could do to help her, to keep her. "No . . . no, I won't let you go. Melody needs you . . . I need you. Please! You can get through this; I'll help you."

She coughed again—more blood. "Love you forever." And then nothing. No chest rising and falling, no movement or life anywhere along her silent form.

I hugged her broken body to me. "Love you forever." Uncontrollable sobs racked my body.

* * *

"Do you want me to answer that?" the nurse asked again. She tucked a thick clump of auburn hair behind her ear and flipped it over her shoulder while she stared at my cell phone on the table beside my bed. "Maybe it's your husband."

"Not married."

She pointed to the ring on my left hand.

"Engaged."

"What's his name?"

"Sean." Even the one-word responses were too much.

She picked up the phone and looked at the display, then held it out to me. "It's him."

I lay back and stared at the ceiling, an unyielding heaviness in my chest. Then I nodded ever so slightly toward the nurse.

"Hello?" the nurse answered my phone.

"She's right here, but she's been in an automobile accident . . . She's physically fine, just cuts and bruises and probably stiff muscles . . . We'd like to release her tonight. Where are you? . . . Oh. I see. Does she have any family I could call? She shouldn't be alone."

Alone, alone, alone, the word reverberated through my mind.

"Um . . . that won't be possible." Her voice grew quieter. "They were killed in the accident. She keeps mumbling, 'No family, no family.'"

I hadn't realized I'd been saying that out loud.

"I'll try, but I don't know that she's up for talking quite yet." The nurse, Betty, according to her nametag, held the phone out to me. "He wants to talk to you." She gave me an imploring look. "Do you want to at least say hello?" she asked gently.

And then what? What could I possibly say to him? Nurse Betty had told him everything I could.

I took the phone from her, put it to my ear, and whispered, "Can't talk." Then I closed the phone and set it back on the table.

Nurse Betty shook her head sadly and marked something on my chart before leaving. Outside the curtain in a low voice, she asked, "How did the two fatalities happen?"

I recognized the EMT's voice, "No seat belts."

"What about the airbags?"

"The airbags failed to deploy. Recalls for Hyundai Elantras matching that year were announced last week."

The pressure in my rib cage made it hard to breathe. I lay back and resumed examining the ceiling. Tears slid from the outer corners of my eyes and into my hairline.

A rattling sound rolled closer, and then the curtain slid open. "Hi, I'm Tina," a nurse with cropped and honey highlighted hair pushed a baby cradle beside my bed. Melody.

The weight pressing on my chest increased.

Melody fussed as Rebecca's last request rang in my ears. I rolled onto my side and pushed myself into a sitting position. I wiped my sweaty palms on the bedsheet, took a deep breath, and stood to peer into the clear plastic hospital cradle.

Miniature fists jabbed the air and a slightly upturned nose and forehead wrinkled. Another whimper expressed her displeasure.

My legs melted. I grasped the metal cart and steadied myself as Tina's arm around my waist supported me. Would Melody want me?

"Whoa there, hon." Nurse Tina looked to be in her fifties, but her iron grip on me revealed youthful strength. "Take your time."

I nodded, closed my eyes, and took a deep breath. How could I possibly be her mother? She needed Rebecca. Why did Rebecca and Ryan have to die? Why not unmarried, childless me?

I leaned over the clear plastic hospital cradle and stroked Melody's tiny brunette curls with a trembling hand. "How is she?" My voice cracked.

Nurse Tina gently moved me toward the bed. "Sit."

I obeyed.

"The car seat did its job flawlessly. I fed her since you said earlier that she was hungry." She rocked Melody's cradle.

I had no memory of telling her Melody was hungry, but I was glad she'd been fed. "Did she take the bottle?" I whispered, fighting for control, fresh tears brimming.

Nurse Tina scooped Melody out of the cradle and turned back to me. "She did, but that doesn't always mean she'll be so willing the next time. Scoot yourself into the middle of the bed."

When I was sitting cross-legged in the center of the hospital bed, Nurse Tina bent over and placed the tiny baby in my arms.

Melody's warmth seeped into my chest and permeated my being with a sudden calm. *This is right*, the feeling said. My heart swelled and a tear slid down my cheek. "Oh, little Melody," I kissed her soft cheek. "We'll get through this, you and I, somehow," I whispered and smoothed the dark curls she'd inherited from Rebecca. Another tear splashed her forehead. I kissed it away as others streamed into her hair.

A moment later the nurse was talking again but I missed what she said. "What . . . what should I do if she won't eat?"

I gathered Melody closer and gently rocked back and forth.

"It's perfectly normal for babies to go on strike for up to twenty-four hours." She laid her arm across my shoulders. "It's very unpleasant for you, but she'll get hungry enough to eat. Be patient and keep trying the bottle."

"Eva?" A quiet voice called. I looked up to see Ryan's mom step around the curtain. A trim seventy-five-year old woman, she wore her long white hair swept up in her usual twist. Deep lines of grief creased her face, replacing the serenity I was accustomed to seeing there. A second figure, nearly identical in size and shape, emerged from behind Suzette—Jayne. The distress marking Jayne's face belied her energetic zest for life even as her spiky red hair intimated her true personality. The anguish displayed by each looked out of place on faces more often given to laughing. "Come home with us tonight," Suzette's quiet words invited.

Suzette lived in the basement apartment of Jayne's home. She and Jayne gazed at me; pain and loss reflected from their eyes and tear-stained faces as they awaited my response.

I nodded. Then their arms were around Melody and me. I shifted the baby to one arm and threw the other around Suzette. I clung to her and let my tears fall.

* * *

It was a long night. When Melody refused the bottle at her next feeding, Suzette patiently held her through her screams and frustration. Melody had sixty minutes of fitful sleep amid four long hours until, at last, she took the bottle and fell asleep. However, sleep evaded me, and I was sure it evaded Suzette as well. I listened to her toss and turn as I lay on the couch, my mind churning.

The bishop and Relief Society president arrived shortly after breakfast. When they left, Suzette agreed that I should go to Rebecca's house. Everything I needed to care for Melody was there. Even my car was there, where I had left it before climbing into Ryan's now totaled Elantra.

We made a quick stop at my apartment before driving to the house. Sooner than I wanted, Suzette pulled into the driveway of the little farmhouse and stopped behind my twilight-blue Astra.

I sat in the passenger seat and gazed at the house, unwilling to get out of Suzette's car and go inside. A wide porch with white rails ran the front length of the house. Three stairs marked the middle of the porch and led to a door flanked by two large white slider windows. A pair of white wicker chairs and a round table sat in a grouping to the left.

Mentally I pictured the brown speckled carpet stretching across the living room and up the stairs to the loft with its master bedroom and nursery. I saw the tan walls and white crown molding Rebecca and I had painted last year. I envisioned the wall of family photos hung under and along the stairs, photos of my deceased parents—and now Rebecca and Ryan too. My sister's impeccable taste and skill as an interior decorator marked each room of her home. She and Ryan had systematically been updating and remodeling the house for the past year and had had plans to continue.

But, like their lives, those plans were over now.

CHAPTER 6

"Ready?" Suzette lightly touched my shoulder after a few moments.

I took a deep breath and glanced at Melody in the back seat. "Mmm-hmm." I nodded before stepping around to lift her out.

I used my new spare key to open the front door then stepped aside to allow Suzette entry. I followed with Melody in her carrier. A faint hint of maple syrup hung in the air—left over from the French toast we'd eaten yesterday morning before leaving. Morning sun streamed through the front window. Its warmth illuminated a chocolate-colored leather couch and the mahogany coffee table Rebecca had bought at a garage sale and refinished to look brand-new. The crowning piece of furniture stood ahead and left of the entry tile—a baby grand piano that had belonged to my mother. Losing my parents had been hard, but not until now did I realize how much strength Rebecca and I had given each other during that awful time four years ago. Having no one to cry with was so much worse.

Next, my gaze stopped on the stone hearth separating the kitchen and living room. My nose tingled and my throat ached. A longing to cross the room, walk around the fireplace, and see Rebecca finishing breakfast dishes filled my heart so full that I was sure it would burst with the next beat. I glanced at Suzette.

Tears trickled down her face. This had been her home too; it was where she and Cal had raised Ryan. With her husband's death not even a year ago, I couldn't fathom the sorrow this homecoming brought her.

"Seems like they should still be here," she whispered.

"Yeah." My throat tightened. I couldn't say more.

* * *

It was barely past eleven when Melody's rhythmic breathing signaled me to carry her upstairs to her room. I leaned over the crib with the sleeping baby just as the doorbell chimed.

My arms jumped, involuntarily jostling her. "Shh, shh, it's okay." I gazed down at the slumbering baby. I needn't have worried—her eyelids didn't even flutter. But who would be here at this hour?

I hesitantly opened Rebecca's front door and stood still as stone.

"I came as quickly as I could get a flight."

I threw myself into Sean's arms, overwhelmed by the comfort his presence brought. I knew now I didn't have to go through this alone.

"Eva, I'm so sorry." He held me tight against him.

My breath came in irregular gasps. I pressed my face into his chest as sorrow threatened to engulf me. My tears soaked his shirt.

He released me, pushed the door closed, and led me to the couch. "Why haven't you been answering your cell phone?" His voice was gentle, concerned.

"I can't talk," I whispered and buried my head against him. More tears spilled down my cheeks.

Sean hugged me to him, stroking my hair. "I stopped by your apartment. I never imagined you'd be here." His fingertips tilted my chin toward his face. "*Why* are you here?" He pulled back and put his hands on my shoulders. His eyes bored into mine. "You can't even talk to me on the phone and I find you *here*?"

"It's easier to take care of Melody here," I whispered.

His eyebrows arched slightly. "Melody survived? I guess . . . I just assumed . . . Eva, what happened? I only know what the nurse told me when she answered your phone for you." His hands cradled my face. "I'm not good at guessing."

I took a deep breath and recounted the horror from last night. I got as far as finding Rebecca when the visual pictures renewed my sobs and made talking impossible. Sean held me and waited. I pulled more tissues from the box on the coffee table.

"So I'm . . . we're going to need a lawyer specializing in family law and adoptions." I settled back into Sean's arms and closed my eyes. "Do you have any friends like that?"

"Yes, Terrence Singleton." His voice began to fade. "I'll give him a call tomorrow."

* * *

"Eva. Eva."

The voice sounded so far away.

"Eva."

A hand shook my shoulder. "Melody is crying."

Now I remembered. Sean. Melody. Rebecca and Ryan gone.

The familiar heaviness thudded into my chest again. I forced my eyelids open, blinking against the light.

"Melody is crying," he repeated.

"What time is it?" I raised my head off his chest.

"One o'clock in the morning."

"She's hungry." I yawned, stood, and then shuffled to the kitchen, where I took a bottle from the fridge and put it in the bottle warmer.

"She eats at one o'clock in the morning?" Sean mumbled as he followed me into the kitchen.

"Yeah, she eats every three hours during the day and stretches to every four hours at night."

"So she'll wake up again at five o'clock?" He yawned.

"Yep." I put my hand on his arm. "You're tired. The key to my apartment is in my purse on the coffee table. Why don't you crash there tonight?"

His eyebrows pulled together, and a frown flashed across his mouth.

I sighed. I didn't have the strength to argue tonight.

He opened and closed his jaw then took a deep breath, and a calm smoothness spread across his face. "Sure, thanks."

"No problem." I started up the stairs then turned back. "I have to go to the mortuary tomorrow with Suzette." I ran my hand back and forth across the smooth handrail. "We have to pick out the headstones." I gripped the railing. "Would you come with me?" My voice had a higher pitch and sounded small. This was a task I dreaded.

He looked up from searching my purse, concern on his face. "Yeah, I'll pick you up. What time?"

"Ten thirty." Relief flowed in my voice. He would be there with me.

* * *

I sat on the couch the following morning contemplating what had to be done. Picking out headstones was a bad enough way to start a Wednesday. I was truly grateful school had ended last Friday and I didn't have to worry about finding a sub for my kindergarten class or the adult English class that had also ended with the school year.

I heard a tap-tap on the front door before it creaked open. Sean called, "Hello?" and stepped into the living room. "I called Terrence this morning."

"Who?" I looked up from packing formula into the diaper bag.

"My lawyer friend specializing in family law."

I nodded. "So what do we need to do?"

"After I explained it all to him he suggested we start with LDS Family Services."

"LDS Family Services?" My eyebrows wrinkled. That seemed an odd starting place. Why would they even need to be involved? I walked to the kitchen.

"It's better to find the adoptive family before drawing up papers. They may have an attorney they want to use."

I stopped with the cupboard door half open and peered back over my shoulder. "Adoptive family. What *exactly* did you tell Terrence?" I enunciated each word with precision.

He put his hand on my back, brushed his lips against my ear, and whispered, "Don't worry, I knew you would want to have contact as Melody's aunt, and that can be arranged with the adoptive parents."

I whirled on him. "Sean, *we* are the adoptive parents." I thumped his chest and then pointed to myself. "You and me." How could he have missed that?

His jaw fell open.

"I promised Rebecca I would raise Melody as my own daughter."

"How—"

I took his hand, needing so badly for him to understand me. "The first time I picked her up in the hospital after the accident, I felt the Spirit so strongly, letting me know she should be with me. I could never give her up to strangers or anyone else." My throat tightened against the pain. I swallowed. "She's the only family I have left."

Sean's eyebrows pulled together. "I'm sorry, Eva, but I didn't understand that from the information you related to me last night."

I pulled a bottle out of the cupboard and carried it to the diaper bag. "How could you even think of giving her away?" My voice rose. Melody, sleeping in her car seat, stirred. I wiped the wetness from my eyes.

"I just never considered the alternative."

His calmness infuriated me. I continued with my still-too-loud voice. "I—*we* are the most logical choice." Melody fussed, and I tapped her seat, gently rocking it.

"Hey, no need to get angry." He raised his hands as if in self-defense. "I didn't see things that way."

I lowered my voice to keep from disturbing Melody and hissed, "How did you see things?"

"At seventy-five obviously Ryan's mom is too old to raise another child." His calm, matter-of-fact way of stating things should have soothed me, but instead, it continued only to rile me.

"Obviously." Sarcasm dripped off my response, and I almost felt as if I were watching this argument from outside myself. I never talked to Sean like this. I climbed the stairs to Melody's room. Sean trailed me.

"And we are leaving for Iceland in two and a half months, remember." His unruffled tone continued.

"What has Iceland got to do with adopting Melody?" I yanked three diapers off the changing table and slapped a package of baby wipes against them.

"Eva, surely you see the implausibility of taking a baby to Iceland."

As if it would be more plausible to rip the last family I had from my arms. "No, Sean, I don't. Why don't you explain it to me." The hard edge in my voice stung my ears.

He took a step back and a deep breath then continued listing evidence in his placating tone. "Who's going to watch her while you teach English?"

This was a most ridiculous excuse, and he knew it. I was teaching English in Iceland to keep myself busy while he worked on his dissertation research. "I don't have to teach. You know we don't need the money. Next." We descended the stairs.

"We don't know anyone there. We'll have to attend a lot of functions, none of which are family friendly. Again, who's going to watch her?" he asked.

"You aren't making any sense. Other parents have successfully dealt with these issues and we will too." I put the diapers and wipes in the bag and zipped it closed.

He inhaled slowly and glanced at his watch. "Eva, I'm sorry I misunderstood your intentions. We've both got a lot on our minds right now." He crossed to the front door and held it open. "Let's talk about this later. We have to leave now or we'll be late."

My jaw tensed. No. I couldn't leave the discussion like that, without seeing him even consider the role I was asking him to accept. I picked up the car seat with Melody cradled inside and walked to the open door. She slept, her lips shaped into an O.

I gazed up into Sean's deep azure eyes and felt tears collecting in my own. "Sean, don't you see? You're going to be a father." I balanced the car seat on my hip between us and took his hand. "She *is* my daughter. I really did—and still do—feel that. I love her." I placed his hands around her head with my hands atop his. "She's ours. You're her daddy." I looked up to examine his expression. I read nothing in his eyes, but a wet warmth traced paths down my cheeks.

Sean wiped my eyes. "I don't want you to cry." He sounded worried. "This has just kind of blindsided me, Eva. I need some time to absorb all of it. I'll call Terrence and clarify your wishes." He moved us forward and pulled the door closed. "Please though, let's not talk more about it now. You've got a long day ahead of you."

Choosing headstones and caskets was a blur made all the more confusing as I fought to keep my composure after Sean's shocking assumption about putting Melody up for adoption. I felt betrayed even as I tried to convince myself it was only a misunderstanding. How could he even consider doing that? Why wasn't his first instinct to adopt her or think that I would want to adopt her? He knew how important children and a family were to me. Or did he? And what about Suzette? Did he think she wanted to give up her only grandchild to strangers? She, like me, had lost everyone. She needed Melody as much as I did.

* * *

Back at Suzette's apartment, we made all the funeral arrangements. Memories of my parents' funerals flooded my mind. These recollections brought more pain as I remembered how Rebecca and I had clung to each other to get through the details of those days. My eyes settled on Sean seated on the couch, remote control in hand. At least I had Sean.

Another worry pressed in on me as I watched Suzette making phone calls. She had lost her husband, Cal, a year ago and now her only child and daughter-in-law. How could I take her only grandchild so far away from her? First to Iceland and then Montana?

She finished her last call and made a check next to a name on her list.

"I'm sorry," I murmured.

"What are you talking about, dear?" She looked up from her notepad.

"I'm taking Melody away from you."

"Yes." Suzette sighed, reached across the table, and placed her hand on mine. "She needs a family. A younger mom."

"But you need your granddaughter."

She looked down at Melody sleeping in her car seat. "It won't be easy," she agreed.

"We could set up a webcam for you and check in every week." Excitement colored my voice as the idea came to me. "Then you would get to see her quite a bit."

"Web what?" Her nose wrinkled as she tried to make sense of my words.

"Webcam. It's a camera we hook up to our computer and transmit the picture to your computer."

"I don't have a computer."

"Sean and I will get you all set up." I looked over at Sean.

"Sure. It's easy," he said then went back to flipping stations on the remote.

"I don't know if I'll be able to use it." She sounded wary, but there was hope in her voice.

"Sure you will." I placed a reassuring hand on her forearm. "We'll practice until you can do it."

Suzette smiled. "I would enjoy seeing her grow."

I nodded, happy to know the separation would be tempered at least. My thoughts turned to the last issue that needed resolving today. I had three days left until I had to be out of my apartment, and while I had originally planned to move in with Rebecca until my wedding anyway, it now seemed the easiest place to be to care for Melody. From my own experience, I knew that all of Ryan and Rebecca's assets would be placed in a trust for Melody. Still, I wondered what to do about the house. I didn't know how much Ryan and Rebecca owed on it. Ryan had grown up in it. Would Suzette want it?

Suzette nodded when I brought the subject up. "Something you may not realize is that my late husband, Cal, left the house to Ryan as his inheritance. He stipulated that Ryan had to pay sixty thousand dollars and then the house was his."

Understanding dawned. "Rebecca used her ten thousand dollar trust. That's how they could afford all the remodeling they've done."

"Yes. Ryan knew the house would need extensive updating. We'll have to find the paperwork, but I think they took out a loan for eighty thousand dollars. They needed more than Rebecca's ten thousand dollars for remodeling. You remember how the loft used to be. It was in pretty bad shape. Ryan closed it in and added a master bedroom and bathroom up there." She glanced up at a picture of Cal helping Ryan hold a fishing pole, and then back at me. "Cal and I planned to use the down payment money from Ryan to remodel the house on the north side of you. It was supposed to be our home, but then Cal died and I sold it."

"That's why you live with Jayne."

She nodded. "I didn't want to do the remodeling without Cal."

"With all the updates Ryan and Rebecca made, you might want to move back into your old house instead."

"Perhaps. There'll be time to decide that later." She patted my hand.

I still needed to talk to her about living in Ryan and Rebecca's house until August, but I hated to ask. It was such an awful time to bring up moving, but I had no choice. "Could I live in the house until my wedding in August?" I couldn't read Suzette's expression so I continued, "I have to be out of my apartment by June 1—next week. And since I'm not renewing my teaching contract, I have to get all my stuff out of the school by then too. I was planning to move in with Rebecca until the wedding . . . and now with Melody . . . it would be so much easier than finding a new place. That is, if you don't mind. I could pay rent, or the mortgage payment, or whatever you want."

"It would make your transition with Melody easier," Suzette agreed as her toes gently rocked Melody's carrier. "And it would keep Melody close to me for the summer at least."

That simple statement revealed Suzette's fear of losing Melody. I silently vowed to be vigilant about keeping those two in contact. "You're welcome anytime, you know. Melody needs you too."

CHAPTER 7

SEAN MADE ARRANGEMENTS TO HELP me pack and move my apartment and classroom over the next two days. Suzette had agreed to watch Melody for me, and so we were able to work quickly. Working with Sean also helped me focus more on the future instead of my present loss.

Thursday we moved nearly everything from my apartment into Rebecca's basement, leaving only a skeleton of furnishings. Sean would sleep in my apartment until next week when he could move into a cabin at GBEEC for the summer. I placed my mother's rocking chair in the living room. Rebecca had her own rocking chair, a Christmas gift from Ryan, in her bedroom, but I kept that door closed against the painful memories within.

I also made a concerted effort to help Sean get to know Melody better. When we picked up Melody that evening, I nestled her in Sean's arms before picking up the car seat. Then I walked through Suzette's apartment, gathering Melody's things into the baby carrier. When I returned to the front door, I found Sean holding a fussing Melody at arm's length.

I bit back a frown as I held her against me and swayed until she settled. "A little movement seems to calm her," I said to Sean.

"She's probably ready for an evening nap," Suzette said as she packed the things I'd gathered into the diaper bag.

I settled Melody in her car seat. "Thank you, Suzette. We'll see you about the same time tomorrow if that's okay?"

She nodded, but I noticed the fatigue in her pale blue eyes. Even her natural tranquility couldn't hide the weariness that came from caring for such a tiny baby. We'd have to be back by noon tomorrow so Suzette could rest before the viewing.

Sean carried Melody to the car and we drove the couple of blocks to Rebecca's.

Once inside the little farmhouse, I warmed a bottle for Melody. "You want to feed her?" I held the bottle out to Sean.

He hesitated. "Not really."

"I'll fix our dinner while you give Melody hers." I led Sean to the rocking chair.

Sean eyed the rocking chair. The skin between his eyebrows creased. "I can wait."

"Don't be silly. She won't hurt you. She'll even be happy—you're giving her just what she wants." I slid Melody into his arms and waited for him to sit down. "Rock her a little while she eats. It soothes her." I turned toward the kitchen.

I pulled out some leftover casserole a ward member had brought by and fixings for a salad. Just as I finished, Sean quietly asked, "Now what?"

I turned to see tiny Melody sleeping in Sean's huge embrace.

Warmth seeped into my chest, lessening the pressing weight there. They looked so beautiful like that. "Come with me." I walked past the two-way fireplace back into the living room and up the stairs to the nursery. "Just lay her on her back as gently as you can," I whispered, pointing to the crib against the wall to the right.

"See, that wasn't so bad," I said, sliding my arm around his waist as we walked out of the room.

He nodded but made no comment.

I scooped some macaroni casserole onto two plates and put one in the microwave.

Sean set both our phones on the table. "I know it's bad timing, but tomorrow and Saturday are going to be really busy with the funeral, and then I'll be moving up to GBEEC. Do you think we could pick a day to take wedding announcement pictures?"

I flipped through the calendar on my phone, then closed the application. It felt too soon after Ryan's and Rebecca's deaths to be making plans, but if we didn't do this now, it would only add more stress later. "Just pick a day. School's out. I'm not going anywhere." I knew I could rely on Sean to take care of everything.

"Okay. I'll talk to the photographer. And there's one other thing . . ." Sean uncharacteristically cleared his throat. "Your wedding dress. Or lack of one."

I sighed. "I don't want to think about that right now." Showing up for pictures I could handle, but dress shopping would be nothing less than painful without my mom and sister. Rebecca and I had made it a girls' day out when we shopped for hers. We hadn't had my mom, but we'd had each other. We'd concocted some story about a double wedding, embellishing it with fresh details at each new shop. Giggling like adolescents, we left a wake of exasperated sales clerks. I smiled at the memory, and then a lump rose in my throat. My dress-shopping day, in stark contrast to that memory, loomed ahead like some dreadful chore.

"The wedding is two and half months away," Sean said quietly and placed his hand on mine.

I blinked my eyes, clearing the memories. "Sean, I can't. I just . . . not yet."

"I understand."

I tried to stifle a yawn.

Sean scooted his chair out and came to stand behind me. He began messaging my neck. "Tired? We moved a lot of boxes today."

I relaxed, letting my head fall forward. Sean's hands gently eased the tension from me. "It's not so much the moving as the not sleeping through the night." *And worrying about you and Melody*, I thought. "I just get worn out faster."

"Melody's not sleeping?"

"She sleeps like a baby, which means she wakes up every four hours," I explained again. "She's good about going back to sleep after she eats. It's the broken sleep that makes me tired." I lifted my head and covered another yawn.

I felt his lips on my neck at the same time I heard Melody's cry.

"That was a short nap." I reached up and squeezed Sean's hand. "Just a minute."

His hands briefly balled into fists then relaxed as he muttered, "Sure."

On my way up the stairs I called back, "That first plate is done. Can you stick the other one in the microwave for me?"

I returned with Melody and set the salad on the table before sitting down.

"My mom could go dress shopping with you," Sean suggested.

I froze with my fork midway to my mouth. "I don't think your mom would enjoy going to the shops I'm planning to visit."

"Nonsense. She lives to shop."

"Our budgets are a little different."

"You know my parents have offered to help pay for your dress." Sean stuffed a large forkful of casserole in his mouth. "What is this?"

I shrugged. "Noodle surprise? A ward member brought it over."

Sean picked through the casserole examining the ingredients before taking another bite. He swallowed and continued, "I'm only trying to help you find someone to go shopping with. No bride should have to shop for her wedding dress alone."

Melody began to fuss. I took another bite and bounced her on my knee. "No, but it would be a really awkward situation with your mom." Sean's mom had elegant taste, which wasn't necessarily bad, but I preferred simple styles with a touch of elegance. Simplicity wasn't her forte, and she assumed I opted for uncomplicated designs due to a lack of money. Which wasn't the case.

"I could go," Sean offered.

I shook my head. "This is one thing the groom *shouldn't* help with. Especially you." I tried to give him a smile, but my mouth wasn't cooperating.

Melody's fussing intensified. Sean tried to say something else about dress shopping, but I couldn't hear. Melody serenaded us with her screams as Sean quickly finished his last few bites. He stood abruptly. The tendon along his neck popped in and out as he said, "I've got to make some last-minute arrangements for the search parameters next week." He bent down to kiss me as Melody arched her back with another wail. Sean jerked back as if Melody had struck him. I grabbed his hand and pulled him back. He hurriedly kissed me—his lips just grazing my cheek—then walked out the front door.

I bristled at his rushed good-bye kiss. He was running away after being with Melody for less than an hour today. True, she was pretty fussy tonight. But how was I going to help him adjust to Melody if he bolted whenever she wasn't silently sitting in her carrier or asleep? He wasn't the only one who had to adjust. Melody had lost both her parents. I was sure she was confused and missing her mom. Just like me. *Rebecca, why did you leave me?* An overwhelming emptiness pressed in on me, lodging thick in my throat. My heart ached as I stood alone in the doorway. The tears collected, threatening to fall. I moved to the living room to rock Melody in our mother's chair. On the wall under the stairs, Rebecca's photograph collection elicited visions of our family whole and complete. Memories cascaded through my mind while tears stung my cheeks. Could Sean and I make those kinds of memories for Melody? More time. Sean needed more time to adjust.

* * *

Friday, as we packed my classroom, Sean tried to distract me from thinking about the viewing that evening. He kept up a steady stream of commentary about the summer's anticipated expeditions. First he related the Indian and mountain-man myths that spoke of the legendary hot springs. When he began to fill me in on Icelandic culture and the places he wanted us to visit, I realized Sean had been there for me all week, but all I cared about was his relationship with Melody. How could I be so selfish? I resolved to make the day more normal for Sean at least while we were moving my classroom.

He'd even brought brochures detailing different Icelandic points of interest. During lunch he spread them out on the floor for us to look at. Something about seeing the place in color photos stirred up the adventurer in me. My family never traveled beyond a few of the western states, but my dad made every new place exiting. When he wanted the family to go somewhere, he'd bring home a stack of books from the library. We'd all sprawl out across the living room floor searching through pictures for *the place*. This scene wasn't so different, and that reassured me and helped ease my worries. I felt lighter than I had all week.

Sean grabbed a stack of paper cups from the shelf we were packing. "Get two pieces of paper. Write your name on one and mine on the other."

"What are we doing?"

"I'll make a list of touring days. Whoever's name we draw out gets to pick the destination for one day."

I wrote a name on each paper, folded them in half, and placed them in the paper cup. "Ready."

Sean drew a paper out and opened it. "Eva"

"I get the first day? Great." I picked the closest brochure. "Too bad we didn't get married in February because I would have loved going to the Food and Fun Festival in Reykjavik." The pamphlet pictured a man and woman clothed in white terry robes relaxing in front of crystal-blue water. "So I think we should start with the Blue Lagoon."

"Really? You just went from food to mud."

"What's not to love about white mud and mineral salts? And this says the water is warm." I held up the pamphlet.

"I'm writing it down." Sean put my name back in the paper cup, covered the top with one hand, shook the cup around and held it out to me.

I pulled a slip of paper from the cup and opened it toward Sean. "What does it say?"

"Eva."

"I get the second day too? Let me think."

"I'm taking golf clubs." Sean showed me the pamphlet with golfers on a green and snow-streaked mountains towering in the background. The caption proclaimed twenty-four hours of sunlight for golfing every day in June and July.

"You're going to miss the midnight golfing in June and July, so that's no fun." I brushed the pamphlet aside.

Sean started to protest, but I waved him off with the paper containing my name.

"I can wait till it's my turn." Sean held the pencil ready to record my choice. "What are we doing the second day?"

"Let's see . . . how about the Mýrda glacier hike?"

"Mýrda?"

I picked up a brochure showing a hiker in climbing gear crossing an ice field. "This place." I pointed to the word *Mýrdalsjökull* and noticed that no children under ten were allowed. What was I going to do with Melody in Iceland? "I call it Mýrda for short. You might want to write *Mýrda* for short."

"You forget where I served my mission."

"Do you know anyone in Iceland who could watch Melody for us a few times?"

Sean stopped writing. "On our honeymoon?"

Oops. I shouldn't have mentioned Melody. "I just realized we'll have her." I placed my paper back in the cup and shook it again. "Your turn." I held the cup out to Sean.

He didn't even look at the cup. "Melody? On our honeymoon?"

"We won't be honeymooning the entire three months. You have to finish that geothermal pump while we're there. Forget it for now, okay? We'll talk about it later." So much for making this day more normal for him. I shook the cup at him. "Draw another name."

He pulled out a slip of paper and silently read it then said, "Again?"

"Me again! This one I already know. The horseback riding lava tour."

"Horses. Did you see the tour with four wheelers?"

"You already have four wheelers. You don't have a horse. This is something new. The lagoon was something blue."

"What about something old?"

"Iceland itself is old."

"And something borrowed?"

"I'm working on it. Draw another name."

Sean took out a paper, opened it up and instantly crumpled it. He pulled out the next paper, but I had already stood up and bolted for the door.

I wasn't fast enough. Sean grabbed me around the waist and said, "It's a pity a kindergarten teacher can't spell my name right," He held a partially full bottle of water over my head.

"I know how to spell your name. S-E-A-N. See?" I struggled to pull Sean's arm from around me.

"E-V-A. On both papers." He began drizzling a bottle of water over me. "How else would I get to go all the places I wanted?"

"How will you get to go if you bring Melody?" He released me suddenly.

I stumbled but caught myself before falling. Bringing up Melody had been a big mistake.

* * *

Saturday, the day of the funeral, dawned bright and warm in stark contrast to my disposition. Sean had said remarkably little yesterday after my blunder in mentioning Melody. Taking her as our own would require a leap of faith on Sean's part. My dad had always believed taking a leap of faith was more like falling into faith than leaping. I didn't quite understand what he meant by that. The scriptures taught that faith without works was dead so wasn't faith more like an action, like leaping? I wished Sean would take some faith-directed action. But I wasn't going to think about it today. Whatever Sean did or didn't do wouldn't bother me. Today was for saying good-bye to Rebecca and Ryan.

Midway through the prefuneral viewing I excused myself to go change and feed Melody. Another woman already occupied the mother's room. Not wanting to talk to anyone, I searched out an empty classroom.

Melody was halfway through her bottle when the door opened. "Sean said he saw you slip in here to feed Melody." I looked up as Peter, dressed in a shirt and tie with his neatly trimmed goatee and caramel hair pulled back into a low ponytail, quickly crossed the room and sat beside me. I hadn't seen him since before the accident, and for some reason the sight of him brought fresh tears rolling down my cheeks. His eyes brimmed with tears as well. "Eva, I'm so sorry." He put his arm around my shoulders.

Emotions I had so tightly controlled this morning now streamed down my face.

"I can't even imagine how devastating this must be for you," he finished in a whisper.

"It's all too much the same from my parents' funerals." I carefully wiped my eyes, trying not to smear my makeup. "Two caskets, all the same family and friends. I can't bear to be out there. I miss her so much." I looked into his tear-filled eyes, searching for answers. "Why her? Why them? They had everything to live for—each other, a daughter." I looked at Melody. "It doesn't make any sense." Peter gently stroked Melody's short curls. Her eyelids stuttered open for a brief second and closed again. "Why couldn't it have been me?" I asked the question that had plagued me since the accident out loud. Unmarried, childless me.

He put his arm around me and patted my shoulder. "Sean's certainly grateful it wasn't you."

A sob flew out before I could contain it. The mention of Sean's name reminded me of my concerns about him and Melody. I was annoyed despite my determination not to let Sean's actions bother me today. I balanced Melody's bottle against my chin and retrieved a tissue from the diaper bag.

"Here, I can take her for a minute." Peter expertly transferred the baby to his arms while holding the bottle and allowing her to drink it uninterrupted.

Sean poked his head in the door at that moment. "It's time for the family prayer." Then he was gone again.

I dabbed at my eyes, hoping my make-up wasn't running, and took Melody from Peter. I needed to hold her right now. She gave me a glimmer of hope, something to cling to. Without Melody I knew the aching heaviness pressing in on my chest would engulf me. "Here we go," I said more to myself than Peter.

Peter grabbed the diaper bag and followed me out.

* * *

Late that night I rocked Melody. My irritation with Sean's behavior was growing. Where had he been while I fed Melody during the viewing? He probably thought there wasn't anything he could do to help with Melody, I reasoned, but *I* had really needed someone there. The echo effect of my parents' funeral had sent my emotions reeling. And then Peter had appeared. He'd understood my complete desolation, even voluntarily held Melody for me. I wished Sean would at least make an effort to interact with Melody. I was tired of telling myself he needed more time. If he had a whole year instead of two months, it wouldn't make a difference if he didn't try. And that was the crux of my frustration with him. He didn't appear at all motivated to bond with Melody.

I peered at Melody's angelic face snuggled tightly against my shoulder. She'd lost so much in her two months of life. I would have to provide her the security and love of two parents while Sean worked through his reservations.

* * *

Monday morning I heard a light tapping on the door and Sean called "Hello?"He turned the doorknob. "Eva, I know how we can handle having Melody in Iceland. I don't know why I didn't think of it before. It's the perfect solution."

I was a bit wary. "What's that?" I thought the perfect solution was for Sean to accept Melody as his daughter, and then we'd go from there. But I shook that thought away and tried to keep an open mind as I entered the kitchen and pulled out the frying pan to start breakfast.

"A nanny. We can hire a nanny to come with us to Iceland. Then you don't have to give up your teaching position over there and we will know Melody is in good hands. It's perfect."

I caught my breath. "Sean, there is absolutely no economic reason for me to work." I cracked four eggs into the pan, inhaled deeply, and turned to face him. "You know I was planning on quitting when we had children. It's just come a little sooner than we expected." I paused then added, "But that doesn't change me wanting to be a full-time mom."

He raised his hands as if he expected nothing less. "Okay, if you don't want to work, that's fine. We can still hire a nanny though."

"But—"

He put his palm against the side of my face and peered into my eyes. "That way we'll know Melody is in good hands when we're out."

The conflict-accompanying nausea started. "You want to hire a nanny we'll only need a few times a week?" I turned away and put bread in the toaster.

"It could be more. Just think, we—or just you—could leave whenever . . . or we could be home together . . . without interruptions." His hand was on my back and he kissed the top of my head.

I walked to the stove, hoping the distance would calm my stomach. "What will the nanny do the rest of the time?"

"Some agencies have nannies who also do housework. We could interview from those organizations."

"Then what would *I* do all day? A nanny is completely unnecessary." I flipped the eggs, keeping my back to him.

"It wouldn't be so bad. Just think about it."

Spatula in hand I slowly turned around, unable to keep myself from asking the question that burned in my mind. "Are you suggesting a nanny just because the baby is Melody?"

The accusation surprised him. "What do you mean?"

"I'm not blind. You don't like interacting with Melody." My tone caught him off guard. He opened his mouth, but I waved the spatula and took a deep breath. Then, in a more sympathetic tone, I said, "I also realize that this whole thing kind of blindsided you."

"True, this was unexpected." His words were measured as he tried to decipher my mood.

I slid the eggs onto two plates and placed them on the table. "But what if she were our baby?"

He started to protest.

I placed my fingers over his lips. "What if she were biologically ours? Would you still want a nanny?"

"Eva, that's not a fair question."

Undaunted, I gazed up into his eyes. "It'll help me understand your point of view."

Sean pulled me close. "Please, just consider hiring a nanny."

I searched his sapphire eyes and laid my hand against his cheek. "Not if you won't tell me what you're thinking." Melody's first fussing before she really woke stirred the air. Automatically my head turned toward the stairs.

Sean dropped his arms and mumbled something incomprehensible.

"What did you say?" I asked

The tendon along his neck tightened and relaxed. "Nothing."

I hesitated then said, "The toast should pop up any second. Go ahead and start. I'll be down in a couple of minutes."

Sean finished his breakfast and left for GBEEC before I made it downstairs with Melody. The queasiness hadn't entirely subsided so I scraped my breakfast into the sink. Melody had lost both her parents and he wanted to trust her with some stranger all day, every day? I couldn't do that to her after all she'd been through. It irked me that Sean had suggested such a thing. Thinking about it only increased the nausea. I needed a distraction, something to do, and gratefully, I did have some work to do.

I took Melody with me to clean my apartment. Sean had insisted I hire someone to do it. I'd tried calling someone earlier in the week but the line was busy and I forgot to call back. Sort of. I didn't know if I could spend an entire day alone in Rebecca's house. I had decided Melody could sit in her carrier while I cleaned and it would be good for both of us to get out. That's where I was wrong. Half an hour into cleaning, Melody let me know she was done with the car seat. For once I was grateful I only had a two-room apartment to clean. We made it home around six and collapsed on the couch. When Sean appeared on the doorstep with red roses and two Subway sandwiches, I knew he was sorry about leaving so abruptly this morning. I took the roses from him and inhaled their sweet fragrance. "These are beautiful. And how did you know I didn't want to cook tonight?" I asked as he stepped through the door.

He tapped his forehead knowingly. "I thought we could use some down time. It's been a busy week full of big changes. How about we go see a movie?"

"Maybe a rental would be better, or Rebecca has some movies." I nodded at Melody. "She's been kind of fussy today. I don't want her to start crying in the theater."

Sean let out a loud breath. "Right."

"You know where the movies are. Why don't you pick one out while I put these roses in some water and get a bottle for Melody." I turned toward the kitchen.

"Rebecca sure liked the chick flicks." Sean called from the living room.

"Try the second drawer down," I answered from the kitchen sink.

"Ahh . . . this must have been Ryan's drawer."

"He has some pretty good thrillers in there." I put two plates on the coffee table and slid the sandwiches out of their bags.

"And one I've been wanting to see." Sean slid the DVD into the player, sat down next to me, and grabbed his plate.

Just as I took a bite, Melody decided she wanted her bottle. I exchanged my sandwich for Melody and her bottle while the opening credits flashed across the screen. After drinking her bottle, Melody refused to go to sleep and objected to being rocked or me sitting down with her. I spent most of the movie standing behind the couch swaying with her in my arms. With fifteen minutes left, she began to wail.

Before I could leave the room, Sean stood and headed for the front door. "I've got to get back to GBEEC." He exited without a backward glance.

I instructed myself not to cry. He was not adjusting well. But worse than that, I felt sure he wasn't even trying.

CHAPTER 8

Tuesday morning the hours stretched before me. I lay Melody on the changing table in her room and considered my options. How would I fill an entire day? Feeding and changing Melody wouldn't take twelve hours. I finished changing her diaper and headed out the door when I glimpsed a stroller leaning against the closet's back corner. We could go for a walk.

The late morning sun climbed higher in the clear blue sky as I buckled Melody into her stroller. At the edge of the front walk, I looked left toward fields green with new growth and then right at the tree-lined street with houses spaced unevenly along its expanse. Cheerful birds chirping enticed me south toward the homes.

Soon I spied a retired couple out planting their garden. The wife dropped seeds at regular intervals while the husband followed behind pulling and pushing soil over the furrow of seeds. Memories of my father dragging a hoe along string tied to stakes at either end of the garden flashed through my mind. I pushed the stroller closer to them. "What are you planting?" I asked remembering that Ryan and Rebecca had planted peas, lettuce, and spinach early this spring.

"This is another row of corn," the man answered, pausing to rest his hands on the hoe's handle tucked under his chin. "You ever planted a garden?" he asked.

"Only with my parents, but my sis—I have a garden spot this year." I quickly steered the conversation away from Rebecca. "Any suggestions on what I should plant?"

"We're past the last frost so you can plant whatever you like," the woman replied with a smile.

"Even tomatoes?"

"Yes, tomatoes, peppers, melons, whatever you want," her husband said.

I knew I probably wouldn't be around for much of the harvest, but Suzette or someone else could enjoy it. After deciding to plant some beans, corn, tomatoes, and cucumbers, I made a quick trip to the local nursery and then gathered the necessary tools from the garage. I placed the baby carrier in the shade of an old tree near the garden's edge. The fresh air, bright sun, and change of scenery excited Melody. Even I couldn't resist feeling lighter in its influence.

A carpet of green stretched across the garden plot, making it difficult to discern rows among all the weeds. The neglected peas, lettuce, and spinach needed attention, but first I had to clear a place for the new transplants.

I thrust in the shovel and brought up brown earth. Repeating the action eventually yielded a row of freshly turned soil ready for starts. The exertion felt good. Work always brought a sense of purpose that helped me relax. I dug a small hole, then carefully removed a tomato start from its planter and dropped it in.

I knelt in the garden and wiped the back of my hand across my face. Through wisps of sweat-dampened hair I admired evenly spaced tomato and pepper plants amid the recently turned soil. They looked so tiny, but with some care they would grow.

It occurred to me that Sean and I were not unlike these starts. We too had been thrust into a much larger environment. With time and attention, we too would thrive. The thought gave me hope, and I smiled for the first time in a while. I'd been so overwhelmed with grief and the responsibility of caring for Melody that perhaps Sean was feeling neglected. I stood and brushed the dirt from my jeans.

Melody waited at the garden's edge happily kicking her now sun-kissed feet. I wasn't finished, but it was enough for today. Right now I needed to leave a love note on Sean's voice mail. He'd hear it the next time he was somewhere his cell phone could get coverage.

* * *

A pattern of life developed over the next week. Each morning I worked in the garden or yard, and in the afternoons Melody and I went for a walk. Evenings brought some variety. Either we visited Suzette or Sean visited us. Nights still stretched long in Rebecca's house surrounded by family photographs. The tears still flowed while I fed and rocked Melody in the dark hours before sunrise.

Not all of my tears were for Rebecca and Ryan, however. Sean's reticence toward Melody weighed heavily on my mind. He still didn't volunteer to hold Melody or even interact with her unless I initiated the contact. I tried to be patient, giving him time to acclimate. I held on to that moment of clarity in the garden, hoping he was just going through a difficult transition. But nagging doubts in the back of my mind made me wonder whether more time would improve the situation.

Saturday night Sean insisted we leave Melody with Suzette and have a *real* date. While I had to admit it was nice to be alone together, it did nothing to assuage my growing apprehension.

At church on Sunday, I asked Sean to hold Melody during sacrament meeting.

"She prefers you," he whispered then focused on the speaker.

I stared at his profile for a moment. "She just needs to get used to you," I whispered back and shifted Melody toward him.

His hand pushed her back. "Not here."

My jaw dropped open. "What's wrong with here?" I hissed.

His eyes surreptitiously swept the faces of those seated closest to us. "I don't want everyone looking at me," he said out of the corner of his mouth.

Looking at him? Baffled, I gave up until we got home. "How about holding the baby now?"

"Eva, why are you always trying to push her on me?"

"I'm trying to help you get to know her. She's going to be your daughter." I buckled Melody in her swing and started to set the table. The plates banged down giving voice to my annoyance.

From behind me Sean slipped his arms around my waist and rested his chin on my head. "I'd rather hold you."

* * *

Tuesday night Melody came down with a cold. She didn't yet know how to navigate breathing through her mouth and sleeping, so if I laid her down, she cried. I sat in the rocking chair with her nestled against my chest, which seemed to help. She didn't cry in this position but only slept fitfully.

At her 1:00 a.m. feeding she latched on to the bottle and began sucking then pulled away and whimpered while milk ran down her chin. She gulped in air and latched on again then sputtered and gagged. Her head tossed side to side, but she didn't inhale.

My heart pounded. I sat her upright. CPR techniques raced through my mind, but none seemed appropriate for this situation. I patted her back in quick, urgent strokes.

Melody coughed and gasped, then moaned.

My heart slowed. I wiped her nose amid her frustrated cries. Worry gnawed at my mind—worry she couldn't breathe, worry she was hungry, but mostly worry of the unknown. Was this normal or something more serious than a cold?

I finally called the doctor's office. A recording related normal office hours and then gave the hospital's number in case of an emergency. *Was* this an emergency?

Melody tried to drink from her bottle again but turned her head away to breathe. I placed my cheek on her forehead. It was warm but not hot. She probably had a cold, nothing serious enough to call the hospital about. A frustrated whimper came from Melody as she struggled to eat once more.

I felt helpless to relieve her symptoms until I remembered how steam from the shower helped clear my nose when I had a cold. Pulling the rocking chair into the bathroom, I closed the door and turned on the shower. It seemed to help some—before the hot water ran out. Melody and I camped out in the bathroom for the night. When I thought the water heater had had enough time to recover I turned the shower back on. In between heating cycles, we paced the house.

There had to be another way to help her feel better. I vaguely remembered all infant cold medicine being taken off the market as I prayed this was just a cold and nothing more serious. I resolved to call Suzette in the morning for any ideas to help Melody breathe.

As early as I dared, I dialed Suzette's number. She told me how to make a saline solution from salt and water and explained how to use the baby's aspirator bulb to squirt a small amount into the nostril, wait for the mucus to break up, and suck it out with the aspirator. Despite Melody's objections to the process, it worked so well that she was able to eat and finally sleep. Suzette also suggested I get a humidifier for her room and buy some saline drops, but first I wanted to sleep.

As I reached the last stair on my way down from Melody's room, a knock sounded at the door. I smoothed my pajamas and ran a hand through my blonde mass of tangled hair. I knew my eyes were probably bloodshot and surrounded by dark circles, but I figured I wasn't trying to impress anyone.

I opened the door and squinted my eyes against the morning sun. "I saw your lights on when I got home around three." Peter looked me up and down. "Is everything okay?"

My cell phone rang. "Melody caught her first cold yesterday." I explained to him. "It was a long night." I swung the door open wider to let Peter through. "Come in." The phone rang again. "Just a minute."

I snatched my phone off the coffee table. "Hi, Sean." I yawned.

"Just waking up, eh?"

Peter stepped through the door and stopped.

"Not really." I told Sean. "I haven't gone to bed yet."

"What? Why not?"

"Melody's sick." I motioned for Peter to have a seat on the couch.

"Oh."

I waited for him to ask what was wrong with her. He didn't. "It's just a cold, nothing serious, but she's miserable," I explained anyway. "I need to get a humidifier and some saline drops."

"Sure. I'm just calling to nail down tonight's schedule."

Tonight? What day was it? I searched through the fog invading my mind. Wednesday. Oh, Wednesday! The opening barbeque at GBEEC. The last of the geologists, geochemists, drillers, and engineers had arrived last night. I was supposed to get up early today. I glanced at the clock and groaned. The cheesecakes should already be made and chilling in the fridge.

"Are you okay, Eva?" Sean asked apprehensively.

I flopped into a chair across from Peter. "Yeah, but I don't think we can have cheesecake for dessert. I was supposed to get up early to cook them." I twisted my head around to read the clock on the mantel. "There won't be enough time for them to chill if I start now."

"How long do they have to chill?"

"Four hours. But that's after they've cooled for at least an hour and they take that long to cook. With preparation time that's seven hours from now," I counted on my fingers, "or four thirty."

"The dinner doesn't start until six thirty. You don't have to leave until five thirty. I think it's still doable."

I held up one finger to Peter and walked to the kitchen. Rounding the hearth I stopped in my tracks. "Didn't you schedule the photographer to meet us up there at five-thirty for our engagement pictures?" Stress made my heart beat faster. I was supposed to find a babysitter for Melody since Suzette worked in the Manti Temple on Wednesday nights. Larry and Jayne were staying with his brother over in Nephi helping him recover from surgery. I completely forgot to ask around about good babysitters at church. Now Melody was sick and I couldn't comfortably leave her with anyone but Suzette.

"Yes, but I still think there's time. You said four-thirty, right?"

"Right." My stomach tightened. Should I tell him I didn't have a babysitter? "I don't know if I can leave Melody with a sitter when she feels so awful," I said slowly as I put butter in the microwave to melt and began mashing graham crackers.

"I'm sure Suzette can handle it," he replied smoothly. "That's what grandmas do."

"She's working at the temple tonight."

"Jayne is just as capable."

"She's in Nephi helping her brother-in-law."

"Teenage girls like to babysit. I'm sure she'll be fine."

I found four spring-form pans and began pushing a graham cracker crust into one. "You have no idea how frustrating it is when she can't breathe and won't eat and just cries unless you hold her and walk with her. I don't think a teenager is the solution with a sick baby."

"Eva, we're counting on you as the caterer tonight. I thought you liked doing this."

I stacked eggs and sour cream on the counter. "I do, Sean. You know I won't leave you in a mess. I'll figure it out." Melody's whimper carried over the baby monitor. How was I ever going to pull this off? She'd only been down for twenty minutes, and the cheesecakes were nowhere near ready to bake. "I have to go."

"Love you."

"Love you too." *Or I would never do this.* Melody fussed some more. I snapped the phone shut, leaned over the counter, and rested my head in my arms. *Heavenly Father, please help Melody to sleep a little longer. Just long enough for me to get the cheesecakes in the oven.*

"Do you want me to get Melody? It looks like you're in the middle of baking something."

I jerked upright at the sound of Peter's voice. I'd completely forgotten he was there. "Uh . . . sure. That'd be great. I don't think she's hungry; she just can't breathe. I really need to go to Walmart and get a humidifier for her." I put the crusts in the oven and began combining the filling ingredients, grateful that I had backup for the moment.

Peter reappeared holding Melody vertically against his chest, a grin on his face. "She doesn't like my goatee. Watch this." He took her tiny hand and brushed it along his chin. Melody instantly curled her fingers into a fist and pulled them away at the same time she wrinkled her nose.

I smiled. "I think you're right. Here, let me clean her nose." I reached to take Melody, but Peter moved her away from me.

"Tell me what to do. It doesn't look like you're done here." He nodded toward the bowl of filling.

"It'll be easier to show you." I started toward the bathroom. "Lay her down here." I indicated a towel folded in half spread atop the dryer. Oh, what a mess that nose was. Yellow mucous oozed over a layer of dried white mucous. I demonstrated how to apply the saline solution and clear her nasal passage. When Melody tried to turn her head away from the bulb, Peter gently place a hand on her forehead. I paused. "That's a lot easier when she doesn't move around so much. Thanks."

When I was finished, Peter picked up Melody and cradled her against his shoulder. "There, that makes a girl feel better, huh?" he crooned.

I stared at Peter, amazed. He rubbed her back and gazed into her upturned face while quietly comforting her with soft and soothing words.

He looked over at me. "You better get those cakes in the oven if you're planning on getting a humidifier sometime this morning."

The timer for the crusts was beeping. Peter's demeanor toward Melody had captivated my attention so much that I hadn't noticed. I hurried to the kitchen. Once the cheesecakes were in the oven I mixed the marinade for the steaks and put them in the fridge. I'd have to remember to turn them after lunch. In the living room Melody whined briefly, and I heard Peter walking the floor.

I tried to sort through the to-do list in my sleep-deprived mind. What else did I need to do? Sean and his dad would get the dutch oven potatoes going before I arrived. The watermelon was already up there. *The green salad*, I realized. I washed the leaf lettuce and spinach while the pan for the bacon heated. The bacon sizzled as I sliced the red onion and grated some mozzarella.

I glimpsed Peter carrying Melody to the bathroom, presumably to clear her nose again. With the vegetables washed and chopped, that just left the poppy seed dressing.

As I was pouring dressing from the blender into a canning jar, Peter sauntered into the kitchen. "Are you about done?" he asked.

Warmth spread across my cheeks. "Sorry, I shouldn't have taken advantage of your being here. I did a little more than finish the cheesecakes." I stirred in some poppy seeds into the dressing.

"No, no. I didn't mean it like that. I just meant that I think Melody is searching for something to eat."

"It must be ten o'clock," I said, glancing at the stove clock for confirmation as I measured formula into a bottle.

"Straight up." Peter surveyed the dirty dishes filling both sinks. "Must be a big dinner tonight."

"Thirty people. Everyone is here, even Sean's dad." I held out my arms. "I can take her now." My eyes met his gaze and held there for a split second.

I relaxed. "Thanks so much . . . I never would have been ready for tonight without you."

His eyes skimmed my disheveled hair, pajamas, and bare feet. "I'm going grocery shopping this morning. I'll pick up a humidifier." Before I could respond he glided out the sliding glass door and jogged down the four steps and across the yard to his house.

"Well, okay, then," I said, surprised but grateful. I cleaned Melody's nose then sank into the rocking chair with the bottle. My heavy eyelids fell closed with the slow back and forth motion. Peter had been a godsend this morning. The food was miraculously ready. Now if only I could find a babysitter. Maybe Melody wouldn't mind a drive this afternoon. I could just deliver all the food. Sean and his dad could certainly grill the steaks.

Pictures, on the other hand, would be another matter. Melody might be okay for a little while in her stroller. At least she would be upright and able to breathe easier. Dragging a sick baby up a mountain seemed unreasonable, but I had no alternative. That's the way it would have to be—and hopefully Sean could accept the situation with some grace.

CHAPTER 9

I JERKED AWAKE, STARTLING MELODY. She sniveled and rubbed her face from side to side on my shoulder. Peter poked his head through the front door. His knocking had awakened me. "Sorry I woke you," he apologized.

"It's okay," I mumbled, struggling to keep my eyes open but failing.

"I brought the humidifier." I heard a plastic sack rustle as he walked to the couch.

I peered through half-open eyelids. "Thanks."

"I'll just fill it up and put it in the nursery, 'kay?" His footfalls grew faint, and then I heard the kitchen faucet running.

Someone shook my shoulder. I tried to open my eyes, but they refused to cooperate. "Eva, I'll put Melody in her crib. The humidifier's going; she'll sleep now."

Finally my eyelids obeyed. Peter was bent over in front of me with arms outstretched. "Just put her in my arms."

Barely comprehending the request, I slowly handed Melody to him and watched him ascend the stairs. I rubbed my eyes and stretched.

Peter returned. "You should get in bed while she's still asleep."

Finishing a yawn, I nodded. "Thanks, Peter." I waved and he closed the front door.

I shuffled to the kitchen and waited the last minute and a half for the cheesecakes to finishing cooking. Once they were cooling on racks, I collapsed onto my bed.

Melody's full outcry penetrated my sleep. Even with daylight filling the room I had slept through her first stirrings entirely. I squinted at my watch. Two o'clock. It'd been four hours since she ate, but only three since I'd fallen into bed. And the cheesecakes were still on the counter!

Melody's cry grew more anxious.

Summoning up some willpower, I dragged my legs over the edge of the bed and sat up. First I made room in the fridge for the cheesecakes. They would have to chill in half the time today. Then I changed Melody and brought her down to the bathroom to clear her nose. As I laid her on the dryer, a small white bottle caught my eye. Saline drops. Peter must have bought those too. The receipt lay tucked under one edge with writing on it. I pulled it out.

Heard you need a sitter. Be back at 4:15.
                              —Peter

I swallowed the lump rising in my throat. I would have to do something really, really nice for him. What was that saying I had learned in Primary so many years ago? Go the extra mile. Peter definitely put that principle into practice. He was my own personal miracle today when I most needed one.

* * *

As I positioned the salad in the box, I glimpsed Peter bounding up the back porch steps, a folder clasped in one hand and a plastic grocery sack in the other. I needed to leave in five minutes—I was beginning to wonder if he'd forgotten about his offer to babysit. I slid the glass door open.

"Wow." His eyes moved up and down approvingly. "You look amazing. That's quite a transformation from this morning."

Warmth spread up my neck. "Thanks. Engagement pictures, you know." I turned and walked back to the fridge.

"So is Sean all color-coordinated with your lavender and purple outfit?" he asked with a wry smile.

"Should be. He picked it out." I carefully arranged the cheesecakes in another box then looked at Peter. "I want to say you don't have to do this, but I'm so desperate for a babysitter I'm just going to settle for—well, I really appreciate you doing this."

"No problem. Melody *is* practically my niece."

"Even so, not everyone would be so willing to spend an evening with a sick baby." I thought of Sean's less-than-eager attitude.

Peter gave me a quizzical look. He must have discerned the annoyance in my tone, but to his credit he didn't pry.

"I'm leaving dinner for you. There's a potato in the oven." I opened the fridge and indicated three containers. "There's a steak in one of those you can grill and a salad and slice of cheesecake in the other two. Somewhere in the fridge door is some raspberry and chocolate syrup for drizzling if you want."

"Mmm, that sounds much better than my yogurt." He set his plastic grocery sack on the counter.

"Yogurt? For dinner? Don't guys usually eat a little more than that?" Sean called yogurt chick-diet food.

He shrugged and glanced at the bag. "They were on sale. I've got like three different flavors in here."

I opened my mouth to respond but my cell phone interrupted. Sean's name appeared on the display. "Hi, Sean."

"Glad I caught you. I forgot to tell you that you'll be riding up with the photographer. She wasn't sure she could find the place on her own."

"Where do I pick her up?"

"She's coming from Provo so she'll pick you up any minute now."

"I hope she has room for all the food." My eyes measured the boxes stacked on the kitchen floor.

"Shouldn't be a problem. The gravel road freaked her out a bit so she borrowed her brother's Explorer."

"So you're going to bring me home, then, right?"

"Of course."

"See you soon." I snapped the phone shut and situated the last container of steaks. I explained how much and how often to feed Melody and gave Peter my cell number just in case, though I didn't know how much coverage I would have in the mountains. As I gathered up the food, a white Explorer turned into my drive and I bid Peter and Melody a quick farewell.

* * *

My hand registered a gentle squeeze. My eyes fluttered open and I peered into the darkness of Rebecca's front yard. "We're here," Sean said.

"Sorry about that." I shook my head. "I just couldn't keep my eyes open."

"You were out before we passed through the gate to the canyon road."

I yawned and opened the door. We grabbed boxes from the back of the Escalade and ambled across the grass to the back of the house. Strains of piano music floated on the breezy night air. Peter must be listening to a CD. The sound of the sliding door opening silenced the tune.

Peter appeared from around the rock fireplace. "Melody's been asleep for an hour, and she ate about three hours ago," he reported to me, nodding at Sean and then walking over to grab a few boxes.

We stacked the boxes next to the fridge. "How's her cold?" I asked, rubbing my eyes.

"The same, except that the humidifier helps her breathe easier. My sister-in-law always puts a pillow under one end of the crib mattress when her babies are sick so I put one under Melody's. Hope it helps." He crossed to the still-open door.

Why hadn't I thought of that? "Thanks, Peter." I said sincerely and brushed his arm before he turned.

"No problem." He gave me a quick smile and a wave then disappeared into the night.

I began loading dishes from the boxes into the dishwasher.

"That can wait." Sean clasped my hand and led me to the swing on the back porch. We rocked in silence, arms around each other, gazing up at the star-scattered sky. "I miss you, Eva. I think it's harder having you only thirty minutes away instead of two hours or more. Maybe we should move the wedding up." He leaned down and kissed me.

"So we can spend our honeymoon hiking with the five researchers staying at GBEEC this summer?" I giggled as I imagined myself clutching a GPS and trudging up a hill in hiking boots behind Sean and the researchers.

"They'd give us more privacy than we'll have with Melody," he said as he stared straight ahead into the dark night.

My body tensed as the mood grew serious. "What are you talking about?"

"Eva, we leave for Iceland the day after we get married." A frown pulled at the corners of his mouth.

I nestled my head against his side. "I've been thinking about that, and I've come up with two alternatives."

"Oh?" He sounded intrigued. "Does one involve a nanny?"

"I can't leave her with a stranger."

"So that door is closed?"

"Sealed."

"What are your two alternatives?"

"First, if we moved the wedding up a week or a couple of days, we could have a honeymoon before we leave for Iceland."

"Remember the struggle we had synchronizing schedules to find that day in the first place?" He sounded doubtful.

I nodded. "Yes, so that's why I came up with plan B."

"Go ahead."

"Our plans now are to spend the first week in Iceland honeymooning since you don't officially have to report to work until nine days after the wedding, right?"

"Correct."

I lifted my head to peer into his eyes. "Is it possible to change our plane tickets to a week after the wedding and spend that week on a honeymoon somewhere in the States?"

He smiled. "A week all to ourselves? Just you and me?" He hugged me tighter to his side.

"Just you and me." I kissed him.

A grin brightened his face and he nodded. "So after hearing that, I think you're ready to consider another option."

"Another option?"

"There are going to be several social functions to attend in Iceland."

"More than what you've told me about?"

"You never know, and with Melody we won't be able to be flexible. I think we should leave her here with family while we're in Iceland."

My stomach clenched. How had we made the jump from a one-week honeymoon to leaving Melody for three months? "Leave her?" The words came out in an unnaturally high pitch, like they always did when I was upset.

Sean didn't seem to notice. "All your plotting to find time for us to be alone is quite appealing." He kissed my neck behind my ear. "It took awhile, but my Eva's come back to me," he whispered, his breath hot in my ear. "We need time to become us before we add a baby to the mix." His words tumbled out into the cool night breeze. "Iceland will give us a breather."

The queasiness in my stomach began its advance. "Sean . . . " I stood and moved to the edge of the porch with my back to him, then wrapped my arms around my middle against the uneasy stirrings there, "I can't leave her for three months."

He stood behind me. "You're tired. Admit it—you need a break from her."

I rotated to face him. "We can do this. It's not how we thought our life would be, but we can make it work. She's already lost so much."

"What about me, Eva? What about what I've lost?"

I gaped at him. "Lost?"

"I'm losing you." He unwound my arms, took my hands in his. "Melody's taken over your heart and pushed me right out."

"That's not true," I said, taking a half step back.

"You are consumed with her. Think back to what *our* plans for this summer were." His voice grew louder with impatience. "How you were planning to come to GBEEC a few times a week and participate in the search. All that is gone now."

"I told you I would still come up a couple of times this summer."

He dropped my hands. "Yes, I know. A *couple* of times."

"Sean, a lot has changed since we made those plans," I said.

"*You've* changed Eva. Being a mother is all that matters to you. Where do I fit in?"

I laid my palm against my chest. "Right here where you always have."

"*Is* there room? Because it feels crowded." Bitterness laced his words.

I swallowed, willing the nausea to go away. "You know I want to be a mom. I've never hidden that from you." I slipped my arms around his waist and hugged him to me. "And as for room in my heart, there is more than I ever thought possible. Melody has increased my capacity to love."

He tentatively put his arms around me.

I looked up, searching his face. "If you would let her into your heart, you would understand this." I took a deep breath. "If she were ours, would you love her?"

I felt him tense again. "Eva, that's not a fair question. If she were ours then we would already be married and I wouldn't—" He stopped.

"Wouldn't what?" I probed.

Melody's cry carried through the open windows.

Instinctively, I turned toward the house.

Sean threw up his arms and stepped back. "That!" He jabbed the air. "*That* is what I'm talking about. If she were ours then we would already be married and I wouldn't have to share you for the first year of our marriage, or at least nine months."

I felt my mouth fall open. "Share me?"

"Eva, I want time with *you*. Just you and me." He put his arms around me and pulled me close.

I remained stiff, arms at my side.

"We need time together, to get to know each other." He cupped my chin in his hand. "A baby takes away from us. Our relationship. You can understand that, can't you?" His other hand stroked my back. "Already we've been apart so much, working in different states."

"I understand we wouldn't have chosen this as plan A, and I know it's a lot to take in, but please, Sean. I can't ask someone to watch her for three months. Babies grow so fast. She wouldn't even know me after that long."

He pulled me into his embrace. "All of Peter's brothers are married. They could take turns. I'm sure they'd understand," his voice soothed. "None of them started a marriage with someone else's baby."

"Someone. Else's. Baby?" The words were technically true, but he was making it sound like Rebecca had been some random person off the street—instead of my only sister.

"Remember how upset you were when I bought china without you?" Sean asked.

I nodded, though I didn't understand his abrupt change of topic.

"Picking out dishes without your fiancé is one thing, but you accepted guardianship for your niece without consulting me."

My throat ached, my nose tingled, and tears welled up in my eyes. "So you don't want Melody."

The baby's wail pierced the air.

I grabbed his arms. "Sean, please don't make me choose," I whispered.

He pulled back and put his hands on my shoulders. "I know you haven't hidden your desire to be a mother. But somehow I thought you wanted *me*, loved *me*—"

"I do want you." I gripped his arms tighter.

He held up his hand. "I can't live with being second place in your heart."

"There isn't a first and second place," I pleaded.

"It feels like it to me."

I released his arms and wiped away a single tear. "Three months is too long." My voice quavered. "My love for her doesn't turn on and off like that."

Arms at his sides, he clenched his hands into fists. "But your love for me does."

Air expelled from my lungs as if I'd been sucker punched. "You really feel that way?"

"Unequivocally." He clenched his jaw and stared at me. Light from the stars played in his eyes like flames in a fire.

"So where does that leave us?" The nausea returned tenfold as I forced myself to ask the question.

"Are you hearing me?" Bitterness laced his tone. "In your current state there is no us."

His words thudded into the pit of my stomach. "My state?"

"You're the one who's changed." His mouth closed in a hard line.

My palms began to sweat. "But I haven't changed, Sean. Maybe you're just seeing me clearly for the first time."

"Are *you* seeing clearly? You say motherhood is important to you, that you want to be a full-time mom, but do you realize if we lose us, there might not be a wedding and you will end up alone *and* a working mother?"

I gasped. "What are you saying?"

"I'm saying that this is serious, Eva. I don't like the change that's come over you. I keep hoping things will get better, but they don't. You grow more and more attached to that baby," he flung his arm pointing toward the house, "and distance yourself from me. You won't even consider steps that could save our relationship. What guarantee do I have you'll work any harder at our marriage?"

"Is this an ultimatum? Leave Melody or call off the wedding?" A violent shiver ran through me.

He crossed his arms on his chest. "Yes."

Emptiness shuddered through my body. I took a step back. "Then our differences go far deeper than I imagined." My voice cracked. "Leaving Melody for three months isn't going to fix our marriage. I know she's supposed to be my daughter. I can't deny that witness." I swallowed against the pressing tears. I knew what I had to do. I examined his features for a clue I was wrong. I saw only a hard mask. My heart raced. I took a deep breath and continued, "I can't ask my daughter to grow up bereft of her father's love. I can't live every day wondering if my husband thinks I love him enough." I pulled the ring off my trembling hand and held it out to Sean.

A look of disbelief flashed across his face before his carefully composed public face reappeared. "That's your choice?"

"No, it's your choice, Sean. I'm trying to make this family—"

"We are *not* a family." He plucked the ring from me and carefully placed it on his open palm. His hand trembled ever so slightly, and for a moment he watched the moonlight dance off the diamond's edge. Slowly he brought his gaze back to me and swallowed hard as he closed his fingers over the ring. He walked away without another word. A moment later an engine roared to life and faded away.

I gulped the air around me, but it wedged in my throat. My hands clenched into fists, and I squeezed my eyes tight, but the hot liquid seeped through my lashes anyway. I crumpled to my knees. "Not Sean too!" I screamed into the night. "Not Sean too. You can't take everyone I love away from me. You can't . . . You can't," I finished with clenched teeth and pounded the wooden slats beneath me. Tears streamed down my face, and then chagrin spread through me; I knew deep down that this wasn't God's fault. "I'm sorry . . . I'm not blaming You," I whispered. "But why . . . why?" Another haunting wail burst through my lips and I sobbed into the still blackness. Alone.

Someone's hand pulled my arm around their shoulder as their other hand grasped my waist and pulled me up to a standing position. "Eva, are you hurt?"

Without even wondering who it was, I leaned into the desperately needed support and suddenly became aware of Melody's frenzied crying.

"Oh, Melody, I'm sorry," I whispered.

"What? What's wrong with Melody?" The person gently propelled me into the house.

I wiped a hand across my eyes. "Peter?" Robotically, I mixed a bottle of formula.

"I was loading my car to leave when I heard you scream something and then start to sob. I ran the whole way. Are you hurt—is Melody?" He put a hand on my shoulder and looked into my eyes.

"No one is hurt." I swallowed. Not physically anyway. I started up the stairs. Peter followed. More soundless tears spilled down my face. Inside Melody's room I tripped over a rocking chair.

"Sorry, I should have told you I moved the chair from Ryan's room in here to feed Melody. It was easier for her to drink and breathe with the humidifier," Peter said.

"Oh." I picked up Melody and tried to soothe her frantic cries on the way back downstairs. Peter trailed us. I placed Melody on the dryer and put saline drops in one nostril. I looked up to see Peter staring at my hand—specifically my naked left ring finger.

He lifted his head to meet my gaze, a question in his eyes. "Did you lose your ring outside? Is that what's wrong?"

"Sean's gone," I whispered. My throat tightened and I swallowed hard. "Melody was too much for him."

A look of shock froze Peter's features for a split second before he recovered. "Maybe he was just upset that he didn't have something to match your outfit tonight?" he tried to tease. He offered a lopsided grin, which fell when I didn't smile back.

Shaking my head, I carried Melody into the kitchen. I shook a few drops from her bottle onto my wrist. "Thanks for checking on us, Peter. We'll be fine." I brought Melody into the living room and sat in the rocking chair.

Peter stood watching us. His mouth opened and closed without a sound. He looked at the piano and back to me. "I'll just get my music and go. I left it earlier." He crossed to the baby grand piano that had once belonged to my parents, picked up some papers, and put them in a folder. But instead of taking the folder with him, he slid it into place on Rebecca's music shelf. He opened the door to leave and said, "I'm really sorry, Eva . . . and thanks for dinner." The door closed behind him.

Melody turned her head away from the bottle and struggled to breathe. Peter was right. She needed the humidifier.

I climbed the stairs alone, wondering as I did so if I would always be alone. I would have Melody—but I had wanted to give her a father, a family.

Fresh tears cascaded down my cheeks and onto Melody's blanket.

CHAPTER 10

In the black of night I rocked Melody. The throbbing ache of losing first my parents, then Rebecca and Ryan, and now Sean ripped through my heart, rupturing any last remnants of calm and control. *Why, Heavenly Father, why?* My shoulders shook. Another wave of cries surfaced.

I finally calmed myself enough to rock Melody to sleep and lay her in the crib. Then I descended the stairs, collapsed onto the couch, and buried my tears in the pillows. *Why did I fall in love with Sean if it was just going to end like this? Why, why, why?* My fists pounded the cushions. I'd learned to lean on him. After my parents died, I had to be strong for Rebecca, but with Sean I didn't have to be in charge. I didn't have to be the decision maker. Except tonight. He'd crossed the line with Melody. I wouldn't let him treat her as an unwanted interruption to his carefully planned life. I knew he didn't want a large family, but to treat Melody like that was unacceptable. I inhaled a jagged breath, remembering Sean's words: *someone else's baby.* I curled up on my side clutching a pillow as new tears fell.

A while later, Melody woke. I once again cleaned her nose, fed, and rocked her with tears still slipping down my face. Cradling her tiny form against me, I wondered at this plan of *happiness.* Losing my parents hadn't brought happiness. Losing Rebecca hadn't brought happiness. And losing Sean? This could never be mistaken as happiness.

Melody stirred, turning her head to the other side. I reflexively smoothed her curls, kissed her forehead, and a little piece of joy tiptoed into my heart. Melody brought me happiness. And she'd brought happiness to Rebecca and Ryan. And Suzette. Rebecca had entrusted me with Melody. With Melody's happiness. And I couldn't even give her two parents. I felt another tearful episode boiling up my throat and I swallowed hard. I should have died in that accident. Everyone would have been happier then. I concentrated on taking steady breaths so as not to disturb Melody as I stood and carefully laid her in the crib.

I made it to the dark leather sofa downstairs before tears enveloped me once again. And the questions persisted. Why *had* I survived? What was the point of all this pain? It was too much. Too much!

Sometime later, I sat up, grabbed a Kleenex, and wiped my nose. I fought for control over my ragged breathing but lost to another volley of sobs. Now I wept for lost expectations, for the comprehension that I might never have a whole and complete family. Visions of my childhood complete with two parents and a sister contrasted sharply with the lonely life ahead of me.

In her crib, Melody protested. I used the saline drops and refilled the humidifier before changing her diaper. My tears flowed freely, but my convulsive sobbing diminished as I rocked her back to sleep with a warm bottle. Eventually I traded the bottle for a fresh Kleenex and wiped away more tears. Gazing down at the sleeping babe in my arms, I realized she and I were each other's only surviving family, with one exception: Melody had a grandmother. I clutched the soggy tissue and determined to make the best life I could for Melody. My upcoming marriage had caused me anguish over separating Suzette and Melody. With its disintegration I vowed to stay close. At least Melody could have a grandma. My snuffling subsided as the sky lightened. When I placed Melody in her crib at dawn, my tears ceased. I slid between the sheets of my bed and slept.

The sweet smell of maple syrup gently roused me hours later. Then I heard the sizzle of liquid hitting a hot pan. My breathing came quick and shallow as I wondered who was in my house. Half asleep, I staggered into the kitchen, reasoning that anyone making something with maple syrup couldn't be dangerous. I glimpsed a familiar white twist of hair as Suzette poured another pancake onto the griddle.

"How . . . Why . . . What are you doing?" The words tripped out of my mouth.

Suzette finished pouring a pancake and turned. "Making breakfast."

"Okay . . . but why here?"

"Aren't you hungry?" She set two plates on the table.

I inhaled deeply. The sweet maple scent made my mouth water, and I found my stomach did indeed feel empty. "I think I am."

"Good. I didn't want to eat alone."

I sat at the table. Suzette turned three pancakes onto my plate and three onto hers. I drizzled syrup over the stack and took a bite. "Mmmm."

"I miss making pancakes." She put a bite in her mouth.

"Why—why are you here?" I stuttered.

"Breakfast first." She pointed to my plate. "Then we'll talk."

I was hungrier than I'd expected. When I finished the three pancakes, Suzette piled three more on my plate. Finally, I swallowed my last bite and remembered some manners. "Thank you. Those were really good. Did you put maple syrup in the batter?"

"My secret ingredient." She put down her fork. "Peter called me this morning and asked me to stop by." She studied my face.

"Oh." Great, the news was out already. I looked down and smoothed my wrinkled skirt, realizing I had never changed my clothes last night. I ran my fingers through my knotted hair. Was my make-up smeared too or had all the tears completely washed it away?

"He was really worried about you, you know. He couldn't stay, but he didn't want you to think you were all alone."

"I'm fine."

"I'm a good listener."

"There's nothing to talk about," I insisted. "Sean doesn't want to start a marriage with a baby, and I won't give up Melody."

"Is that really what he said?"

I sighed. "He wants to leave Melody with family while we're in Iceland."

Suzette's even expression gave away nothing. "Why not try it?"

"We'll be there for three months. She's already lost one mother. I can't do that to her." My rising voice betrayed my frustration. "Besides, it's just an excuse for him not to be a father to her."

"This has all hit him pretty fast you know."

Is she on his side? I wondered incredulously. "It's more than him wanting to leave her here," I said. "Sean didn't want kids for a couple of years and then only one or two. I convinced him not to wait because I'll be twenty-nine this fall. We don't have the same commitment to a family. Melody just brought it all to the surface again . . . more sharply." I swallowed a lump in my throat. I didn't think I could possibly cry anymore. I was wrong. A single tear slid through my closed eyes. "I realized I can't be the wife Sean wants. He wants a wife, a social partner, not a mother. I want a family and a husband who enjoys his family. I won't leave Melody for three months. I love her and want to be her mother. I just hope that's enough." I used my napkin to dab at the fresh tears and wiped my nose. "She deserves a father—a family—but now that may never happen."

Suzette stretched her hand across the table and placed it on mine. "It's only been two weeks since the accident. You and Sean both need a little time to adjust to your new roles." She patted my hand.

I appreciated her sincerity. It made me glad I had decided to keep Melody close to her. "Sean is stubborn, and once he makes up his mind there is no going back." I watched out the sliding glass door as a robin pulled a juicy worm out of the ground. "He's right though," my voice faltered, "I gave away my chance of being a full-time mom to Melody when I handed him the ring." I rubbed my forehead. "What have I done?" Once again, the tears fell.

CHAPTER 11

THREE WEEKS AFTER SEAN LEFT, a loud *thonk* outside interrupted breakfast. I opened the front door as a motor roared to life. Squinting through the sun's morning rays, I spied Peter's sister-in-law, Marie, standing on the front porch. Thick, shoulder-length brown hair framed her round face and dancing dark eyes. Jeans and a plain T-shirt hid her curvaceous figure this morning. She and I had talked easily at Melody's blessing. Her husband, Rick, pushed the mower past the porch.

A wave of guilt hit me—I should have noticed how long the grass was getting. I had immersed myself in taking care of Melody and little else, venturing outside only long enough to check the mailbox each day.

"I've come to invite you to the Manti pageant," Marie said. "We're taking Pam and David and all the kids tonight. We want you to come with us."

"I don't think so." I moved to close the door.

Marie's hand stopped it. "Eva, it would be good for you to get out."

"Suzette's been talking to you," I mumbled.

"Jayne. But yes, Suzette is worried too."

"We're taking you by force if we have to. But you *are* coming with us." The glint in Marie's eyes belied her solemn tenor.

I looked down at my track pants. I would have to change, maybe even shower. I had pretty much lived in these pants for the last week. I didn't bother to change into pajamas at night. Each morning I exchanged my T-shirt and I was good to go. Maybe I *should* get out, I considered. I'd never seen the Manti Pageant and tonight was the last performance of the season if I was remembering right. Going with the Finch clan presented certain advantages. Rick and Marie with their six children and David and Pam with their three would certainly provide enough conversation to hide my waning social skills. It would also help me keep my mind off Sean. I sighed. "All right."

"Good, we'll pick you up at eight." She smiled. "Any luck with the job search?"

"How—"

"Suzette told me you couldn't get your position back because of declining enrollment."

They certainly were a social family. "I made my last call yesterday. All teaching positions in Sanpete County are filled. Both districts agreed to keep me on file in case anything opens up, but in the meantime, I'll have to submit my application to other districts. I've already called my old school in Boise, but they don't have any openings either. That means moving Melody away from Suzette." It was just one more way I had failed Melody.

Marie frowned. "Doesn't Melody get social security survivor benefits?"

I sighed. I figured since she seemed to know a lot about what was going on anyway, I might as well be straightforward. "I've run the numbers. If I take over the loan on this house and use my trust money to pay off my car, I'd have just enough to pay the bills and buy groceries. No insurance. That's the worst part. As much as I hate relying on government programs, I could get CHIP for Melody. But if the car needed a repair . . . Financially teetering on the edge, ready to fall anytime is stressful. I need a job with benefits or one that pays enough for me to buy insurance."

"I wish I knew how to help."

My cell phone rang and I turned slightly back toward the doorway. "I better get that."

"Remember, eight o'clock tonight."

I nodded my head as I closed the door and looked down at my phone. A 208 number flashed across the screen. Who would be calling me from Idaho? Certainly not Sean. "Hello?"

"You've got an interview."

"Linda?" Her voice brought back whispered conversations during many a faculty meeting.

"You can come, can't you? Because I sure talked you up."

"What? Oh! When?"

"I know the district told you there weren't any positions, but May Williams decided to retire. We have a new principal, Mr. Tyler, and I told him all about you. He wants to see you Monday at 2:00 p.m. So can you make it?"

There was no need to consult my calendar. Monday would look the same as the last twenty-one days—empty. "Sure, I'll be there. Do you have a number I can call to confirm the appointment?"

"Get your pencil."

If I couldn't find a job here, Boise was the next best place. Living there again would be familiar, almost comforting.

* * *

I spied the Manti temple, majestic and serene in its creamy limestone exterior, rising barely east of the highway. David snaked through the residential side streets searching for a parking place, and at last we pulled onto a street only half filled with parked cars. David parked the car next to Rick's suburban; parents and children poured out all four doors. Gravel crunched and doors slammed as we set off for the pageant.

I hoisted the diaper bag over my shoulder, clutched a blanket under the same arm, and nestled Melody securely into the crook of my other arm. Each adult, plus Rick's oldest boys, grasped the hand of a young child with one hand and a blanket with the other and commenced walking toward the temple hill. The soft breeze carried chatter from various clusters of pageant goers along with harsher voices. Marie stopped and gathered the children around her. "Okay, kids, stay close to us and don't talk to the people yelling things in the street or take any papers from them. Just ignore them. As soon as we put blankets on our chairs, we can go across the street and play in the grassy area by the distribution center for a while."

I looked ahead. Bunches of friends and families merged into a babbling brook of sorts, parting and darting around individual boulders to preach a torrent of anti-Mormon sentiment. The abrasive declarations being spewed out directly contrasted the peaceful feeling that surrounded the holy refuge—the backdrop to their melodrama. We pressed forward. I focused my gaze beyond the cacophony, never allowing my eyes to rest on their faces. As we passed through the gates onto the temple lawn, I relaxed.

A sea of silver folding chairs stretched across a flat, expanse of green. Near the temple, the ground rose sharply. This steep incline served as the stage for the pageant. I found the east wall where Marie reported that Samuel the Lamanite would stand to deliver his prophetic words. Pam pointed out the temple tower where the angel Moroni would make his appearance.

We laid our blankets across the necessary number of chairs and then strolled across the street. Pam found an open spot of lawn where the children could play, and I steadied Melody in my arms and dropped cross-legged to the ground. Being out of the house felt good. Marie was right. I needed to get out and stop thinking about what could have been with

Sean. Pam's preschoolers, Nora and Kilee, toddled over to Melody and began caressing the baby's head.

"Beebee," Kilee said.

"Soft," said Nora.

"Your mama's going to have a new baby too, isn't she?" I said

"Beebee," Kilee said again.

"Hey, you made it!" eleven-year-old Craig sang out, and I lifted my head to see Marie's girls, Ruth and Leah, rush Peter, each hugging one of his legs.

He smiled and said, "Hi there," while patting their heads. Peter, hair pulled back into a low, tight ponytail and sporting a neatly trimmed goatee, sank to his knees in front of me. He caressed Melody's cheek with the back of his finger. She instinctively turned openmouthed toward his touch. "It's good to see you, Eva."

In contradiction to the usual ache in my chest, I felt myself relax.

"Hey, it's Uncle Pete!" thirteen-year-old Tim yelled as he ran up behind Peter. "You're late as usual."

Peter half turned to focus on Marie's sons. "Hey, guys. So what kind of message was that anyway?" Peter, eyebrows pulled together, eyed his two oldest nephews. "It sounded more like a threat than an invitation."

"The boys really wanted you to come," Marie explained.

Tim pulled a football from behind his back. "Are you up to the challenge?"

Peter stood and stepped toward Tim. "Five hundred, right?"

"He's looking pretty slow, better give him a hundred points or he'll never catch us," Craig said.

Peter streaked by Tim, leaving him empty-handed. It took Tim a split second to recover and then both boys raced after Peter. Rick and David followed with two more boys.

Marie and Pam plopped down on either side of me to watch the game. Seven-year-old Ruth herded the preschoolers into a line and demonstrated how to toss a grapefruit-sized foam ball into an open diaper bag. Mostly, she spent the game retrieving their wild throws.

Pam absently rubbed her basketball-like tummy. "You and Peter seem to have hit it off."

Marie gave her a stern look.

"Hey, it's pretty obvious. I'm sure I'm not surprising anyone by saying it, especially not Eva."

Marie gave an almost imperceptible shake of her head.

"It's okay, Marie," I said. "It doesn't bother me." I looked at Pam. "Yes, Peter and I get along well. Ever since Ryan and Rebecca's deaths he's been like family to us." I looked down at Melody. "I'm kind of like the sister he never had."

"His . . . sister. *That's* what you think?" Pam's expression was incredulous.

"I th-think so. He does so much for me." Did it bother Pam that Peter considered me a sister? "He's more than a friend."

"I think we can all agree on *that*." Marie said then quickly asked Pam, "So have you had any luck finding another preschool?"

Pam shook her head. "Have you?"

"Nope. Well . . . there's one accepting new students, but I don't like it. It's more like daycare than preschool. The teacher is a little too out there for my taste. I wish Lori wasn't moving. She ran the best preschool I've seen, even if it was in her home," Marie said.

"Don't tell me that. I was hoping to start Nora wherever you found a place for Leah. Lori was *so* good," Pam said.

"She's left a lot of parents wondering what to do."

Peter jogged up to our little circle, but he was looking behind us.

"Did they wear you out already?" asked Marie.

"Not exactly."

"Here. Sit." Pam patted the ground next to her.

Again Peter's gaze briefly focused behind me. His eyebrows met momentarily then smoothed. "Marie, can you hold Melody? Eva wants to play." He held Marie's gaze longer than necessary and then his eyes darted to a spot behind me again. Marie's eyes followed then locked on Peter's for a fleeting half second.

I shifted Melody and started to turn when Peter's hands gathered Melody up. Instinctively, I pulled back. "I'm fine, really."

"Nonsense. Take advantage of an extra pair of hands when they're around," Marie said extending her arms.

Peter, his hands still around Melody, raised his eyebrows at me.

"All right." I released my hold and watched Peter hand Melody to Marie. She snuggled Melody comfortably into her arms.

Peter grabbed my hand and pulled me up and toward an open patch of green. His calloused, work-worn hand pressed comfortably against my palm. Peter's brother, David, and four nephews stood in a half circle facing his other brother, Rick, who cocked his right arm back behind his ear before sending the football flying. Immediately, the half circle of figures sped toward the ball. David reached and stretched his fingertips, ready to receive the pass. Just before his hands touched the worn leather, Craig leaped up and swatted the ball away then landed in a heap on the lawn. "Way to go, dude!" Tim praised Craig, bumping knuckles with his brother.

"Give an old man a break," David said.

"Rick is throwing now. He'll call out a point value before throwing the ball," Peter explained. "If you catch it, you get the points. When you get to five hundred you can take his place."

"Yeah, I played this in college."

"Great, find a spot, then." He released my hand.

I found an empty space behind two of the boys.

"Seventy-five," Rick said and launched the ball over Craig and Tim. It spiraled straight toward me.

Adrenaline surged through my legs and carried me forward.

Simultaneously, Craig, Tim, David, Ben, and Peter all turned and sprinted after the ball's trajectory.

I raised my arms heavenward. Pigskin brushed against my fingertips before a solid *thunk* hit my legs. I strained to stretch over Tim's crumpled form as I fell forward. Then, chin tucked to my chest, I rolled down my spine, landing with a sprawling thud on the carpet of jade.

I lay there for a moment not moving, afraid to disturb the airy feeling lightening my chest. A small giggle bubbled up my throat. The laugh faded, but a wide grin remained. It felt good—this cheerful feeling. Peter's shadow fell across me.

"That smile looks good on you," Peter said, extending a hand and pulling me up.

"Woo-hoo!" David yelped and ran over to us. The others weren't far behind.

"What was that?" said Craig.

"You gotta at least give her some points for style!" Peter said.

"No ball, no points," Rick said.

Tim, standing off to the side, said, "Sorry, Eva, I tried to stop, honest."

I finger-combed grass from my hair. "No worries."

Five year-old Adam chased the wobbly ball. "I got it, Daddy!"

"Good job, buddy. Give it to Uncle Rick." David tousled Adam's hair.

"Come on, let's go!" Craig said.

"Sixty." Rick pulled back and fired once more.

I felt pretty good that I had ended up with a hundred and eighty points when David caught the final pass to earn his five hundred. Crickets serenaded and twilight shadows danced long and lean by the time we claimed our blanket-covered seats.

"Are those two seats taken in the middle of your row?" A woman with luxuriantly thick, dark-auburn hair and a trim yet shapely figure stood next to me. Dark brown eyes contrasted with her flawless ivory skin.

Something about her seemed familiar. I squinted to get a better look. Maybe not. It was nearly dark, after all. "Excuse me?"

"Those two seats, are they taken?" She pointed again with her left hand.

My gaze stuttered at the ring on her finger, the ring I thought I'd never see again, and I inhaled sharply. A heavy flowery scent jolted my memory as waves of nausea cascaded over me. Florence . . . of course I knew this woman! My mind suddenly flashed back to the memory—crystal clear now.

"What do you mean there are no refreshments?" a deep male voice hissed.

"There was a little confusion as to who was actually supposed to place the order and it just never happened," another man answered, less sure of himself.

"The elementary school choir opens the ceremony in five minutes with a five minute introduction followed by a twenty minute speech, which gives you thirty minutes to come up with something to serve ninety people."

"Sean, that's impossible," the nervous man said.

"Florence, could you help us out here?"

"I don't know what you want me to do. We should be in our seats. People will start staring," a woman's melodic voice answered.

I swiveled my music stand to the left in order to match faces to the voices. One man in a well-cut black suit with thick black hair towered over another man who was wiping his bald head with a folded white handkerchief. The woman named Florence, wrapped in a black leather blazer with deep red-brown hair framing a porcelain complexion, hung on the taller man's left arm—Sean, I assumed.

I held up my hands, cautioning my students to remain seated and silent, then crossed to the trio. A flowery perfume assaulted my senses. Florence's presumably. "I overheard your dilemma," I began, "Perhaps I could help. I'm in charge of a party this weekend and have the refreshments for it at home in my freezer. It's pineapple slush with a variety of home baked cookies. I live five minutes from here. After the choir sings and the children are seated with their parents I could hurry home and get the food."

"Perfect. Lou, you go to the store and pick up napkins, and . . . " The man looked at me. "What do we need?"

"Clear plastic cups."

"Darling, we have to take our seats now." Florence pulled Sean to the chairs reserved for dignitaries.

"Flori, I found . . . two seats." The voice faltered on the last two words as I snapped back to the present.

My cheeks burned. I clutched Melody tighter and buried my face in her blanket, clenching my teeth against the sudden queasiness in my stomach. I didn't need to turn my head to know Sean stood just behind me.

"These are so much closer, darling." Florence stepped in front of me, enticing Sean to follow.

Please just go. Please just go. Please just go.

A jean-clad leg moved into view next to Florence, and the nightmare suddenly got even worse. "Eva. What a surprise. I'd like you to meet my fiancée, Florence."

I forced my chin up and met the steady gaze of his deep blue eyes.

"Florence, you remember Eva?" His ever-polite voice intoned.

"No." She shook her head slightly.

"She saved us at the Boise project unveiling," Sean prompted.

A sharp pain stabbed my chest. Not only was he engaged to this woman after three weeks, but he hadn't even told her about me. About our engagement and upcoming marriage that should have been six weeks from now. It was as if I never existed in his personal life, only as a rescuer in a business setting. Would he remember me only as a caterer for other events we had attended as a couple?

"She did?"

"She magically provided refreshments for ninety people, remember?"

She wrinkled her forehead. "I still can't place you."

"Are you going to teach kindergarten here again next year?" Sean asked as if we were old friends who had happened to cross paths. Nothing more.

I started at the question for a different reason though. No, not at the question, but at the sincerity in his voice. Just for a moment he was the Sean I fell in love with, the Sean I had planned to spend eternity with. His tone quieted my rioting stomach, dulled the pain under my rib cage. I swallowed. "No, enrollment is down so my position is . . . unnecessary."

Concern flashed in his eyes.

I refused to have him pity me. Worse yet, if he had moved on to the point of another engagement, I wouldn't let him know I'd spent the last three weeks wearing a single pair of track pants and that I had only left the house to get the mail or turn the irrigation water into my property. Summoning all my emotional strength, I said, "I'm interviewing in Boise next week." From the corner of my eye I caught movement as Marie looked up from the book she was reading to Joseph and Leah.

Shock then a sudden curiosity registered in his deep sapphire eyes. "You are?"

"Now I remember." Florence flipped her hair back over her shoulder and pointed a perfectly manicured finger at me. "You conducted the children's choir."

"So the old and new fiancées meet." Peter's voice sounded flat. I hadn't noticed when he'd appeared at my elbow.

Florence turned to face Sean, a question forming on her open lips. Sean gave Peter a piercing look then clutched Florence's elbow and led her up the aisle.

CHAPTER 12

"You okay?" Peter asked as he sat in the seat next to me that had been mysteriously vacated sometime during the exchange.

I watched my hand tremble as it rubbed Melody's back. "You didn't need to do that," I whispered through clenched teeth. I couldn't trust my voice.

"You're upset with *me?*"

"The situation was awkward enough already!"

"I'm sorry, Eva," he said quietly.

I searched the diaper bag for a bottle, saying nothing.

"I was watching out for him, but not her. I didn't want you to have to go through seeing him tonight."

Watching him? Suddenly the pieces fit together. I faced him. "He's been here all evening. You and Marie before—with the eye conversation—you asked me to play five hundred to divert my attention!"

"I was coming to ask you to play when I saw him. Then I just didn't take no for an answer."

"And you've been *watching* him. Why?"

"I told you. I knew it would be hard for you to see him so soon."

"I don't need a big brother."

He rolled his eyes, and in that instant, another puzzle piece slid into place. Peter had said "her" like he had known there would *be* a her. Had he known about Florence? "You knew he was engaged! How?"

Peter sighed. "I passed them on the way in."

"And he told you they were engaged?"

"No. I didn't talk to them at all."

"How did you know, then?"

"I didn't know they were engaged."

"Then why were you so worried?"

"Let's just say it didn't look like a first date."

I quickly dismissed that visual picture. "Oh."

Peter mumbled something that sounded like, "I thought an engagement this soon was a little far-fetched, even for Sean."

"He was dating her pretty seriously when we met." Why was I defending him? If I had driven my car, I could have escaped by now. "They've known each other a long time."

"So I gathered from his *introduction* of you." Peter sounded more than a little disgusted with Sean's formality.

How long had he been listening? "Let's talk about something else."

Peter's eyes scanned the rows in front of us then said, "So Boise, huh?"

"Pride made me blurt it out." I swallowed hard. I *would not* cry here. I measured formula into a warm bottle of water. "I couldn't let Sean think I hadn't moved on when he obviously has."

"I'm not so sure about that."

"She's wearing my—his ring."

"I saw his expression when he realized it was you sitting here."

"So much for a new topic of conversation." And so much for an evening free from thinking about Sean. I replaced the bottle's lid and shook it vigorously, watching the powder dissolve.

A crewman dressed in black jeans and a black hoodie scaled a mini Eiffel Tower.

"So why Boise?" Peter asked.

"That's where I taught before moving here. Plus, it's the only place I've been able to get an interview." I positioned Melody comfortably in the curve of my right arm and began feeding her.

"Do you have family there?"

His words stung my conscience. "No. I wanted to keep Melody closer to Suzette, but all the surrounding districts have finished hiring."

"Things can always change."

"Yes, but I can't wait and hope for a job. I have Melody to think about." I wiped the milk drizzling down the corners of her mouth then looked back at Peter. "Wherever we end up I'll have to find a babysitter. That may take some time."

Worry, along with the residual nausea from my encounter with Sean, troubled my stomach. I dreaded moving to a new town and trying to find someone I could trust to take care of Melody.

The music faded and reminders against flash photography resonated over the audience. The opening prayer was given and a soloist sang "The Star

Spangled Banner." Determined to regain some portion of peace tonight, I took a deep breath and pushed my concerns to the back of my mind to deal with later.

"You sure you're okay?" Peter asked.

I shrugged and focused my attention on the actors flooding the hillside. A young couple dressed in 1800s attire paused in the spotlight trained on the steeply sloping temple hill.

Suddenly, Peter put his arm around me, gave my shoulder a little squeeze, then relaxed his arm across the back of my chair.

My heart jolted, and my mouth fell open. I stared at his profile while he kept his eyes on the story unfolding on the hillside. I had to be honest with myself. Nothing about Peter's arm around me made me uncomfortable. Shouldn't it, though? I was only three weeks out from a breakup—from calling off a wedding!

Marie turned just then, and after taking in Peter's arm and my startled expression, she grinned.

Peter looked over at my stunned face and quickly removed his arm.

Then an image of Sean and Florence filled my mind, along with a spark of anger. If Sean was *engaged*, I didn't need to feel guilty about an arm around the shoulder. Besides, it was only another one of Peter's brotherly gestures. He knew the whole Sean and Florence episode had upset me. It wasn't like we were on a date. Not one he or I had initiated, anyway.

When the pageant ended, I gathered the diaper bag and tucked a quilt securely around Melody. As we left the temple grounds, I kept my eye on Dave and Pam trying without success to remember which way the car was. I listened to the two families chatter about people they knew in the pageant. Melody fussed, and I stopped to check her. Discovering she had spit out her pacifier, I helped her latch onto it again before looking up. Unfamiliar voices now surrounded me. I looked ahead expecting to see the Finches, but they weren't there. I turned my head to the left, then the right. Only strangers. I wished I had a better sense of direction. It seemed like I was always getting turned around. I walked a few steps forward searching the crowd of people, not wanting to get further behind, then wondered if I should bear a little right as part of the throng nearest me was doing. Still, I recognized no one.

A feeling of apprehension swept over me. *Stay calm; they can't be that far ahead. Concentrate. Think about the walk from the car to the temple lawn.* Faces and bits of conversations flashed through my mind but nothing indicating what route would lead me back to the cars. Perfect. Pam and David were surely wondering where I was. Maybe they had a cell phone. I could call them . . . if I knew their numbers. Which I didn't. "Perfect," I mumbled.

"It *is* a pretty night."

I jumped at the sound of Peter's voice.

"Looking for Dave and Pam?"

"Yeah. I lost track of them," I said, startled.

"I told them I would take you home since I live next door." He put his palm on my back and guided me through the human maze.

"I need Melody's car seat."

"Got it," he said swinging his left arm so I could see the carrier he grasped. "Do you get lost often?"

Chagrin warmed my face. I hoped the darkness hid the color from Peter. "More often than I'd like," I answered honestly.

He smiled and led me through the jumble of cars and people.

* * *

Peter's car came to a stop a few feet from the garage door. "Stay there." He held his hand up as if stopping traffic. Then he quickly exited the car and reappeared at my door and opened it for me.

An SUV pulled in front of the house as I emerged from Peter's car. My stomach rolled. Even in the dark of night I knew that car. "Sean." I chewed my fingernail.

"You don't have to talk to him, Eva," Peter said, his gaze solemn as he watched the car come to a stop in the driveway.

I opened the back car door and reached inside for Melody.

"I can send him away," he added.

I squared my shoulders. "I'm not afraid of him. Will you take Melody inside, please?" I handed the baby carrier to Peter. "I want to get this over with." I wiped my sweaty palms on my legs and moved toward Sean's Escalade.

Sean got out but stopped about a dozen feet from his car when he saw me approaching.

I spoke first. "What do you want?"

Sean's eyes looked beyond me, following Peter. "Be careful. Shaggy seems a bit protective."

"Consider me warned." I spun and began walking back toward the house.

"Eva, wait."

I stopped and turned around. "Is Florence in the car?"

"You know she is."

I measured each word carefully. "Why are you here?"

He held out a business card. "I just wanted to give you the contact information for Terrence Singleton. I'll help you with any fees."

I took the card with a trembling hand and quickly jammed it in my pocket. "I don't want your money."

"How about a job?"

I pivoted, preparing to leave.

His words came in a rush. "I need a dinner catered the second Saturday in August."

Of course he did. But still, I couldn't bring myself to simply say no. "I don't know."

"Everywhere I've tried is booked that weekend. I'll pay you ten percent more than the going rate."

I faced him with clenched teeth. "I don't need your money."

"Please . . . I need you."

"It's painfully clear you don't." I nodded toward the Escalade.

He took a deep breath. "Eva, you're a better caterer than all of them."

"Is that what you told Florence?"

The carefully controlled mask dissolved. The tendon along his neck tightened. "Did you expect me to pine away forever?"

"A month would have been nice."

"You moved on pretty quickly yourself." He bobbed his head toward the house.

"Peter is just a friend."

He laughed. "Open your eyes."

"I did that three weeks ago!"

"You—" The sound of the passenger door opening cut him off. He momentarily closed his eyes. When his eyelids opened, he cleared his throat. "This summer hasn't been what either one of us expected. I need an answer. Will you do the dinner?"

I hated that he knew I needed the money. I also hated to leave him in a bind. If we'd still been engaged, this would have been one of the three dinners I'd agreed to cook for this summer. He must have found a caterer for the other two. I lowered my voice to a menacing whisper. "Only if you tell Florence about us. She deserves to know, and it should come from you." At normal volume, I added, "When you've done that, have your assistant call me with the details." I spun around before Florence could greet me and strode toward the house.

Quietly I closed the front door and crossed to stand in front of Peter, who was sitting in the rocking chair.

"What was that all about?" he whispered while he rocked Melody.

"He gave me the business card for his friend specializing in family law." I held my hands out for Melody, and he passed her to me. "Thanks, Peter. I'll see you at church tomorrow."

"It looked like he upset you." I glanced though the window directly across from the rocking chair. Peter had left the lights off while rocking Melody, so the full moon had clearly illuminated our confrontation.

I started up the stairs. "He wants me to cater a dinner." I turned away quickly, not waiting for his response. "I'll be back in a minute. I need to get Melody to bed."

I was surprised to see Peter sitting at the piano when I returned from putting Melody in her bed. He began softly playing a tune I vaguely recalled hearing before. I stood at the corner of the baby grand trying to remember where I'd heard it. "That was you playing the night Sean brought me home, wasn't it?" I asked in amazement. "I thought it was a CD."

He nodded. "Rebecca didn't play it for you?"

A twinge of pain contracted my chest. I shook my head. "Is it one of her compositions?"

Peter stopped playing. "Wait here. I'll be right back." Deftly, he stood and walked to the bookcase where Rebecca stored her music.

I stared at the empty piano bench as if seeing it for the first time in the five weeks I had lived here. I never had learned to play very well, not like Rebecca. And now I avoided the piano—a reminder of her absence. Music was Rebecca. Slowly, I sat on the bench and tenderly picked out notes from the sheet music that had been there since the day I'd moved in. It was the song Rebecca had written on the last Christmas before our parents' deaths. She had played it whenever one of us needed comforting. Peter stepped behind me with a folder. I stopped playing.

He set the folder down, sat on the bench next to me, and began playing. I stared. "When did you learn that?" I asked.

"After I heard Rebecca play it at our Christmas party. She loaned me the music." He picked up the folder.

I recognized it from the night he had tended Melody. "Is that the music you were playing before?"

"I guess Rebecca wanted to surprise you. She asked me if I would play it at your reception." He opened the folder and handed me a half sheet of paper. "This is the note she gave me with the music."

I looked down at Rebecca's flowing script. Loneliness engulfed me. I took a breath to calm the ache and then tried to swallow the lump forming in my throat.

Pete,

Watching you and Eva entertain the cousins at Melody's blessing inspired this song. The children's faces were radiant with delight (and I might add, so were yours!). To me this piece expresses Eva's giving and joyful nature. I know it might be a little awkward for you, but I'm hoping you might still consider playing this at her reception. Please, for me Pete?

Love you like the big brother I never had,

Rebecca

A tear spilled over, ran down my face, and dropped onto the crisp white paper. "Sorry." I quickly wiped my eyes. I could feel Peter watching my reaction. The pieces of the puzzle slowly came together as Pam's words and disbelieving face from earlier tonight echoed inside my head—*His . . . sister. That's what you think?* I raised my eyes to meet his. "Playing this song at my wedding would have been awkward for you?"

Peter slowly nodded. "Remember how your ring surprised me at the Christmas party?"

I nodded, although the word *stunned* would have been more accurate.

"After I helped you move in August, I decided to ask you out the next time I saw you." His voice was low, careful.

"We didn't see each other again until Christmas," I said, understanding dawning on me.

His hands made fists. "I was in New Mexico for work until December." He took a deep breath, uncurling his fingers. "Eva, I know you're going through a lot right now. I'm gone more than I'd like, but if you'll let me, I'd like to be here for you."

"You already are, Peter."

"I want to be more than your friend."

I looked down at the ivory keys. "I don't know if I'm ready to date anyone."

"I wouldn't bring it up so soon after all you've been through, except I'm only home two or three days a month, and I know you may be moving soon."

I turned back to him. "That wouldn't change if we were to start dating."

"We can continue like we have been. I don't mean to make dating a big production. I just want you to know I'm interested in you as more than a neighbor." He took my hand in his.

My pulse hastened.

"I want to get to know the giving and joyful Eva, not just observe her."

His hand on mine coupled with my pounding heart made concentrating difficult. "Why the hurry?"

"One day soon Sean is going to realize what he gave up and come back."

"He's moved on. Remember Florence?"

He looked down at my hand in his. "The self-centered woman wearing your ring?" His thumb rubbed my empty ring finger.

My stomach twittered. "The strikingly beautiful woman Sean almost married before he met me?"

His warm brown eyes met mine. "Almost. That's the danger."

"Do you really want to take on an emotional wreck right now?"

"If it means I can hold your hand, then definitely, yes." He winked at me and squeezed my fingers.

The teasing released a bit of the ache inside me. My mouth twitched as I felt myself begin to smile. I remembered how I'd felt playing five hundred with him in Manti. "You're sort of impossible to resist."

"That's what I'm counting on." He stood, crossed to the door, and looked back. "I'll be over to walk you and Melody to church in the morning. Plan on dinner at my parents' after church. Suzette will be there too." He winked at me and left.

I remained at the piano, too astonished to move. My hand still felt warm where Peter had squeezed my fingers. A tiny spark of happiness had lighted in my heart, but I felt as if I were reaching for a flame just out of reach. I wanted to bring my spark closer to the flame, but it would require leaping, and I was scared. I didn't want to get burned, not again. *It's not leaping, Eva, it's falling,* my dad's voice counseled. *You must fall into faith.* I must be getting tired if I thought my dad's counsel on faith could apply to dating. Peter had said he wanted to keep things casual. So that's what I would do. I'd focus on getting to know Peter, learning about his work. Since he was home so infrequently, that ought to take a while. His constant business trips were another worry. Sean had constantly conducted business on the phone afterhours, but at least he hadn't been gone most of the month. Did Peter have to be gone that much, or did he prefer it that way? If he had a family, would he be home more? I needed to know before I let myself be anything more than friends with him.

CHAPTER 13

I was buckling Melody into her stroller when Peter arrived dressed for church, his low ponytail and goatee an odd juxtaposition to the white shirt and tie he wore. I was finding his outdoorsy, rugged look more and more appealing.

Peter lifted the stroller down the porch steps and immediately began peppering me with questions. What was my favorite holiday, movie, book, band? With each question I persuaded him to answer too. At least I was learning something about him, even if it wasn't how he felt about balancing work and family. Peter paused a moment, but I was too slow at forming a question before he asked another. "What was it like growing up with only one sister?"

"We were either best friends or couldn't stand each other. Sometimes both in the same day."

Peter maneuvered the stroller around a parked car. "Did you split everything fifty-fifty, like chores and time with parents?"

"One time we did use masking tape to put a line down the middle of our room. I don't remember counting up chores or anything like that."

"I'm guessing you didn't get along as teenagers."

"I don't remember fighting much then. We're four years apart so I was seventeen when she turned thirteen. But when she was eleven and twelve and trying to wear my makeup, I wasn't the most understanding big sister."

"My older brothers didn't have make-up; they had Legos. They could make cool ships with them. I'd come home from kindergarten and play with their creations and make a few modifications. When they saw what I'd done . . . hoo boy!" He turned the stroller up the walk to the church doors.

"My turn to ask something." There was one question I had been particularly curious about since he had avoided it when I asked before. "How does your consulting business work?"

He glanced up at the doors before answering. "There's not time to explain it right now." He glanced at his watch. "Church is starting." He held the door open while I pushed the stroller inside. Raising an eyebrow to let him know I'd be asking again later, I followed him inside.

Midway through sacrament meeting I repositioned Melody and straightened my cramped arm. Right away Peter transferred the baby to his arms. She fussed. I watched, tense, ready to take her back. He softly rocked her until she grew quiet. Peter appeared completely at ease holding Melody. I sat back and breathed deeply. Peter looked over at me. "Thanks," I whispered and rubbed my elbow, sore from holding Melody so long in one position.

"You know we've started a massive gossip chain by being seen together at church," Peter said as we walked to his parents' home after church.

Here was the opening I needed to find out about his work. "Is that why you travel so much? To escape the gossip?"

"Work is definitely not an escape. I'd rather be here with you and face the gossip."

That was something at least. "Why can't your clients come to you? Then you wouldn't have to travel so much."

"When I'm on site, I learn things I can't get any other way."

"Couldn't they set up a camera or something?"

"I need to be inside their organizations, interacting with the people, gaining their trust."

"Do you have two personalities?"

"What do you mean?"

"The Peter I know is pretty easygoing, but the Work Peter you're describing sounds more intense." Was that side of Peter more like the ladder-climbing Sean?

"Maybe I do. At work, a lot of people are depending on me to get it right, to fix things. So when I'm there, I'm completely absorbed. And when I come home, I come home. I leave work."

I liked that idea, but I was becoming ever more curious about why he was so reticent to share anything about his occupation. "Can you give me some specifics about your job? Like, what are the most common behaviors you work on correcting?"

"Oh no you don't. I told you, I'm home." We turned up the walk to Jayne and Larry's home. The smell of roasting chicken welcomed us from the front porch. Once inside, Suzette claimed Melody, and Jayne fired off instructions to Peter and me. We set the table and listened to Jayne relate the latest giggles from her grandchildren. Energy danced from her dark brown eyes and spiky red hair. I loved the way her face showed signs of frequent smiles and laughter.

Peter's father, Larry, also smiled often but seemed content to watch Jayne take center stage. When Jayne took Peter in the other room to show him something, I asked Larry, "So who does Peter work for?"

"You mean which government agency?"

"He has a government contract?"

"Sure. That's how he gets paid."

"What other clients does he have?"

Larry looked surprised for a split second but recovered so quickly I wondered if I'd read his expression correctly. He gave me half a smile. "Oh, that's a question better answered by Peter himself."

"I've tried a couple of times but he always deflects my questions."

"He probably finds you more interesting than the people he works with."

Peter reentered the kitchen just then. "Right, Pete? Eva's much more fascinating than a description of your paperwork."

"Yeah, by a long shot." A look passed between father and son, a silent communication I didn't understand. "Mom said to get everyone to the table. Dinner's ready."

Dinner conversation was lively, but it never steered too close to the topic of Peter's work. I found myself surprisingly at ease. Everyone wanted a chance to coax Melody's newest development, a smile, but only Suzette was rewarded for her effort.

Suzette beamed when Melody's face at last erupted into an open-mouthed smile. As I watched her softly talking and cooing with Melody I wished again that we could stay close. This was what Melody needed. I couldn't give her a father, but I wanted to keep her near her grandma.

After dishes and saying good-bye, I pushed the stroller ahead of Peter down his parents' front walk. At the sidewalk I turned right.

"Taking the long way home, or do you have an errand to run?" Peter paused where the front walk and sidewalk merged.

Immediately, I turned the stroller and started down the other way then wished I hadn't when I saw Jayne's and Suzette's puzzled expressions.

Warmth flooded my cheeks. I walked faster. My own actions betrayed my miserable sense of direction.

"It's a good thing Ephraim is small . . . you'd eventually find your way home," Peter whispered as he fell into step beside me.

I didn't respond as my mind turned back to finding a way that I could stay near Suzette.

"Did dinner upset you?"

I blinked. "Far from it."

"You haven't so much as looked at me since we left."

I turned my head and looked at his face that I was finding increasingly handsome. I didn't have to tilt my head back to gaze at him like I did with Sean. "Sorry. I'm a bit preoccupied right now."

"Sean?"

"What? . . . No." I noted the worry swimming in his eyes. "Back there . . . watching Suzette with Melody. I don't want to take that away from either one of them." Or myself. I desperately craved a sense of family too. I sighed. "I don't know how to magically make a teaching position open up."

Peter smiled.

"What?"

"I'm just glad to see you deliberating how to stay close to me." With one swift movement he acquired control of the stroller and was holding my hand.

My stomach fluttered, and I chastised myself. I couldn't become attached with my future so uncertain—and with my past so close on my heels.

"What do you like to do in your spare time?"

"The interrogation continues?"

"I only get to see you a few of times a month so I have to cram two weeks' worth of getting to know you into a couple of days."

And so his questions continued right up to the porch. My porch. I was beginning to consider Rebecca's house my home. The minute the stroller stopped, Melody complained.

As I lifted her from the stroller, Peter opened the front door and asked, "Did you serve a mission?"

"Hold on. I need to change Melody before I answer any more questions."

Peter was gone when I brought Melody back downstairs. I walked around the stone fireplace and into the kitchen to see him rummaging through my fridge.

I smiled. "Hungry already?"

"Just looking for a bottle to warm up for Melody. It's about time for her to eat, isn't it?"

"I don't have any premade bottles." With my free arm I pulled a bottle out of the cupboard, filled it with hot water, and scooped in the right amount of formula. Peter shifted Melody to his arms and wandered back to the living room while I shook the bottle.

As I stepped around the fireplace, I heard Peter's hushed velvet voice serenading Melody. He stood in front of the picture window looking across the shade-covered lawn of early evening.

Hearing my approach, he turned. "I'd hoped to continue the interrogation, but it's time for me to go."

"Work?"

He nodded and slid Melody into my arms. Then he placed his hands on my shoulders.

A feeling of calm settled over me as I looked into his eyes.

"Don't forget me while I'm away."

"Where are you off to this time?"

"It's a wilderness retreat of sorts in a remote place few people know about." He looked at his watch. "I'm out of time. I'll see you as soon as I get back." He opened the door.

"When will that be?"

"Probably the middle of next week." He bounded down the steps, then turned and waved at me before jogging up the slight incline toward his house.

Loneliness replaced the calm. I stayed frozen in the doorframe, visually retracing Peter's empty path. I already missed him. Had I learned enough about his work to be more than friends with him? Thinking back over our conversation I realized Peter hadn't given me any information beyond generalizations. His job description didn't include a single company name, behavioral technique, or specific place. But I had learned that when he was home, he was truly home. And that's all I needed for now.

* * *

Melody woke at five as usual. Only this morning I had already been up for an hour, showered, and eaten. Suzette would arrive soon, but I wanted to feed Melody before I left for Boise.

I carried a warm bottle in one hand and a note from Peter in the other. I'd found the note taped to the milk jug when I pulled it out of the fridge this morning. I sat in Rebecca's rocking chair. I had finally moved it out of her room and into the nursery for convenience at night. I lightly tapped the lamp sitting on the dresser so I could read his words again.

Eva,

I've enjoyed learning more about you. And I've noticed a few character traits we share. I've hidden two other notes around your house explaining these qualities. Hopefully, you'll find this note first so the others will make more sense.

1. Per-sist-ent: adj. tenaciously or obstinately continuing despite problems or difficulties

When I was five years old, I decided I wanted to ride a bike like my older brothers James and Rick, so I asked my dad to help me. One summer evening he spent the better part of an hour following me around the neighborhood with his hand securely holding the back of my bike seat. It wasn't until we reached our driveway again that he let go and I learned I still didn't know how to ride. In dismay, I watched my two brothers turn around and head back out. I looked at my dad, who said, "Sorry, son, you're on your own now. You know how balance feels. It's your turn to try it out." Two hours later, after several falls accompanied by scraped knees and elbows, I rode out of our driveway and down to the corner all by myself.

That lesson of working toward a goal, even when the going is rough, has stayed with me. In my line of work, unforeseen circumstances regularly present themselves. Persistence, with an eye on the goal, gets me through.

As I think about all you've gone through, with the deaths of your parents and now sister, and then breaking off your engagement, I see persistence in you to keep moving forward no matter what. I've seen the heartbreak losing Rebecca has caused you and yet you remain faithful in your testimony of the restored gospel. More than that, you are committed to Melody as if you were her birth mother, even at great personal sacrifice. She's really blessed to have you as her mother on earth.

I'll think of you often,
Peter

I smiled, imagining a five-year-old Peter racing to catch his brothers. His words warmed my heart and I wished I could thank him in person for them.

* * *

A feeling of homecoming spread through me as I exited the freeway for Boise. I'd made good time—only taking one wrong turn along the way. Familiar businesses dotted the landscape. Memories of the three years I'd spent teaching here bounced across my mind, and memories of friendships that

I'd neglected this last year brought a yearning for belonging again. Some of my students' moms babysat, if I remembered correctly. Two in particular I could feel good about entrusting with Melody. I could be happy here again, I decided.

I parked the car and offered a silent prayer of thanks for this opportunity and asked for help to present my best self in the interview. I grabbed my portfolio and exited the car. A wave of heat greeted me. I smoothed my skirt and took a breath to steady my nerves before opening the school door.

A short time later, I sat in the office with Mr. Tyler—who had now checked his watch for the third time in the last five minutes. He absently glanced over at a file on the corner of his immaculate walnut desk.

Anxiety pulsed through my veins and sweat slicked my palms. My explanations must be boring him. I finished my answer.

Mr. Tyler stood, signaling the end of our interview. "We'll let you know." He extended his arm.

"How many more interviews are you conducting?" I asked.

"You're the last."

"Can I expect your decision within a week then?"

He stared at his watch and cleared his throat. "Actually, I have to be honest with you, Eva. The position is filled. The new teacher signed her contract this morning and should be arriving momentarily."

Confusion stalled my response. "How . . . what . . . why interview me if you already hired someone?"

He lifted his hands slightly. "Linda highly recommends you and I respect her judgment."

"That still doesn't explain hiring another teacher before interviewing me," I said, feeling a bubble of anger rise in my chest.

He took a breath and let it out slowly. "The high school hired a new basketball coach. His wife is an elementary school teacher."

Mr. Tyler didn't have to finish; I could guess the rest.

"I'm sure you understand the district's position. She needed a job and our school had the vacancy."

Eager to leave, I extended my hand. "Thank you for your time and honesty."

"Linda was right. You have exceptional skills. Being fluent in Spanish should help you find a teaching position soon. I'll keep you on file in case anything opens up."

"Thank you." I walked out the door hoping to escape contact with the new teacher. My old friend Linda, dressed in her signature fuchsia top, was exiting her car as I entered the parking lot. She waved energetically even as her round figure bounced toward me.

"Eva!" She ran over to me. "So how'd it go? What do you think of the new principal? He's a little stiff but he means well. We'll loosen him up. I can't wait for you to get the choir going again. I was thinking we could cast a musical this year. What do you think?"

I swallowed. "They already hired someone."

"What?" She fairly shrieked. "Oh! He hired you on the spot!" She slapped my shoulder. "You are such a tease. I've missed you. We all have. The other day Walt—"

"They hired the new basketball coach's wife."

Linda drew in a sharp breath then threw her arms around me. "Oh, Eva! I'm so sorry."

I climbed back into my car ten minutes later despite Linda's opposition. I was in no mood for friendly conversation. Pulling onto the freeway, I recalled my optimism of an hour before. It was all gone now. Did Mr. Tyler know how far I'd driven to hear him tell me the position was filled? What a waste of a day. Now I would have to begin applying anywhere I could find an opening.

* * *

Driving up the road to Rebecca's house, I spotted Sean's SUV in Peter's driveway. The garage door was always open so Sean had to know Peter wasn't there. What was Sean up to? I parked in the garage and dashed through Peter's side yard, behind his house, and came out between the house and garage in time to see Sean exiting what I guessed to be Peter's kitchen door. "Taking your own personal parade of homes?" I hoped he registered the venom in my voice.

Sean turned at my words but didn't have the decency to look embarrassed at being caught. "Believe me. This place wouldn't make the cut."

"I never believed you were capable of this."

"Have you seen inside that hovel?" he asked.

"Is the lack of leather sofas and granite countertops offensive to you?"

"So you haven't been inside. Maybe there is hope," he mumbled. "By the way, there *is* a leather sofa. At least I think it's leather under the dust and pile of jeans."

His superiority irked me. "What does the American Bar Association think of attorneys breaking and entering?"

"The door was open." He opened it now. "Take a look around."

I bit back my curiosity to peek inside. "I wasn't invited and neither were you."

"You're so obviously on the rebound, someone has to look out for you."

"Snooping around my neighbor's home when he's gone is creepy."

"Shaggy himself is pretty creepy."

"You don't even—"

"If you don't believe me, take your own little tour." He gestured to the open door.

"It's been a really long day and I need to get back." I pulled my cell phone from my pocket. "So can you please leave or do I have to call the police?"

"Will you open your eyes! I'm trying to help you."

"Oh, you've opened my eyes today. This little stunt . . . I have no words for it." I punched nine on my phone. "Now would be a good time to leave before I hit the two ones."

"Just take a look," Sean pleaded.

I made sure he was watching and pushed one.

He reached in the house and pulled the door closed. "Okay, okay. I'm going." He got in his Escalade and called, "Remember, the door's open. You can take a look anytime."

Sean drove away. I stood there trembling from the encounter but strangely free from nausea. I had stood up to Sean and won. Maybe this day hadn't turned out so bad after all. I was halfway to Peter's door before I realized what I was doing. If I went inside, then Sean would win. What was it that had upset him so much? Sean's apartment was fanatically neat, but even he realized that was unusual for a man so it couldn't have been a little dust and some dirty laundry. Sean had called it creepy. Really? Peter's house? I took two more steps toward the kitchen door and halted. This wasn't right. If I wanted to see inside Peter's house, I could wait until he came home. I spun and crossed the yard back to my house where Suzette waited with Melody.

After Suzette left, I needed something to keep me from wandering back over to Peter's house so I was grateful when I remembered Peter had left Rebecca's last composition for me to learn. Now was the perfect time. I opened the piano bench and a little flutter of excitement came over me. Another note from Peter lay atop the music. I picked it up and sat on the bench. Quickly I drank in the message penned on a white sheet of paper in Peter's careful black script.

2. Pa-tient: adj. The ability to endure waiting or delay without becoming annoyed or upset or to persevere calmly when faced with difficulties

When I was ten years old, my parents put me in charge of four rows in the garden. I had to plant, weed, and harvest them. I decided to plant a row each of peas, beans, carrots, and corn. I excitedly planted the seeds and watered them in. Then the waiting began. After a week of checking and finding nothing, I promptly forgot about my seeds for three weeks (it's a good thing it rained a lot during one of those weeks). When I finally remembered to check my rows, the little plants were choked with weeds. My mom helped me weed the first row and then left me to finish the other three by myself. With Mom's help, the first row only took half an hour. But it took me three days to weed the other three rows.

The pattern of weeding, forgetting, weeding continued until harvest. My mom helped me wash and prepare the vegetables for freezing. I was so proud of my shelf in the freezer that winter.

By helping me exercise patience, my parents instilled that value within me. It serves me well at work and in my personal life. I see you persevering patiently, even faced with your current challenges, and I know that when Rebecca placed Melody in your trust, she knew this about you too.

Wish I could be there,

Peter

His insightful words stirred something deep inside me. Our childhoods had been very similar. Maybe that was why I felt drawn to him after such a short time. Or maybe it was the way he noticed so much about me. He'd picked up on my directional dysfunction right away. Not even Sean knew about that. Peter grasped things about me I tried to keep hidden from others, as well as qualities that others simply didn't notice much. It felt comforting in a way. Rebecca was the only one who really knew these things about me, and now she was gone. I reread the note and smiled. My gardening habits were similar to ten-year-old Peter's. I needed to do some weeding this week.

CHAPTER 14

Friday was the fourth of July. Marie had grown up in Mount Pleasant and her family gathered annually for the celebration beginning with a community Pancake Breakfast at the park. Once again I found myself swooped into their plans. I was grateful for Marie's friendship. More and more I realized I had never put down roots in Ephraim by establishing any relationships beyond work. My whole life had centered on Rebecca and Sean, and both were gone now.

After breakfast Monday morning I decided to reclaim the garden from the weeds overrunning its rows. I strapped Melody into her stroller and headed out. A gentle breeze stirred the summer sun's hot rays. A white square of something flapped on the end of the hoe hanging on the garage wall. I took the hoe down and removed a piece of paper taped to its handle.

My heart twittered in anticipation, hoping it was a note from Peter. It'd been a week since I'd found his last note. The one that reminded me I needed to weed the garden, and I still hadn't done it yet. Maybe Peter should have extolled the patience of plants waiting to be weeded. The garage's dark interior made reading impossible. Outside in the bright sunlight I squinted to make out Peter's words.

3. Trust: n. Confidence in and reliance on good qualities, especially fairness, truth, honor, or ability. Also, responsibility for taking good care of somebody or something

The summer I turned seventeen my dad's older brother had knee surgery. His children were grown with jobs of their own and couldn't come back to run the farm for him so he asked me to help out. Up to that time I had only worked on the farm occasionally when we visited. I didn't know very much about how it operated. My uncle said he trusted me to get the job done because he knew I was a hard worker. He placed a lot of responsibility on my young shoulders, but he was always there to teach me how to do something new. His confidence in my ability to learn and get the job done created a willingness in me to live up to the trust he placed in me.

    Trust is an important facet in both our lives. My colleagues trust me implicitly and I them. Rebecca trusted you to raise her daughter. And I trust that you are missing me as much as I am missing you.

    Missing you,
    Peter

I read the note twice, absorbing every word. Carefully, I folded it in fourths and slid it into my back pocket. Peace was the feeling I associated most closely with Peter. I missed him and the peace he brought. And yes, I admitted to myself, I missed Peter. I gazed at Peter's house. What was in there that could have disturbed Sean so much? I set the hoe aside and turned Melody's stroller toward Peter's house. I had to know. Besides, I told myself, I wanted to check his fruit trees to see how close the apricots were to ripening. I hesitated a few feet from the back door. Peter's note burned in my back pocket. Spying on Peter was how I showed my trust? I turned to go home, but not before the back door opened and Neil appeared.

Where was his truck? "Neil?"

"Hey, Eva." Shock registered across his face.

"Unbelievable. Sean dropped you off, didn't he?"

Neil pulled off a very good confused look.

"Neil, you've got to talk to him. He can't be checking up on my neighbors like this."

"Why does he want to?"

"I don't know. Because he has long hair, a goatee, and apparently dust. Sean couldn't get over the dust in the guy's place. Oh, and the dirty laundry. He said it was creepy."

"You didn't go inside?"

"Why would I? He's not home. He never is." He didn't need to know I'd come over to do precisely that. I wasn't behaving any better than Sean and Neil. Melody fussed and I began moving the stroller back and forth.

"That would explain the dust. But it still doesn't explain why Sean would go through this guy's house. I think you're dating him."

That was something I'd never admit to Neil. "Neil, I'm a mess. The last thing I need right now is a boyfriend—including Sean. I'm desperate to find a job. I even interviewed back up in Boise."

"But here you are at this guy's back door."

"Melody needed a walk, and," I pointed to the fruit trees in Peter's yard, "I was hoping I could harvest some of the fruit from these trees since he's never around. I wanted to check and see if the apricots were ripe. So will you talk to Sean? He might listen to you. I nearly had 911 called before he would leave."

"Yeah, I'll talk to him. But you and Melody should seriously stay away from this place."

Neil too? I must have looked puzzled because he said, "It'll be easier to convince Sean if you promise to stay away."

"He's starting to scare me."

"You don't have to worry, Eva. I'll talk to him. He won't come back, but you've got to keep your promise."

How would either of them know if I didn't? But I said, "*I* don't go through other people's houses when they're not home. Now if he invites me over, I—"

"He won't. Not in there." His cell phone rang. "That'll be Sean wondering where I am. He arranged to pick me up a couple blocks away so you wouldn't see his car." Neil fetched the phone from his pocket and answered it, "*Espere.*" He shoved the phone back in his pocket.

"Sean would understand wait better if you used Icelandic or English."

"I like to mess with him."

"I don't understand why he sent you. He's already seen the place."

"He wanted a second opinion."

"So what's your opinion?"

"You should stay away from here, and Sean too. I gotta rock-n-roll." Neil turned and jogged away, leaving me to decipher the confusing mass of anger, fear, and curiosity tumbling around inside my head. The thought of Sean sending Neil to check out Peter's place had at first angered me. But maybe I should be afraid. Was this how stalking started? I knew no woman had ever rejected Sean before—and wasn't that what I had done when he had given me his ultimatum and I'd given him the ring back? I didn't want to believe that was possible. But if that's not what was happening then I had to believe there was something terribly disturbing inside Peter's house. And that didn't make sense either. Nothing in my interactions with him and his family led me to believe there was anything twisted about him. And then there was the peace I felt whenever I was with Peter. Sean's (and now maybe Neil's) perception of Peter didn't mesh with my experiences. I remembered Peter's note. Trust. Peter would be home in a day or two. I could be patient and talk to him then. I could trust him and stay out of his house until then. But when he did come home, I could also be persistent in finding out why Sean and Neil had both warned me off his house. As I turned to take Melody back home to weed the garden, I noticed Peter's garage door was now shut and locked. Odd, it had been open when I found Sean over here last Monday. Neil must have closed it, I decided.

* * *

A week and a half had passed since my Boise interview and I remained unable to get another interview in the state of Utah. Teaching school would give me more time with Melody, but if I couldn't find a teaching position, I would have to secure other full-time employment. This morning these worries clamored for my attention, and I paced the front room with Melody, softly rubbing her back while I pondered our circumstances.

My last paycheck would be direct deposited in three and a half weeks. It was time I considered other options—the most immediate being the dinner Sean wanted me to cater. As much as I hated to accept money from him, I knew it would be foolish to refuse. It was too bad the area couldn't support another full-time caterer. A restaurant/catering business had just closed its doors last month, and I was positive that had contributed to Sean being desperate enough to ask me to do the dinner later this summer.

Still walking the floor with Melody, I began reviewing bills and options. I could use my ten thousand dollar trust fund to pay off my car. Then Melody's nine hundred dollar monthly social security benefit would probably cover the house payment, groceries, and maybe utilities. But how would I pay for car and medical insurance? And if I needed to repair anything or buy clothes for Melody . . . I needed a job.

I was weary from mentally cataloguing finances and employable skills while repeatedly wondering when Peter was coming home and if I should explain about Sean and Neil rummaging around in his house. With a sigh, I paused. Without knowing it, I had walked to the kitchen. Cool air from the swamp cooler moved past me toward the barely open front room window. Ninety-eight degrees, the local radio station reported at ten o'clock this morning. It was quite a bit hotter now at four o'clock. The mulberry tree towered just off the back porch, blocking the sun's scorching rays. I only had to turn off the cooler for ten minutes to feel the temperature rising to meet the outside heat.

I glanced at the sunlit garden then turned back to the oven, deliberating. Baking always melted away my anxiety. Knowing July was a terrible time for my preferred stress reliever, I set Melody down in her swing and assembled flour, sugar, salt, oil, and a few recipes on the counter next to my Bosch. The mixer had been an expensive acquisition, but I'd never regretted the purchase. I attached the dough hook and measured ingredients into the mixing bowl to start the sponge for bread. While I waited for the yeast to do its job, I retrieved my largest mixing bowl and started a triple batch of muffins. Pam's and Marie's children would certainly enjoy those. I looked over at Melody; she was happily playing with the toys on her swing's crossbar while I worked.

When the sun dipped behind the mountains, I put Melody to bed and opened all the windows to move the evening breeze through the house. Even then the kitchen hovered above eighty degrees. I used a paper towel to mop the sweat from my forehead and down the back of my neck. A loose French braid kept my hair up.

"Smells good," Peter called through the kitchen window.

My heart gave a little leap at the unexpected voice from the dark outside my kitchen. Peter was back.

"Hungry?" I tried to sound casual.

"What are you baking?" Peter stepped through the sliding glass door, hair pulled back in his usual short ponytail.

"Um, bread, cinnamon rolls, muffins, rolls, and some cookies." I turned a muffin tin upside down.

"That's quite a welcome. I could smell it all the way over at my house when I pulled in an hour ago." He picked up a freshly glazed cinnamon roll. "May I?"

"Sure." I hadn't seen his headlights through the kitchen window. I must have been rocking Melody to sleep. "So it took you an hour to work up the courage to come over, huh?"

He bit into the still-warm roll. "Mmm, that's good." He swallowed then continued. "Hardly; I've been traveling all day. I really wanted a shower first."

I could smell a trace of his aftershave amid the chocolate chip cookie aroma.

"What's going on?" He gestured to the bread covered counter, cooling racks piled with cookies on the table, and pans of rolls and cinnamon rolls balanced atop the stove burners, not to mention the baskets of muffins filling the sink cavities.

"When I'm stressed, I bake."

"Stressed?"

"The Boise position was filled before I got there."

Peter opened his mouth as if he were going to say something but stopped and grinned instead.

"What are you smiling at?"

"Boise's too far away." He shrugged and took another bite.

I busied myself scooping dough onto a cookie sheet. "I have to find work. I only have one more paycheck from last year's contract." The oven timer beeped. I took out a tray of cookies and replaced it with the one I had just finished. I shut the oven door and turned around. Peter was standing inches away from me.

"You'll find a spot," his tenor voice assured.

I looked into his warm eyes and breathed in his aftershave. It smelled fresh and woodsy. Suddenly, I wanted him to understand my frustration. "I don't want to take Melody away from Suzette. I didn't want to be a working mom, but now I am. It just seems like I try so hard and come up against a wall every time." I walked around him to the table and began lifting cookies from the pan onto the cooling rack.

Peter followed. "It'll all work out. Patience, remember?"

I smiled as I remembered his letters. "Like planting a garden?" I set the cookie sheet down and turned toward Peter. "Thanks for the notes. That was a fun way to get to know you better."

He took my hand and squeezed it. "I didn't want you to forget me."

My heart gave a flutter. "Have you had dinner?"

He looked at the cinnamon rolls.

"That's not dinner. I have some leftover lasagna." I rummaged through the fridge until I found the casserole dish. "Want some salad too?" I asked, snagging the bowl of lettuce before the door swung shut.

"Sure."

"Hand me a tomato."

His eyes searched the room.

"The bowl on top of the fridge." I motioned with my head while I scooped lasagna onto a plate and then placed it in the microwave to heat. Oregano and garlic mixed with the bakery smells. I cleared a spot on the crowded table and set down the hot lasagna, bowl of salad, and a glass of water.

Peter inhaled deeply. "You should open a restaurant."

"You're just hungry. Sit. Eat." While Peter ate, I prepared another cookie sheet for the oven. Having Peter there calmed me immensely. Could Sean have really seen something disturbing in Peter's house? It was more likely that Sean was trying to scare me away. There was nothing creepy about Peter. Sean's recent actions, however . . .

Peter drained the last liquid from his glass. His plate and bowl were now empty. I sat in a chair next to him. "So . . . you're not rushing off anywhere tonight?"

"Nope. What are you doing with all of this food, by the way?" His arms made a wide arc.

"Freeze some. Give away the rest. You should sample everything and take what you want. Since you don't have to rush off tonight, I have something to tell you, but I don't know where to start."

"This sounds serious." He picked up a cookie. Shouldn't he be worried if he were hiding something? Instead he was mindlessly eating.

"It's the other reason I had to bake tonight. I couldn't think about it anymore. So here goes." I took a deep breath and plunged ahead. "Sean went through your house."

His hand stopped midway to his mouth. "He did what?" Peter shouted.

I winced, hoping he hadn't awakened Melody.

He looked at the baby monitor. "Is Melody asleep?"

I nodded. "He went—"

"I got it the first time." Peter snapped the cookie in half. He took a deep breath and then slowly spread his fingers wide on the tabletop. "Did you go through it with him?"

"No. I couldn't. Not without you. Sean said the door was open. I know that's no excuse but—"

"What he saw disturbed him," Peter finished for me.

I felt all the blood drain from my face. "I wanted to believe it was the dust and dirty laundry," I said more to myself than Peter. Sean had been right.

"So you did go in."

"N-n-no. S-Sean—" I couldn't stop stuttering. What was it Sean had seen? I'd trusted Peter. He'd babysat Melody for me. An urgent need to get him out of my house came over me. I willed myself to speak normally. "I'm really tired. All that baking . . . I need to go to bed. Can you go? We can talk tomorrow."

"You look like a fish that just found out the fly he swallowed was a hook. Whatever Sean told you . . . I think you better see for yourself." He stood and held his hand out to me. "Trust me one more time, Eva, please?"

I wanted to know what Sean had seen—but could I trust Peter? I looked at his outstretched hand and stood. "Let's go." I hated that my voice shook.

I stepped past Peter's hand out into the shadowy night and continued to his now familiar kitchen door. "I'm supposed to be helping remodel this house as part of my rent." He turned the knob and stepped through the door. I followed. Peter flipped a light switch revealing skeletal kitchen cupboards. Unhinged cupboard doors balanced at odd angles along the lower cabinets and walls. The upper cabinets exposed barren shelves coated with sawdust. The counter next to the sink housed Peter's entire kitchen collection. A small frying pan balanced precariously atop a saucepan of similar size. A stack of paper plates and cups and various utensils completed the set. The stark contrast against Sean's carefully designed kitchen was accentuated even more by the lack of appliances. A tackle box and a few spools of fishing line decorated the top of a dorm-style fridge squatting in the far corner. Three fishing poles rested between it and the wall. A hot plate served as stovetop.

"In here," Peter said.

I followed Peter past the dining room table—a table saw—and into the living room. The dusty leather couch and a card table sat on bare floorboards. "This is it." Peter pointed to the lone wall decoration. A cork board hung at a peculiar angle secured with what looked to be five two-inch nails placed irregularly around its border. Above it, red spray paint screamed the word *Remember*. Newspaper clippings covered the bulletin board. I skimmed the headlines: "Beheadings Used As Scare Tactics by Mexican Drug Cartels," "Zetas Drug Cartel Killed Rivals," "Mexico's Drug-Related Violence," "Mexico's Drug Cartels Have New Target," "Bodies Hanging from Bridge in Mexico," "Brutal Mexican Drug Gang Crosses into US."

I felt as though an invisible slime were slipping down my spine. I shuddered. This is what Sean didn't want me to see.

"Eerie, huh?"

I didn't say anything. One of the articles was dated this last Sunday. I looked down at the table to see what newspaper he'd cut it from. There were no newspapers, scissors, or pushpins.

"I'm researching the criminal mind, specifically the scare tactics they use," Peter explained.

"Scare tactics?" I asked.

"These Mexican drug cartels behave like a pack of wolves." Peter pointed to the bulletin board. "The leader is the alpha male. The rest of the gang falls into order behind him. But they're always conniving and fighting, trying to impress the dominant leader, even if they've never met him. The alpha is careful about revealing himself. Usually only a handful know him by sight." He paused for a moment and I tried to reconcile all the feelings swirling inside of me. Then he continued. "They're pretty animalistic. Oftentimes it's the second in command who overthrows the alpha. Because of this, the alpha has to constantly keep his 'family' in line with threats or scare tactics. He might withhold payment for a job, claiming it wasn't done right, or leave ominous messages, even kidnap family members. Whatever it takes to keep everyone in line."

My head was spinning. Peter seemed so casual about the whole thing. Keeping newspaper articles to study was one thing, but displaying them like this was more than creepy or eerie.

"But why hang it like that?"

"To remind me how dangerous these people are. They have a kill-or-be-killed mentality." Peter studied me like he was calculating the effect of his words on me. He needn't have worried; the solemn intensity of his words convinced me he spoke the truth.

"And the spray paint?"

"The owner wants that wall covered anyway." He gestured to a pile of wainscoting leaning against the opposite wall.

Peter seemed so normal, not anxious or upset. As he spoke my fear began to dissipate. "This research is for work?" I asked.

"All my research comes back to work one way or another."

"What client are you doing this research for?"

"You *are* persistent. I'm glad I was right about that." He took a deep breath and looked at the ceiling and back to me, contemplating, I supposed, where to start. "It's not for one specific client. It's personal."

The dichotomy between the alarming wall décor and the calmness I felt whenever I was with Peter mystified me. Was this how his clients felt? "What do you do as a behavioral consultant?"

"Well . . . put simply, in my job I do a lot of observation, then I get really involved in a hands-on sort of way, and when the timing is right, I call in my team."

I started to ask another question but he put a finger over his lips, silencing me. "The values I shared with you in my notes are an integral part of not just me but my work." Then he pulled a small box out of his pocket. "There's one more I waited until tonight to tell you about. And since you've seen this," he gestured to the sinister bulletin board, "I think now's a good time."

I stared at the tiny box and swallowed. "Is it in that box?" I wasn't sure our relationship was at the gift stage, especially jewelry-box-looking gifts.

He took the lid off and handed the box to me. "A little reminder for you that I am always true to my word." A sterling silver locket with an ornate swirl design lay against a black velveteen background.

The back of my throat tightened. "Thank you, it's beautiful. But how—"

"How is it a reminder? Open it."

I opened the hinged cover to reveal a tiny compass no wider than one of my fingers.

"A compass always points north. It's always true. You can trust it just like you can trust me." He pulled the locket out of the box, unclasped the silver chain, and walked behind me to fasten it around my neck.

I touched the cool metal, tracing its design.

"And now for tonight's date."

"Date?" I asked, confused.

"The Finch family reunion is a week from Saturday, and we're in charge of an activity."

"*We* are?"

"Yep. I'm not missing a date with you just because it's my family reunion. My mom would never forgive me for skipping it, so you and I are hosting the Saturday afternoon activity." He pointed back and forth between us. "Besides, Aunt Sue is coming up for the activities on Saturday, and if she's invited, so are you and Melody."

"Where exactly is all this taking place?"

"They're all camping up Fairview Canyon by one of the lakes." He took my hand and led me outside. "We're organizing an orienteering course for the teenagers and adults and a simple compass maze for the younger children." As we neared my house the smell of chocolate chip cookies greeted us. Peter added, "Your bakery will provide the incentives. We just need to teach you how to use your compass." He indicated my locket.

"This really works?"

"Sure does. Although for the orienteering course, I'll lend you one with degrees on it. But tonight I can teach you the basics doing a children's course."

"In the dark?"

"A compass knows which way is north even in the dark. Something you should remember about me, also, but I brought a light." He picked up a flashlight off the porch swing. "Hold your hand out flat with the palm facing up toward the stars and put your compass on it."

"Are you sure you're not trying to keep me from getting lost all the time?" He chuckled. "This compass charm is going to help you in so many ways."

"That lost hiker could have used one of these."

"What lost hiker?"

"The one up Ephraim Canyon last week. You must not have heard since you've been gone. A hiker went missing for a few days. He was pretty banged up from a fall. He's convinced someone pushed him over the edge of a really steep, rocky hillside. The authorities aren't so sure. They think he may have had heat exhaustion and stumbled over the edge himself."

"Does he have any broken bones?" Peter asked with real concern.

"I don't think so. At least the article didn't say."

"Heat exhaustion wouldn't make you think someone pushed you. I'm glad I convinced the family to camp up Fairview Canyon for the reunion," Peter said. "Sounds like it's a good year to stay away from Ephraim Canyon."

Peter taught me the basics of charting a course and following it with the compass, which was a fairly easy concept to grasp. I retrieved some paper and pencils from the house with a few home-baked goodies for the treasure part of the hunt, and we tested our courses on each other.

"Think you can handle this?" Peter asked in between bites of his cookie. We were sitting hand in hand on the porch swing after several successful maze attempts. "I think I've got it. It's kind of fun. It's something I'll have to try with my students—wherever I teach next year." I sighed.

"You'll find a job." He squeezed my hand. "So . . . were you serious about me taking what I want out of there?" He jerked his head toward the kitchen.

"I think you'd better. I've seen your cupboards."

He pulled me up. "A cinnamon roll for breakfast sounds good."

Peter helped me package the baked goods and take them downstairs to the freezer I'd brought from my apartment. Then we loaded the dishwasher and hand washed what was left. When the kitchen was at last clean, Peter picked up his plate of goodies and placed his free hand around my shoulders.

My arm tingled with his contact and I yearned to relax into the hollow of his arm, but I resisted the impulse. My life was too uncertain to rush into a relationship.

He gave me a gentle squeeze. "It's good to be with you, Eva. See you in the morning." He slid the door open and disappeared into the night.

Melody would be waking soon so I wandered to the living room to wait. I'd experienced so many emotions tonight. Joy that Peter was home. Apprehension to tell him about Sean. Fear that Sean was right. Even a streak of terror when I viewed Peter's spine-chilling research. If tonight had happened to Rebecca, I would have told her to stay far, far away from Peter. Why was it different when it happened to me? I sensed Peter wasn't telling me everything, but I couldn't deny the peace I felt when we were together. I felt safe with Peter. Besides, I hadn't committed to anything more than getting to know Peter. I stroked the locket between my thumb and forefinger. A feeling of comfort filled my heart, and a smile played at the corners of my mouth. Tomorrow we could start fresh, without Sean's interference hanging over us.

CHAPTER 15

THE NEXT MORNING MELODY WAS sitting in her swing watching me unload the dishwasher when Peter tapped on the door before sliding it open.

"I thought we could pack a picnic and head up Fairview Canyon to learn some orienteering." He looked at Melody. "Will she be okay with that?"

The thought of carrying the baby up and down the mountain while learning to navigate with a compass made my biceps burn. I remembered the ache from Sunday when she wouldn't let me sit down all through Sunday School and Relief Society. "It's more a question of how long my arms can handle hiking around with her." I opened the fridge. "So . . . by 'we could pack a picnic,' do you really mean me?"

He looked sheepish. "I'll help." He picked two apples out of the bowl on the table. "These look good. You tell me what to get and I'll go to the store. My fridge doesn't have anything but a quart of sour milk. I haven't been shopping yet."

"Let's see what I've got." I pulled out some leftover chicken, mustard, Miracle Whip, and lettuce.

"Do you have some sort of chest pack you strap on to hold Melody?" Peter asked as he sliced four pieces of bread.

"Good idea. I think Rebecca got a Snugli at her baby shower. Finding it is the tricky part." I fished a tomato out of the bowl on the counter. "Why don't you check Melody's closet while I finish the sandwiches?"

I was in the basement searching for a small cooler when Peter called my name. "I'm down here," I yelled.

The rhythmic thumping of Peter's footfalls descended the stairs. "I think I found it." He held out a tan pocket of material trailing long loops of matching fabric and other straps.

"Now we just have to figure out how to use it." I eyed the contraption as I picked up a cooler.

"No problem," he said, turning the Snugli and tugging at various straps.

Peter eventually deciphered the tangled web of material, and I was pleasantly surprised at how easily I could move around with Melody in it.

As we transferred Melody's car seat to Peter's sandstone Jeep, I asked, "So do you have some sort of fetish with compasses?"

"What?"

"Your car—"

"—Is a Jeep Compass, yeah—I mean no. I mean it's a Jeep Compass but only because the Cherokee cost too much. This works fine for a bachelor."

His line of reasoning sounded like me talking. I ducked in the backseat to buckle Melody in.

After an hour's drive, Peter pulled into a parking lot above Huntington Reservoir. Clusters of pine intermingled with swells of tall grass and patches of dirt surrounded the lake. I positioned Melody in the Snugli while Peter grabbed the cooler and compasses. He led us around the lake and into a stand of aspens before stopping.

"You learned the basic principles of orienteering last night." He handed me a compass. "See how the ring of numbers around the compass star moves? And notice how the numbers end at 360?" He paused while I experimented with the dial. "The numbers represent degrees. For a longer course it's important your path doesn't veer off your destination angle. By keeping your compass aligned with the proper trajectory number, you can make minor adjustments in your trail as you go."

"Uh, okay."

"Keep your focus in line with the target and you'll arrive at your goal." His elbow nudged me. "That's another tidbit about my work for you to consider."

Peter devised several courses using boulders or bushes for objectives. After about the fourth target, I began to comprehend the pattern of directions, degrees and steps. Then Peter pulled out a map and showed me how to apply those skills to a map.

Peter and I traded off with Melody. As long as we walked, Melody was content to be in the Snugli. At lunch I spread a quilt and laid her on her back to play while we ate.

Around two thirty we collected our things and headed back. I hoped to let Melody have a nap before dinner with the Finch clan. Peter glanced at me a couple of times as we made our way down the winding canyon road. His fingers gripped and released the steering wheel in drumming fashion. Finally, he cleared his throat. "Just so you know, Pam can be very enthusiastic." He looked at me out of the corner of his eye then back at the road. "I mean she gets really excited when I bring someone to dinner with me."

"Oh." I was unsure where this was leading.

"Don't be bothered by anything she says." Worry lined Peter's face. "She means well; she's just concerned about me." His voice was so low I wasn't sure I heard him right.

"I went to the pageant with her, remember? I'll be fine."

"I just want you to know there's no pressure from me."

"You make it sound like she's going to propose for you."

"Given an opportunity, she just might." He clenched his jaw and stared intently at the road ahead.

I laughed.

"What?"

"You weren't this nervous to bring me to dinner at your parents' house."

"That's because Pam wasn't there." He continued to stare straight ahead. "Maybe we should play it up. I—"

"No." His tone carried a note of finality. Then his voice softened and turned earnest. "I like to keep things real, Eva. If it's not sincere I don't think my emotions could handle the roller coaster." His eyes bounced furtively from the road to me and back again.

Tender affection for this man swelled my heart. Instinctively, I brought our interlocked fingers up and brushed his hand against my cheek. I closed my eyes and breathed in the warm scent of his skin tinged with cedar. Reluctantly, I placed our hands back beside the gearshift.

He squeezed my hand three times.

I touched my locket. A comforting calm settled over me. Like his reminder, he was close to my heart.

* * *

From a block away I spotted the cherry-black vehicle parked in front of my house. I looked at my and Peter's hands intertwined and a knot began to form in my stomach. I knew when Peter recognized the car. "What?" He said it like an expletive. Sean's unwelcome presence stirred deep reactions in both of us.

I looked over my shoulder to check on Melody. Her chest rose and fell in the rhythm of peaceful sleep. As the car slowed to turn down my drive, I observed Sean sitting on the front porch.

The churning started in my stomach. My hands grew cold.

"What does he want?" Peter came to a stop a few feet from the garage.

I shrugged my shoulders. "Better get this over with." I withdrew my hand from his grasp.

He clasped my hand again. "I'm coming with you."

"No." Peter's presence would create enough of a stir without a face-to-face encounter.

"You're white as a sheet. You obviously don't want to see him." His thumb stroked the back of my hand.

Pulling my hand away, I said, "I don't want things more complicated than they already are." But in my heart I knew it was too late for that now. How did Sean always show up when I was with Peter?

Melody shifted, and Peter and I both turned toward the backseat. His voice dropped to a whisper, "I'll take the baby in and get her settled, and then I'll join you—and Sean, if he's still here." His eyes held mine until I nodded.

I sighed. "Okay." Maybe I could manage to get rid of him quickly and avoid confrontation.

"Let's go." Peter brushed a few errant strands of hair behind my ear before opening his door.

My already nervous stomach fluttered. With shaking hands I opened the car door and headed for Sean while Peter unloaded the car seat with sleeping Melody. I willed my feet to go faster but their sudden weight slowed my forward progress while the firecrackers in my stomach persisted. What could he possibly want now? If this visit was about the catering job, I had specifically told him to have his assistant call me with the details. Or he could have called or texted me. That would have been preferable to this.

"Hi," Sean said as I stepped onto the porch. He brushed back a lock of his wavy black hair.

As awkward as seeing him was, a little place inside me still longed to be the girl who could brush back that errant lock of hair. I pushed the feeling aside and said, "I thought your assistant would call me." I really wished I didn't need the money this job would give me.

He looked at me with a puzzled expression.

"The dinner. In August."

"Right." Without waiting for a response he continued. "Anyway, I'm not here about that. Neil and I were in Boise this weekend, and we ran into Linda."

"Oh." Just what I didn't want—him feeling sorry for me. Why had he even bothered to come here?

"Tough break about the coach's wife and all."

Peter walked up the steps then, and I moved to open the door for him. He stopped, gave Sean a steely glare, and said, "Guess I better start locking my door." Then he continued inside, pushing the door closed with his foot.

"You're still seeing Shaggy?" Sean hissed. "You have no idea what's—"

"Inside his house? You mean the bulletin board covered with newspaper clippings below the red *Remember*?"

Shock registered across Sean's face. "I told you to stay away from there." He frowned.

"He's a behavioral consultant studying the criminal mind."

"Are you sure he's not the criminal mind?" Sean asked.

"You're the one going through another person's property."

"Eva, I'm concerned—"

"You've seen I'm jobless. You don't approve of my current company. I think it's time for you to leave." I moved swiftly away from the stairs and held out my arm indicating his exit path.

"Eva, wait."

"No, you wait." My tone escalated above a polite conversation level. "You and I chose not to make our lives together. Be civil or leave."

He took a deep breath and stood. "I have a lead on a teaching position."

I stared at him without moving. This felt even worse than his pity.

"Aren't you even curious?"

"Why are you doing this, Sean? I can take care of myself."

"I'm just trying to be nice. Neil's sister is a principal in Las Cruces, New Mexico. With recommendations from both Linda and me, Neil was certain his sister would want to talk with you so he called her. When she heard you were fluent in Spanish, she requested an interview."

I spotted Sean's laptop backpack behind his chair. He followed my eyes.

"I set up an interview on Skype for you today at four."

"Today?" I looked at my watch. Four o'clock was in fifteen minutes.

"I've been trying to call since last night. Do you answer your phone anymore?" He picked up his backpack.

"New Mexico?" I struggled to keep my voice even.

"Yeah. We need to get set up." He gestured toward the door.

A sick feeling started in the pit of my stomach. "Why would I want to live in Las Cruces, New Mexico?"

"You need a job." He nodded at the door. "Eva, please. Let me do you a favor. I feel bad for how much pain I've caused you."

I stared at him, not moving. "I don't know anyone in New Mexico."

"You didn't know anyone in Boise." He opened the door. "Besides you do know someone—Neil."

I followed Sean into the house. "Las Cruces is all but in Mexico. Melody will never see her other family members." And I definitely didn't want to see more of Neil.

Sean surveyed the room. An inexperienced person would assume Sean hadn't heard me. I knew better. He'd heard me but wouldn't acknowledge my opposition. "I'll set up my laptop here. That way you can sit on the couch for the interview." He turned to look at me. His eyes took inventory from head to toe. "There's no time for a shower."

His cursory assessment irked me. "You can explain that I've been hiking all day and didn't know about this interview." I chewed my fingernail. Sean could always make me feel self-conscious about my appearance. I never worried about it much with Peter, who would be coming out of Melody's room anytime now, I realized.

My breath came short and shallow. Apprehension rolled through my stomach at the thought of them in the same room, and I sank to a sitting position on the piano bench.

"Just put it up in one of those twist things you do. That should work," Sean decided about my hair.

The door to the baby's room opened and closed. I met Peter's gaze as he started down the stairs—his eyes never left me as mine darted between him and Sean.

"Eva, time is wasting." Sean uncoiled a super long Internet cable. "Where does the Internet come in?"

"In my bedroom."

Sean walked down the hall trailing cable behind him as Peter sat beside me. "What's going on?" he whispered.

I couldn't explain all this to Peter right now. And there was no derailing Sean. It would be easier to agree to the interview now and then send him on his way.

"Sean talked to my friend, Linda, in Boise. They found a new position and set up an interview for me today at four." Maybe if Peter thought Linda was behind all this he would accept the situation.

"In Boise?"

I shook my head. I needed to turn the conversation. "Don't you have some shopping to do? You could do that while I interview."

Peter tracked Sean's movements as he reentered the living room, turned on the laptop, and began typing in his Skype account information. "Can't he see how upset he makes you? You don't have to let him do this."

I took a deep breath. "I'm fine, really." I yawned. "The interview shouldn't take long. And maybe if I can get rid of both of you, I'll be able to take a nap."

Peter studied me. "I'll be back at five thirty." He squeezed my hand then silently slipped out the front door.

Without a word to Sean, I escaped to my room where I exchanged my jeans and T-shirt for a blue skirt and white eyelet blouse with gathered sleeves. I carefully arranged the locket under my collar. My fingers traced the chain and rested on the cool silver. Immediately, I felt calmer. I could get through the interview. It would be good practice for my uncertain future. I stepped across the hall into the bathroom and quickly ran a brush through my hair before smoothing it back into a twist.

"Eva." Sean rapped on the door.

"Ready." I moved past him, ignoring his impatient eyes, and continued to the living room. "Show me where to sit."

Sean handed me a headset and explained the basics. The laptop sat on the coffee table. On the screen, a man and woman each sat in a chair placed in front of a large desk.

"The man is Mr. Ramirez. He's the district personnel director," Sean said. "Ms. O'Keefe is the principal I told you about."

The interview went well enough. I even found myself enjoying the process. Who wouldn't love telling people their opinions and being asked for more? At the conclusion, Mr. Ramirez said I was their final interview and that he would call in an hour with their decision.

I took the headset off. "Guess I better turn my phone on."

"That would be helpful."

I walked to my room, unplugged the cable, and began coiling it as I walked back to the coffee table.

"I think they were impressed," Sean said.

Avoiding his eyes, I turned off the laptop. No energy remained for me to continue this façade.

"I think it's quite likely they will offer you the position."

I placed the laptop in the backpack. "Which pocket does this go in?" I held up the coiled internet cable.

"You don't want to discuss the interview?"

I slid the cable into his backpack. "Where's Florence?"

"Why are you evading my questions?"

My careful control over my temper slipped a little with each word he spoke. I gathered the last of the electronic equipment and thrust it at him. "Why are you here, Sean?"

"Aren't you even a little excited about the possibility of a new job?"

I chose my words carefully. "A new job, yes. You didn't answer me."

"It's rather obvious why I'm here."

"Actually, to me it's not. I got jobs all by myself before I ever met you, and I can do it again." I carried his pack to the door.

"You quit your job to marry me. I thought you would appreciate my help in rectifying the situation."

"My position was eliminated due to changes in enrollment. I would be out of a job with or without you." I handed him the bag.

"Can't you accept some help?"

"Does Florence know you're doing this?" I asked.

He shook his head.

"Have you told her about us?"

"I started to."

I raised my eyebrows.

"She assumed you're married now because of Melody. She thinks we were engaged sometime before she met you in Boise."

"She deserves the truth. A marriage demands complete honesty." I opened the door and Sean finally picked up the cue, slung his backpack over his shoulder, and walked through the door.

On the porch steps, he turned with a frown. "You know, Eva, you're overreacting about this."

"You're one to talk. At least I haven't been sneaking around Florence's apartment."

CHAPTER 16

I QUICKLY STEPPED INSIDE, SHUT the door, and leaned against it. Apparently Sean was suffering from a belated sense of guilt over our breakup. Not enough to accept Melody and try again, only enough to help me get settled into a new life far from Peter. But I didn't need or want that kind of help. New Mexico and Las Cruces, no less!

I curled up on the couch, longing to escape into sleep. Two sharp raps on the door as it opened dissolved that fantasy.

"Eva, turn your phone on."

I sat up. Sean's towering frame was black against the bright light from outside.

"I just tried to call you." His eyes scanned the room for my phone. "Oh."

"Where's your cell?" He didn't wait for an answer but strode past the rock fireplace and into the kitchen.

I followed him.

His eyes searched the kitchen. "It must be in your bedroom." He marched down the hall.

I waited, knowing he would return with my phone in hand.

"Here, keep this by you. Enough of this self-defeating behavior."

I took the phone. After a moment's silence, I said, "You're right, Sean." I stroked my locket with my free hand as new resolve flowed through me.

"Finally, a flicker of hope."

I looked up into his confident blue eyes and met his gaze. "I won't go along with whatever you say anymore. I gave the ring back. You have no obligation toward me."

"We were discussing you setting yourself up for failure."

"Precisely. I only went along with the interview to avoid a confrontation with you. I don't—no, I *won't* work in Las Cruces, New Mexico." I braced myself for the argument.

"Be reasonable. What other option do you have? Most school districts start in five or six weeks."

Stay firm but calm. "That is *my* concern."

"You could teach there for a year while you work to get hired somewhere in Utah the next year."

"I'll handle it."

"Your judgment as of late seems a bit impaired." He hooked his fingertip under my silver chain then let if fall. "Jewelry didn't used to make such a big impression on you, as I recall."

Anger pulsed through my veins, flooding my neck and face with heat. How dare he! Very slowly and through clenched teeth, I said, "You're free to live your life without me. I'd like the same courtesy." I clutched the cool metal of the compass against my palm and instantly knew I would not move from this house. "Thank you for your efforts. It's time you left," I said in an overly polite tone and extended my arm toward the front door.

"I only have your best interest in mind," Sean said with an edge to his voice.

"Melody is my priority now." My hands formed fists at my sides.

"She ruined our life together and now she's going to ruin yours. Is she worth it?" he spat, his eyes filled with skepticism.

A seething fury unlike any I'd ever felt coursed through me. My hands shook. "Get out!" I shrieked.

My shrill tone shocked me but left Sean paralyzed, speechless for once. In all our time together I had never yelled and especially not at him. It was his treatment of Melody—my daughter—that raised such a vehement response.

"Need some help, Eva?" Peter's voice. I hadn't heard his panther-like entrance through the sliding glass door.

Sean focused on Peter. "Look at the guard dog you spend your time with now. What are you thinking?"

I gasped. How could he attack Peter like that? "My life is none of your business."

"I can't stand by and watch you sabotage yourself."

"You have absolutely no right to make decisions for me."

"You need intervention. It's like watching someone run for the edge of a cliff."

Where was all this coming from? Why couldn't he leave me alone? That queasy feeling that always accompanied an argument with Sean began its creep. I wanted him gone. "Go. Now."

Peter came to stand beside me. "It's time for you to leave." Peter's voice was soft, commanding.

Sean turned, appraised Peter's solid stance, glanced at me, and muttered, "Another example of your impaired judgment. You should be kicking Shaggy out. At least take the call." Then he walked around the hearth, through the living room, and out the front door while I stared after him in silence.

As the front door closed with a near slam, I looked at Peter. "Hey." I tried to smile but couldn't quite move it past my trembling lips. I took a step toward the table but my knees gave out. I grasped the back of a chair as Peter put his arm around my waist to pull me up. "No, I want to sit." My insides felt like warm Jell-O. With his arm for support, I pulled a chair out and collapsed into it. Peter pulled a chair close to me and sat down.

"You're early," I managed.

"Um, late really. The dinner starts at five, not five thirty."

I almost smiled at that. Poor Peter, he was always late. My cell phone sounded. I didn't recognize the area code on the view screen. It wasn't Sean. I took a deep breath. "Hello?"

"Ms. Black?"

"Yes, this is she."

"This is George Ramirez. We've made our decision and would like to offer you the fifth grade teaching position at Ms. O'Keefe's school."

I took in a breath and expelled it before answering. "Thank you for your consideration, but I will be unable to accept the position at this time." Peter, who was watching, gave me a quizzical look.

"I don't understand—"

"I have some family concerns that make it impossible for me to move to New Mexico." The slightest trace of a smile played on Peter's mouth at the mention of New Mexico.

"But we spoke only an hour ago."

"I'm sorry about all the effort you undertook to interview me." Peter took my free hand in his. His rough skin was warm and comforting against my clammy palm.

"You're sure there isn't a way to work around these circumstances?"

"Quite sure." I looked into Peter's eyes, drawing strength from their warmth.

"Well, then, good luck to you in your future, Ms. Black."

"Thank you. Good-bye."

"Good-bye."

I clicked the phone shut and set it on the table.

"New Mexico's definitely too far away." Peter grinned.

"Melody would never see Suzette."

"Or me." He stroked my fingers in his hand.

"Or you." I smiled.

"Can I ask what was it that upset you so much about your visit with Sean—besides the obvious?"

My stomach tightened as Sean's words reverberated in my mind. *She ruined our life together and now she's going to ruin yours. Is she worth it?* "Same as always—his attitude toward Melody."

"The mother bear's instincts were awakened?"

"Something like that."

"Were you and Sean planning to have children?" He shifted in the chair. "You don't have to answer that. I know . . . it's none of my business. I just don't get why a baby makes that big of a difference if you were going to have a family anyway."

I let out a long breath. "Me either." I took the butterfly clip out and shook down my hair. "Yes, we planned to have a family—me more than him, apparently. At first I thought he was just having a hard time adjusting to the shock of starting our marriage with a baby, but over time I realized our attitudes about family in general don't mesh."

The baby monitor came alive with Melody's first whimpers. I pushed my chair out and crossed to the cupboard for formula.

"Do you still feel up to going tonight?"

I considered my emotions and mental state before replying. "I think it would be a great relief to be surrounded by Finches tonight."

He chuckled. "I doubt anyone has ever thought that before."

"Besides, you're the one with all of the anxiety about dinner, remember?"

He grimaced. "You don't have to remind me about Pam. I can't forget."

"I don't think Pam is as scary as you think." I shook the bottle, mixing the formula.

"She scared off Vanessa."

"Vanessa?"

"She's someone I dated quite a bit when I lived in Denver. We'd been seeing each other for a few months when I brought her home to meet the family. Well, you know Pam." Peter paused, searching for the right word. "She's really . . . social."

I tried not to smile. That was a kind description of her busybody skills.

Peter continued. "Anyway, Pam did her usual thing, thinking she was being friendly, but it felt really intrusive to Vanessa. She actually accused me of putting Pam up to it like some sort of trial run to see if I wanted to propose. We stopped dating after that. A year later, it happened again with someone else. So now we all try to run what we call 'Pam interference' when I bring someone to dinner. So yeah, to me, Pam is scary." He reached out and touched my hand. "I don't want her to scare you away."

"She won't. I promise."

* * *

Dinner was a casual affair held in his parents' backyard. The smell of charcoal and sizzling hamburgers hailed our arrival. A pile of grilled hotdogs occupied a small portion of the grill where Grandpa Finch stood holding tongs in front of a jumble of grandchildren clutching paper plates. Peter stopped the stroller next to the back side of the wraparound porch. Jayne and Suzette were just coming down the steps, frosty pitchers of lemonade in hand, as I pulled Melody out of the stroller. From the fire pit at the back end of the yard, Marie called, "Peter, grab the cheese off the counter and bring it over here."

He took the porch steps two at a time, pulled the screen door open, and reached his arm inside. It reemerged holding a plate mounded high with cheddar cheese. "Time to finish the potatoes," he said then placed his fingers on my elbow and guided us toward the split-log benches surrounding the fire pit.

"Hi, Eva," Marie greeted me with a smile. "That's a pretty necklace."

"Peter has good taste."

"What's this? Peter's giving you jewelry?" Pam piped up. Peter nearly dumped the entire plate of cheese into the open Dutch oven. He passed the plate off to Marie as Pam continued. "You know what they—"

"How are you Pam?" Peter didn't wait for a response. Hand on my elbow he steered me toward the other side of the yard. "Suzette wants to see Melody," he explained as we passed Pam.

"It's all right. I can handle this," I whispered.

"I can't," he whispered back, picking up the pace. We quickly reached Jayne and Suzette.

"Evasive maneuvers, son?" Jayne handed a bag of buns to Peter. "Put one of these on each of the children's plates. That ought to keep you occupied for the moment.

"And I haven't held Melody yet." Suzette extended her arms. "You can help put ketchup and mustard on the hotdogs for the younger ones."

I handed Melody to Suzette. Her serene eyes met mine. "Pam doesn't bite," she murmured.

"I know that." I rolled my eyes toward Peter. "He's the one who's jumpy."

"Stick close to Marie, then. She's good at redirecting conversation."

Pam's pregnant form ambled toward us. I didn't think Peter was looking in her direction at all, but as soon as she neared us he picked up a second bag of buns and called, "So who wants a bun?"

The head of every child clustered around Grandpa turned. "Uncle Pete!" The path between Pam and us crowded over with children scrambling to hold on to their plates while exclaiming, "I want a hotdog one," and "I'm having a hamburger so I need a squishy one."

Once the children's plates were full, Peter and I dished up our dinners. Walking toward the conglomeration of picnic and card tables with a few lawn chairs scattered between, we determined that only two empty chairs remained—and that they were between Marie and Pam. Marie saw us coming while Pam was turned away from us as she talked to her son. Quickly Marie slid her plate down two chairs next to Pam and grabbed Rick's plate as he lifted a forkful of potatoes to his mouth. His expression said, "I can't believe you just swiped my dinner!" but Marie silenced him with her eyes and slid down two chairs, pulling Rick with her. Peter and I noiselessly squeezed into the vacated seats. When Pam turned back, Marie winked at us then focused on Pam and said, "Ginny registered Mark with the Shooting Stars Preschool."

"With Zoë the gypsy lady?"

"She made it sound like you were sending Nora too."

"Never! I bet Ginny doesn't even want to send Mark there. But she'd rather register him now and hope something else materializes than risk Shooting Stars being filled if she can't find another option."

"Zoë seems nice enough."

"Oh, she's a sweet spirit." Pam's tone dripped with sarcasm. "She's all into this 'letting children direct their own learning path' philosophy. If Adam had been in her preschool, she would have let him sit on the floor and crash trucks together all day. Hello? He does that at home. I don't need to pay her to watch him smash trucks together and make up some gobbledygook about him acting out all the ideas that are colliding in his mind." She stuck out her tongue and pointed to the back of her throat.

"We're all going to miss Lori."

"How many sessions did she run?" I asked. An inkling of an idea piqued my interest.

"Three."

"How did she schedule them?"

"Two morning sessions and one afternoon. The mornings were Monday-Wednesday and Tuesday-Thursday. Her afternoon session was Tuesday-Thursday." Marie said.

"That's a lot of students." I estimated the number of students and tried to calculate a reasonable tuition amount to decipher how much Lori had been making.

"That doesn't even include those on the waiting list, like me," Pam said.

"Hmm, I wonder . . . " My voice trailed off, but my mind was still turning over the new opportunity before me.

Later, after the dishes and food had been cleaned up, we sat on green, plastic lawn chairs scattered beneath an apple tree. Melody was enjoying her nine o'clock bottle as I mulled over the possibility of opening a preschool in my basement. I was calculating income again when Peter said, "You look deep in thought."

I nodded. "Listening to your sisters-in-law talk gave me an idea."

"Mind sharing it with me?"

"I've only been planning this for an hour and a half so a lot of the details are kind of sketchy." How much of my recently conceived plan did I want to reveal?

"Understood." Peter looked at me, waiting for me to continue.

I took a deep breath. "I'll have to find out a few things about the house and Melody's trust." Marie turned to look at me. "I want to finish the basement as a preschool. Ryan finished the framing, plumbing, and electrical. It just needs to be sheet rocked, mudded, and sanded. And since the sheetrock is mostly there, that cost will be minimal. I'll have to replace the sheets that were ruined from the flooding this spring. Then I can paint and bring in flooring and fixtures."

"Will you qualify for a loan if you quit teaching and start your own preschool?"

"I have a fund from my parents' estate that I was saving for a house." I chuckled.

"What's so funny?"

"Rebecca had money from my parents too. We're both putting it into the same house."

"Ironic," Peter agreed.

"I still have a lot to figure out. I don't know if Melody and I can survive on three sessions of preschool. It just sounds like the perfect fit. I wouldn't have to leave Melody with a babysitter every day." I looked down at Melody, her cheeks drawing in and out while she drank. Her little hand clutched a fistful of my hair. Her other hand rested near mine on the bottle. "And she would still be able to see her only grandma frequently." As I talked, I realized that this was what I wanted to do. I could make this work. I had to make it work. A seed of excitement swelled in my chest. My heart beat, not faster, but stronger, invigorated by the challenge. "Everyone tells me that babies work into a morning and afternoon nap schedule around four months. I could maybe even arrange the preschool sessions to run during her naps."

Marie leaned over Peter and touched my arm. "Oh, Eva, that would be wonderful. You could probably run a fourth session if you needed to. Remember that waiting list we were talking about? I don't know how many are on it, but I can find out."

"Would you please? And can I get Lori's number from you? I want to talk to her." Questions and ideas swirled in my head.

"Sure thing. And I'm sure Rick and the boys will hang your sheetrock for you. They're good at mudding and sanding too." I remembered Rick was the brother with the construction company.

"Looks like you're in business," Peter whispered.

"I still have to go over finances to see if this is even feasible." However, I couldn't deny the enthusiastic flutters inside. I wanted to make this work. I bowed my head toward Melody and closed my eyes. *Heavenly Father, please help me make this work for Melody and me. Help me to know what to do. I feel so alive again. This feels so right to me. Help me know if it is right.* A feeling of peace descended, alighting in my heart. "Oh!" I breathed.

"You okay?" Peter asked.

"Better than okay." I smiled. I felt light for the first time in months. For the first time since Rebecca left me.

Peter put his arm around me, and I leaned into him. An indulgence for the moment, I told myself, but I knew it would be harder to resist next time. I felt at ease with Peter. It wasn't hard to let myself care for him. It seemed so natural. But even so, I had to focus . . . tomorrow. For right now I would enjoy being close to him.

Too soon it was time to leave. Melody finished her bottle and we walked home.

"Don't you get tired of coming and going to work in the dark?" I asked as we said our good-byes in my kitchen while I filled a plate with baked goods for him to take.

"I don't have to leave for a few hours, but I need some sleep first."
I yawned.

"So do you." He took the plate of cinnamon rolls and set them on the table, then took hold of my hand and pulled me into his arms. I went willingly.

My heart beat faster as I laid my cheek against his chest. A feeling of security washed over me. I wrapped my arms around him.

"It was good to be with you, Eva."

Confusion suddenly knotted my stomach, leeching away at the peaceful feeling. What was I doing? I couldn't be worried about dating. I had to put my energy into building a preschool for Melody and me.

"I'll think of you while I'm working," he whispered.

I knew I couldn't let myself get too attached for a number of reasons, but unwilling to leave his embrace, I withdrew my arms and curled them against his chest.

Peter moved his hands to my shoulders and pulled back. "Eva?" His work-calloused finger traced a path of moisture from the corner of my eye, down the side of my nose, and ended on my lips, where he gently wiped it away. "Did I do something wrong?" His face held a pained expression.

"No." I buried my face against the warmth of his T-shirt instead of sending him away.

He tightened his arms around me. "I don't understand."

I took a jagged breath, fighting the tears. "It's too soon . . . too much," I whispered. He dropped his arms. "I'm sorry. I'll go."

"No!" It was out before rationality could stop it.

"What is it?"

I took a shaky breath and pressed my palms against each other, rubbing my hands back and forth. At last I met his gaze. "All of my logic is telling me to back away, but my heart pulls me closer to you. Being with you is effortless and I've never experienced that before . . . It scares me."

He took both my hands in his, a spark dancing across his eyes. "Good."

I stared at his pleased expression. His responses were rarely what I expected, but they were refreshing in their simple honesty.

Then he squeezed my hands and smiled. "See you a week from Saturday." He touched my locket. "Remember me," he said before vanishing through the glass door with catlike stealth.

I could still feel the warmth of Peter's arms around me. Last night all I had wanted was more time to get to know Peter without Sean's interference.

Today Sean's presence had intensified my feelings for Peter. When Peter spent time with me, he remembered and included Melody. It felt natural. It felt like family. That was the difference. Peter planned his time to be with family, and that's what I wanted for Melody. Just like I wanted her to stay close to her grandma. I had to make this preschool work so Melody could grow up with Suzette in her life. The garden's produce would be even more important now, I realized. So I would work on the garden and my new preschool to keep from missing Peter so much.

CHAPTER 17

Monday evening I spent a good amount of time bent straddling a gangly row of pea vines, searching their lengths for slightly plump pods. An apple tree bordered the garden, and beneath its branches a blanket sprawled where Melody lay studying leaves quivering in the whisper of a breeze. Muted thumps sounded as I tossed a handful of swollen shells into an old ice cream bucket. I stood, hands in the small of my back, and stretched. Beads of sweat rolled along my backbone. The evening sun blazed behind me hot as the day. I determined to pick peas before breakfast in the future.

The low growl of an engine slowed in front of the house, and a white king cab truck rumbled down my driveway, stopping inches from the garage door. All four doors swung open. In turn, eight pairs of various sized legs descended to the ground and advanced toward the front porch.

A refreshing cheer lightened my chest. Visitors. "Marie, I'm in the garden," I called and waved my arms. She picked up little Joseph and, with Leah in tow, started toward me. Rick herded the others to the back of the truck.

Stopping at the garden's edge, Marie said, "We've come for family home evening."

I glimpsed Rick strapping on a carpenter's apron while his sons Craig and Tim hauled a five-gallon bucket to the back porch. "Family home evening? Here?"

"Yeah. Our lesson was on helping your neighbor. This is the activity." David's gray minivan pulled in behind the truck.

I picked up my bucket of peas. "And I'm the neighbor?"

"Don't stop picking on account of us." Marie turned at the sound of car doors banging shut. "Pam, over here." She gestured then stepped over the irrigation furrow and into the garden. "Pam and I will help you finish while the brothers get started."

"Started on what?"

"Putting up your sheetrock." She retrieved a folded slip of paper from her front jeans pocket. "Here's Lori's phone number. She's so excited that someone with your teaching background is taking over. She's anxious to talk with you." Marie dropped to her knees and deftly snapped a pod from its vine. "This is how big the pods should be, Leah. Feel the peas inside? They're just right." She pressed her thumb along the curved tip and popped the husk open.

"Peas!" Leah grinned.

Marie's thumb slid down the open pod. Peas collected in the palm of her hand. Nora and Adam bounded over the ditch and up to Leah. Marie held her palm out to the three of them. "Want a taste?"

Each child gingerly grasped a single pea between thumb and forefinger. Leah quickly plopped hers into her mouth. Nora used her front teeth to bite the pea in half while Adam rotated his wrist examining the tiny green sphere from all angles.

"Yummy," Nora said.

"It's sweet," said Leah.

"Peas are ucky," Adam said.

"These aren't," Leah countered.

"Can I help Daddy, now?" Adam pleaded with Pam.

"Oh, all right. But do exactly what he says, Adam. And be careful, please." Adam grinned, jumped the trench, trotted across the yard, and headed up the back porch steps. "He has to be wherever his daddy is." Rather than bend over with her expectant stomach, Pam sat down next to the row and began picking.

Seven-year-old Ruth appeared just then and gathered all the little ones into the sandbox surrounding the massive mulberry tree standing sentinel in the center of the deep backyard.

"I'm beginning to feel like a project." I set my bucket next to the pea vines.

"Not a project, Eva—family," Marie explained and dropped a handful of pods into the bucket.

Warmth spread through my soul. Family. I gazed over at Melody working her miniature fists and feet. I was worried about providing a family for Melody, but the reality was that she had provided a family for me. Two more sets of hands speeded the picking along, and we were soon finished. Pam and Marie insisted we pod the peas so I turned on a sprinkler and let the children run through it while we moms sat and podded peas in the shade of the apple tree. *We moms*—I was a mom. Strange how life unfolded. Being a mother was one of my deepest desires. Before Sean came along, I had resigned myself to the fact I might never be a mother.

Pam raked her thumb against a shell. A quiet clinking sounded as the peas struck the stainless steel bowl. "So I hear you're coming to the family reunion," she said.

"Just on Saturday. I'll drive Suzette up for the day."

"What about Peter?" Pam asked.

"He's not sure when he's getting in on Saturday so he'll meet us up there."

"That's quite a step up from a family dinner," Pam pressed for details.

Marie shot a warning glance at her then stood. "Time to check on the rockers."

Melody whined and Marie picked her up. "I'll stay upstairs with the baby. You don't want her to breathe in all the dust down there."

I only stayed in the basement long enough to see that the bathroom was completely done. Rick had explained that they were wrapping things up for tonight but would be back Wednesday to do some more. I gave him some money to replace the damaged sheetrock slabs he had found.

Back upstairs I shook the fine white powder from my ponytail. No wonder everyone working wore those surgical-looking masks. Following Pam's example, I had pulled my shirt over my nose and mouth while viewing the progress. Still, I couldn't escape the dry cough that started in an attempt to rid my throat of the tickling dust.

"Here." Marie handed me a cup of water.

"Thanks." My voice sounded hoarse. "Time for the family night treat now." I raided the freezer for cookies and sent the bag outside with the cousins. When the last cookie was eaten and all the children and tools were loaded in the cars, I thanked David and Rick again and waved good-bye. I watched their cars drive away. As I turned to go back in the house I thought I saw movement in the window of the house to the north of mine. The gentleman who lived there was in an assisted living center now. Maybe someone new was moving in. I situated Melody on my hip and started toward the house. There was no car on the street and none parked in the carport. I knocked on the door and waited. I knocked some more and waited. After a third round of knocking and waiting, I returned home. I must have caught the reflection of a bird flying, I decided.

* * *

Tuesday evening found me back in the garden trying to get a handle on the weeds I had let overrun it. It was slow going, but Melody enjoyed being outside under the quivering tree leaves, and I had to admit I did too. I crouched over the tomatoes, weeding in earnest while my mind cataloged preschool lessons I needed to develop. I was so deep in concentration that I didn't hear his approach, only the "Hi," he murmured in that low, memorable tone.

My stomach lurched. I looked up then and paused. Sean stood three feet from Melody at the garden's edge. His shoulders, usually pulled back commandingly, slumped slightly as he stood with hands in his pockets. "Can we talk?"

"You said quite enough the last time you were here." I gripped a stubborn weed with both hands and yanked. It didn't budge.

"I told Florence about us."

I watched him, waiting.

"She thinks it's too soon, that I'm still in love with you."

"Are you?" I asked nonchalantly as I loosened the dirt around the weed.

"I don't know." He hesitated. "She says I need to figure out my feelings."

I returned his steady gaze without speaking.

"Please, can we talk?"

I sighed then removed my gardening gloves and jumped the ditch.

He took a deep breath and glanced at Melody. "You were right. I didn't give Melody a chance. I don't like people staring at me and I don't know anything about babies. I'm afraid of looking like an idiot." He buried his fingers in his dense, raven colored hair and gave a little tug before his blue eyes met my gaze.

For Sean to admit that, I knew he'd done some pretty serious pondering. I expected relief to flood me, but none came.

"Eva, can we try again?"

My mind raced. How many times had I longed to hear those words? I had planned to spend eternity with Sean, but now . . . I swallowed hard. "Things have changed." Peter was in my life now. Had I really just admitted that? "I'm starting a preschool. I can't just put everything on hold to see if we can work this out. If it goes badly I have to be able to support Melody and myself. I don't want to move her away from her grandmother if I can help it. She needs family. I need family." I knelt on the lawn beside Melody.

He stiffened. "You never said anything about wanting to stay here after we were married."

"You would have been my family then. I—we would have gone with you. It would have saddened Suzette, but she'd have understood." Softly I traced Melody's eyebrow with my fingertip. Looking up, I said, "We would have visited and kept in touch."

He relaxed again, then crossed his legs and sank down beside me.

For a moment I allowed myself to wonder just how willing he was to accept Melody. Could he change? It was a big step for him to be here, to declare this much to me. However, I wanted to confirm a suspicion. "You'll be in contact with Florence, I assume?"

I detected a slight narrowing of his eyes, then a single nod of his head. He clearly hadn't thought I would guess that.

"So I can see Peter."

All softness drained from his features. "How serious is this? Were you dating him before—"

"You know me better than that."

"Sorry."

"It's not serious. But I know he would like to spend more time together."

"Are you interested?"

"He doesn't have issues with Melody. Maybe it's just easier to be around him." I took a deep breath. "So I don't know." Hearing those words I realized I did know. I enjoyed spending time with Peter because of *Peter*; he made it easy to be myself.

Sean's sea-blue eyes appeared vulnerable for the first time since I'd met him. He looked storm tossed on life's ocean. "I'm not used to coordinating date nights with other suitors," he said uneasily.

I bit back a retort. "He's only home for a day or two at a time. I won't see him again until Saturday, so you have the advantage."

"Are you going to wear his locket on our dates? Because nothing has changed for me. I still want all of your heart. Not half of it."

"Why are you here, then?" My last iota of Sean patience had dissolved. He could call Florence who knew how often, and he was worried about a necklace? "Florence was right." I stood up. "You need to figure some things out. Spend some quality time getting to know yourself." *Wow, that felt empowering*, I thought in surprise. I leaped the ditch and put on my gloves. "You fulfilled your end of the bargain; now I'm willing to talk to you about the dinner you need catered. Have your assistant call me."

* * *

David and Rick, along with Rick's two sons, returned Wednesday evening to put up more sheetrock. They finished at one in the morning. I was up with Melody and watched as they pulled out of the driveway. As I turned to go back in the house, I was sure I saw a flicker of light in the empty house on the north, but there were no cars in the carport when I checked in the morning and no one answered the door.

The business of starting a preschool while taking care of Melody and the garden consumed all my time. I was grateful I had planted so much earlier this year. I would need every bit of it to stretch our meager income, especially as Melody began eating solid foods. Marie had explained how she used a baby-food grinder to mash up canned and frozen fruits and vegetables for her little ones. The apple and pear trees that grew along the edge of the garden as well as a peach and several apricot trees that speckled Peter's yard would help too. I was sure he would let me have some.

Rebecca had canned a little bit last fall. Mostly, she had collected quite an array of quart-sized canning jars still gathering dust in the basement. She had a boiling water canner but I needed a pressure cooker and pint jars for the green beans that looked to be ready next week. I made a note to ask Suzette, Jayne, and Marie about borrowing a pressure canner.

Aside from collecting canning supplies, I spent most of my time mapping out preschool units and making lists of materials I needed to purchase. I sketched out how to arrange the basement and determined essential furniture to shop for. Amid all this planning, my mind still wandered to Peter and less and less to Sean. I found myself counting the days until I saw Peter again. When I took Melody for a walk each day, I always walked past Peter's house hoping to see his car in the empty garage. One morning as we walked by, I saw the garage was once again closed and locked. I hurried to the kitchen door and knocked, but there was no answer.

CHAPTER 18

A DUST CLOUD BILLOWED BEHIND the car. We'd only seen one other car since turning off the main road. We bumped along the dirt road until arriving at the Finch campsite, which was abuzz with activity. Three children chased a tumbling dome tent afloat on the stiff breeze while two toddlers waded through sagebrush. Teenagers and adults lugged sleeping bags and boxes toward an array of vehicles whose doors stood wide open, ready to receive cargo. Only Peter's father, Larry, remained untouched by the bustling. Off to the right side of where tents were falling, he raised a horseshoe to his nose, paused, then dropped and swung his arm. The horseshoe sailed through the mountain air and dropped at just the right moment. Metal clanked against metal and Larry's fist pumped the air. A ringer.

"No one has the energy to break camp in the heat of the afternoon," Suzette explained. We stood next to the car, surveying the scene. "Everyone will help break down and pack the kitchen after dinner." She nodded toward the left where a green canopy housed two camp chefs and three banquet tables arranged in an L-shape. Two five-gallon water coolers rested on the far table. Ice chests, Dutch ovens, and boxes were stacked underneath. A nearby cluster of trees rose adjacent to a fire pit surrounded by now empty chairs.

One by one, doors slammed shut and small groups set off to fish or hike. Jayne stayed behind with a handful of smaller children and Suzette and I lounged in camp chairs we dragged under a stand of trees. Jayne filled us in on the reunion's funnier happenings, like the preschoolers using the bucket of gray water outside her trailer to fill water bottles.

The sun's high position marked early afternoon, and I wondered where Peter was. He had said he'd be here in time for lunch. I slouched down in my camp chair battling heavy eyelids while Melody drank a bottle—I had stayed up late detailing lesson plans again. A quiet breeze stirred the sweltering air thick with the scent of sagebrush. A car engine droned in the distance, growing ever closer.

My heart quickened its pace as I scanned the dirt road hoping to see Peter's sandstone-colored car. I grinned as a familiar Jeep Compass crested the last hill and wound its way to the camp.

As Peter approached the campfire circle a horseshoe clanged around a post and Larry called, "How 'bout a game, Pete?"

"In a minute, Dad." Jayne stood and Peter hugged her. "Hi, Mom."

"It's good to see you; Javier had me worried," Jayne said.

Peter appraised his mother quizzically, and I did the same. Who was Javier?

"You look well, son," Larry said, approaching from behind him.

"Hi, Dad," Peter greeted his father. Hands pounded backs in a welcome hug.

Larry's voice grew serious. "Javier says you're in deep."

"He talked to you?" Peter crossed to me, pulled a chair next to mine, and sat down. He took my hand and squeezed it. "Glad you made it." The softness in his chocolate-brown eyes made my stomach flutter.

"Likewise," I murmured as I stared at the rugged features I had pictured so often in the last week and a half. His eyes looked tired.

"Javier was here earlier. Said he wanted to check the place out. He says he's been covering you," Larry pressed, sliding a chair closer to us.

"Who's Javier?" I finally asked.

"He's a good friend and the best partner," Peter said to me then turned to his father. "He's been helping me out on this side."

"So you are in deep?" Larry confirmed.

Peter nodded.

"Is something wrong?" I asked. I had no idea what they were talking about.

Peter let out a loud breath. "It's complicated."

"Time for a game of horseshoes, gals." Larry pulled Jayne and Suzette to their feet.

I propped Melody up to burp her. "So . . . what's so complicated?" I patted Melody's back.

"Human relationships are always surprising, especially in my line of work. But the last thing I want to do today is bore you with details about that."

I rolled my eyes and started toward the car. Peter followed.

"Now you're upset?" he asked when we reached the car.

"I don't find learning about your work boring."

"Eva, I don't like bringing work home with me. I explained this to you before. When I'm home, I'm home. So what's for dinner?"

I noted his change of topic but said nothing, recognizing that today was one of his few breaks from work. "Glad you asked." I opened the back door of Suzette's car. "Grab a cooler."

"You're making dinner?"

"No, *we* are. Just like *we* are in charge of this afternoon's activity."

"Yeah, we better get that started." He scanned the meadow as if taking inventory of who was present.

"First let's get dinner cooking."

He opened the cooler lid and peeked inside. "Barbeque something?"

"Three meat barbeque, cheesy vegetables, watermelon, and dump cake. Does that meet with your approval?" I was trying out the dinner I'd be cooking for Sean's group, but I hadn't told Pam that when I'd offered to make dinner tonight. She'd been elated at the thought of buying the groceries but not actually having to cook the dinner.

"How much chopping do I have to do?"

"None."

"The cheesy vegetables thing?"

"Open the bags of California blend frozen vegetables and throw them in with grated cheese."

"I have to grate the cheese instead of chop, don't I?"

I laughed. "Not if you can find the bag of grated cheese in there."

"Saved."

"It'll be fast and easy, and then we can get the orienteering course going."

He closed the cooler. "I don't have much time today."

I swallowed a lump in my throat. How could I be so attached to a man I rarely saw? "Javier needs you?"

"Yeah." He closed his eyes briefly and took a deep breath. "There's something I want to show you later . . . so could we split up duties? I'll get the course going while you get dinner cooking?"

"Sure. The treats are in the box behind the driver's seat when you need them." I tried to make my voice sound light, carefree. I had been looking forward to seeing Peter more than I realized. "I'd better get dinner cooking if you're going to eat before you go." I wouldn't waste time now. I quickly found Suzette and asked her to watch Melody while I started dinner. Since it was Pam's night to cook, she and David had insisted on getting the coals going for the Dutch ovens while I fed Melody. The large deep kettle was heating up now.

With the ribs browning, I turned my attention to dumping bottled fruit, cake mix, and butter into another two Dutch ovens. The hissing in the first Dutch oven subsided as I drowned the ribs with three bottles of barbeque sauce, then put the lid on and used a shovel to disperse coals across the top. I would have to remember to add the chicken in a couple of hours and get the vegetables going when I put coals on the dump cake.

Small groups of family had begun reappearing every few minutes as I prepared dinner. The reunited children were playing horseshoes or hide-and-seek.

A few minutes later, a long, shrill whistle broke the calm. The grandchildren immediately stopped their games and trotted toward the sound's origin—Grandpa. Larry stood next to Peter just below a stand of aspen that stretched up the mountainside. The adults followed the whistle's command with the younger children on shoulders or in tow. Even Suzette and Jayne complied, bringing up the rear with a few stragglers. Peter motioned me over with his arm.

I arrived next to Peter just as Jayne settled a grandchild onto her hip. "Grandpa says you've broken camp and cleaned up so you're ready for a treasure hunt," Peter called as everyone came to order.

A ripple of approval sounded from the children with a few cries of, "Yes!" and "I knew it!"

"Eva will help the children age ten and under with their course." He handed me a paper. "Here's the key," he explained. "I've made five teams out of the adults and older children." He called out names, separated everyone into groups, and passed out compasses with the first coordinates. "Eva's home bakery has provided the goodies hidden at your final destination." He stretched his arm above his head, held it there for a couple of seconds, and then let it fall, slicing the air before him. "Go!"

Paper rustled amid exclamations of, "What does it say?" and "Where to first?"

I gathered my group of nine around me and explained how to use a compass. I called out a direction and how many steps to take, then en mass, we tried it out. After completing a couple of sample courses, we started on the real trek.

* * *

When all the groups sat lounging on rocks and chairs in the shade after we were finished with the activity, Peter whispered, "Let's go."

"Melody?" I whispered back.

"Did you bring your carrier?"

"It's in the car." A warm hand on my forearm stopped me from standing. I turned toward Suzette, who was still holding Melody.

"Go with Peter. I'm enjoying my granddaughter." She looked down at Melody.

"Thank you."

She motioned me away with the back of her hand.

Peter took my hand in his, his touch sending a quiver of excitement through me. *I feel like a sixteen-year-old!* I thought to myself. But today I didn't care—I rather enjoyed it.

Peter clasped a fishing pole and net in his right hand while he led me to a brook carving its way through the far side of the meadow. The children had waded its icy depths earlier today. "Are there really fish in there?" I squatted close to the water's edge, peering through the shallow water. Rocks of varying sizes lay clearly visible on the bottom of the creek bed.

"They hover under overhanging parts of the bank. There will only be one in any given hole."

"Really? Why is that?"

"Trout are quite territorial." He opened a cargo pocket on his pants, pulled out a plastic box approximately the size of a three-by-five index card, and opened the hinged lid revealing a crisscross of smaller compartments filled with colorful fishing flies. "Kind of like Sean." He selected one and tied it to his hook.

"Marie talked to you." I had told Marie about Sean's latest visit.

"Only to say that Sean stopped by this week." He looked at me expectantly.

I took a deep breath. "He wanted to try again—try to accept Melody this time."

Peter carefully dropped his line into the water near an outcropping of rocks. "And?"

"I told him to spend some quality time getting to know himself."

Peter chuckled. "I'd wager he didn't like that."

"Probably not."

Peter's pole dipped. Reflexively he tightened his grip then began reeling in the line. "Got one."

"So soon?"

"Hold the net." He expertly landed the ten-inch fish inside it a moment later. Its silver body flopped wildly. Faint flashes of color let me know it was a rainbow trout. "Have you ever been fishing?" He clenched the rainbow's body and removed his hook before tossing the fish back into the water.

"Not since I was a little girl. My grandpa and dad used to take Rebecca and me on Saturday mornings. They did all the work of baiting and casting. I reeled in a couple. My dad liked to fly fish but I never tried it. Fishing seems like a lot of waiting."

"Wanna try?"

"Do I have to take out the hook if I catch one?" I shuddered and wiped my palms against my pants.

"Not the first two. But if you catch a third . . ."

I smiled. "I won't even attempt it."

"There's another spot upstream a ways." He picked up his net and pole in one hand and clasped my hand with the other.

A feeling of comfort radiated through me. Being with Peter was so natural. We stopped at another overhang with a deeper pool of water.

Peter handed me the pole. "Hold the line with your left hand and the pole in your right. Look where you want the fly to land on top of the water. When you're ready, flick your pole wrist and let go of the line. If you do it right, the fly will drop where you want it."

"That sounds a lot more complicated than it looked watching you."

"Don't over think it. Pitch it into the current and try to get a real nice drift on it."

I pulled back and flicked my wrist. The pole tip hit the water.

"Cast low and slow," Peter said.

My second cast didn't even make it to the deeper pool by the overhang.

"You'll get it. Do it again."

This time the fly landed where I wanted and began drifting downstream.

"Let her go for a sec. Then pull her out and try again." I felt the pole snag at the same time Peter yelled, "You got it! Reel it in nice and steady." Peter got the net ready. When the little trout broke through the water's surface, he scooped it into the net. True to his word, he removed the hook for me and released the fish. We continued upstream, taking turns with the pole. Peter related stories of his previous fishing trips while I soaked in the serenity of being with him.

As seemed to always be the case, time passed by quickly, and Peter said it was time for him to head out.

"You haven't had dinner." I grasped at a reason for him to stay.

"I've got some snacks in my car."

The circles under his eyes had deepened. "You need some sleep."

"I can sleep later."

"On the plane?"

"That would be nice."

We crossed the meadow hand in hand. Instead of joining the others under the trees, he led me to his car and tossed his fishing pole in the back on top of a black tarp covering lumpy masses of something.

Grocery sacks lined the cargo area behind the last seats. "A few snacks?"

He shut the window. "There was a sale on granola bars and cereal."

"That's what you live on?"

"That and the hope I can give you a hug without making you cry." He pulled me into his embrace.

I wrapped my arms around him, inhaling his woodsy scent. "I missed you." It wasn't fair that he had to leave. We'd barely spent any time together.

He squeezed me for a fleeting moment. "Good." He released me and stepped back, eyeing my locket. "Keep me close." He paused and took a long breath as he tilted his head skyward then brought his gaze back to my face.

I sensed a struggle inside of him.

"I won't be coming home again for a long time."

The loneliness I had felt at his shortened visit paled in comparison to the ache in my chest now.

"It's been a mistake for me to see you so often."

It felt like someone had knocked the air out of me. I couldn't move. "A mistake?" I gasped and fumbled with the clasp on the nape of my neck.

His hands stopped mine. "No, not a mistake."

"But you said—"

"It has been *unwise* for me to come home this frequently." He brought our hands—mine clutched in his—between us.

I barely heard him. A familiar numbness began its creep across my heart. "How long?" My voice sounded dead, detached.

"This is not fair to you, Eva. But my work . . . it can't be helped." He sighed and shook his head.

"How long?"

"I need your patience for a little longer." His hands cradled my face. "Please don't make any decisions to marry Sean and go to Iceland before I get back," he pleaded.

The intensity of his words halted the numbing sensation. The ache returned. The swelling started in my throat. "When will that be?"

He swept a few stray locks of hair behind my ear. "Trust me . . . please? I don't have the time Sean does to be with you, but know this Eva, I am sincere." He picked up the locket. "I am true."

With all my heart I wanted to believe him. I cradled his hand in mine as he held the compass. "More than a month?"

"I'll be back," he said simply as he let go of my necklace. Without answering further he paced to the driver's side and climbed in just as Rick reached the passenger door.

"I'm catching a ride with Peter to finish up a project," Rick explained and got into the car.

I watched Peter back down the dirt road, turn around, and fade out of sight. I tried to swallow the lump in my throat. Taking a deep breath, I brushed my palms against my thighs and turned to make my way back to the campfire as I distracted myself with thoughts of dinner preparations. It was time to add the chicken.

With my back to the cluster of Finches under the trees, I crouched over a dutch oven, carefully sliding chicken pieces into the bubbling sauce.

Dirt hushed the approaching footfalls behind me. Marie's form crouched beside me, and she put an arm around me. "How you holding up?"

"You knew?"

She nodded.

The injustices of the summer ran through my mind, and unwanted tears threatened to choke me. "Just when I think it's okay to relax and become a little bit attached."

"He's been crossing the line for you too long this summer."

"Crossing the line?" I whispered, battling to maintain control of the avalanche of tears waiting to spill over.

"I've been waiting for this to happen because Peter is who he is."

"He said it was *unwise* for him to see me so often."

Marie nodded. "This summer's events have left him extremely conflicted. He doesn't want to lose you, but he is loyal to his work."

"Is he always gone this much?" Was work more important to him than a relationship? A family?

"No. His *consulting*," she added an odd inflection to the word, "requires extensive background work. When a particular project takes off, it requires his full attention."

"So work takes priority over everything else." It figured that I would pick someone just as obsessed with a career as Sean. When would I learn? I had thought Peter was different.

"Eva, you've seen him interact with his family. You know that's not a fair assessment," Marie gently rebuked me.

She was right. He was different. I saw that in his family relationships. But his work . . . "I know," I whispered. "I have to be patient."

CHAPTER 19

I DROPPED SUZETTE OFF THEN drove around for a while. I needed time to think. My heart ached at the lost time with Peter, and now he would be gone for a month, maybe more. Marie mentioned Peter was crossing the line, and Larry revealed that Peter was in deep. His partner had even come up to check on him. It all pointed to trouble for Peter, but what kind of trouble? I pondered this as I rounded the corner to my house and spotted a familiar vehicle parked in front. Sean.

My stomach churned. He knew I would be seeing Peter today. Was he trying to check up on me or interrupt our date? I slowed the car, vacillating between turning around and continuing home. Then, with a firm resolve, I pressed on. I was tired; Melody needed her bed. I wouldn't let Sean chase me out of my own home. I parked in the garage, got Melody out of the car, and headed toward Sean.

As I came even with the Escalade, Sean opened his door. "Hi."

"I told you to have your assistant call me."

"I'm not here about the dinner."

I stared at him.

"Well, not *only* about the dinner."

"How many people?"

"Can we go inside and talk, or is Peter on his way?"

"You knew I had plans with him today."

"So when will he be here?"

"Your interference in my life is not welcome."

"I won't be long, I promise."

"How long have you been sitting in front of my house?"

"Eva, please, I just want to talk to you."

I looked at my watch. "You have five minutes."

"You two going to catch the late movie?"

Without answering, I proceeded up the front walk. Sean didn't follow right away. I heard him open his car door and hoped he might be leaving. Halfway up the walk I heard his door shut and the sound of hurried footsteps behind me.

I stopped at the steps to the front porch. On the round wicker table between the two chairs was a peanut-shaped wicker basket. African violets bloomed from each side.

I caught my breath. It had to be from Peter; Sean never sent anything but roses. I mounted the steps and saw, scarcely visible, the corner of a small white envelope tucked under the edge of the double basket.

My fingers twitched restlessly as I restrained myself. I didn't want to attract Sean's attention to Peter's gift, but my entire heart yearned to read Peter's words. Later, I told myself, when Sean wasn't here to spoil the moment.

"Need help with the carrier?" Sean nimbly carried it up the steps.

"Thanks," I said head down, searching through the diaper bag for my keys. I located them and unlocked the door. Sean carried Melody into the house.

"You smell like campfire smoke."

"Yep." I bent down and unbuckled Melody.

She smiled when she saw my face just inches from her own. Her arms and legs pumped the air.

"Hi, baby. Oh, you're such a good girl," I crooned as I unstrapped and lifted her out. "You need a diaper change, huh? It's been a while." I continued in my singsong voice and mounted the stairs to her nursery in the loft. I looked down at Sean still standing near the carrier. I reluctantly decided that I should at least be polite. "I'll just be a minute."

He nodded.

Once inside Melody's room, I realized that she still needed a bath. I gathered her things and descended the stairs.

Sean looked up from the couch where he was thumbing through a magazine.

"It's time for Melody's bath." I strode to the bathroom without a second glance in his direction.

I had just finished rinsing Melody's hair when Sean poked his head in. "Almost done?"

I grabbed the towel hanging on the hook next to the tub. "Just finishing."

With Melody dressed in her nightgown, I scooped her up and pressed my nose against her hair, breathing deeply. "Mmm, you smell like a baby."

I tickled her chin and she smiled her open-mouth grin. "Yes, you are pretty too. And hungry I think." I edged past Sean and into the kitchen, where I opened the cupboard and pulled out the formula.

"I can hold her while you mix the bottle."

My hand froze as it reached for a bottle. Slowly, I turned around. "You want to hold her?"

"Sure. While you mix her bottle. It will be easier that way, right?" He held out his arms.

This was certainly different. But I was still wary. Offering to hold a baby didn't equal a change of heart. I placed Melody into his waiting hands before mixing her bottle. When I finished, I reached for Melody.

Sean turned her away from me. "I'll feed her. I did that once, remember?"

"Okay," I said, unconvinced. I led the way to the rocking chair. "Here you go." I handed the bottle to Sean and waited for him to get settled. Once Melody was drinking, I said, "So what's all this about?"

He looked up and held my eyes with a steady gaze. "I know I had a hard time accepting Melody." He glanced down at her in his immense arms then looked back at me. "I'm trying. Please, give me another chance."

"It's not just Melody. It's your whole attitude toward family. I knew it was different from mine, and I thought we would work it out as we had children. Now I don't know if that's possible. We value work and family differently."

"Is Peter any different? Where is he?"

"We are talking about you and me."

"If you are dating Peter, he is relevant to this conversation."

"Did you come here to confront him? Is that why you picked tonight to come? Because you figured he would be here?"

He shrugged. "Today was a convenient day to do some grocery shopping. Peter obviously thought so too."

"You saw him?"

"Didn't you?"

"Have you ever been fly fishing?" I asked suddenly, thinking of Peter's territorial reference to Sean.

"Are you trying to change the subject?"

"Are you checking up on Peter and me?"

"I happened to be at the checkout when he walked in. He seemed in a big hurry."

Melody fussed and I got up to take her.

"Tell me what to do," Sean said, holding on to Melody and pulling back slightly.

"You're really serious about this, aren't you?" I acquiesced, looking down at him.

"That's what I'm telling you, Eva. I'm here to make this work, and I can't help it if I'm jealous of Peter's time with you." He reached out and clasped my hand. "He's stealing my girl." Gentleness touched the angular planes of his striking face.

Sean left shortly after Melody finished her bottle, promising to pick me up for church in the morning. I stood on the porch holding Melody as Sean's Escalade faded into the twilight. When I turned to go inside I again glimpsed the tiny blue flowers cascading over the side of a basket atop the white envelope on the porch table.

My initial excitement upon seeing this unexpected gift was clouded by tonight's turn of events. Why did Sean pick now to accept Melody? Why not six weeks ago before I started developing feelings for Peter?

I picked up the white envelope no bigger than my palm and dropped into the closest white wicker chair with Melody cradled in the crook of my left arm. I opened the flap and pulled out a solid white card with a lily embossed across the front.

I moved my fingers across the raised surface of the flower but didn't open the card. It was so small. It wouldn't take long to read and I wanted to prolong this moment.

Absently, I fingered my locket and warmth filled me. I opened Peter's note.

Dear Eva,

I'll cherish the memories of the adventurous gal who spent a day with the entire Finch tribe even though she's not related to them. I'll think of you surrounded by children clamoring for their turn to use the compass. I'll replay the scene of a petite blonde crouched over Dutch ovens preparing dinner. I'll smile when I recall the squeamish woman who refused to remove the hook from her third catch of the day! I'll treasure the hug we shared and hold onto the hope of another when I return.

—Peter

On the bottom left corner Peter had scrawled an address for a website. Curiosity propelled me indoors where I turned on the computer, brought up the Internet, and typed in the address. The title words *Flowers and*

Their Meanings flashed onto my screen. I scrolled down to African violet and read: *watchfulness, faithfulness, I'll always be true, devotion.*

My mind repeated Peter's last words: *I am sincere . . . I am true . . . I'll be back.* He had asked me not to make any decision to marry Sean while he was away. I had dismissed his request as absurd. But now . . . what about Sean and his desire for a fresh start with Melody? Did I still love him? Could he really change?

Sleep evaded me long after Melody was down for the night. My mind replayed the day's events multiple times. I analyzed every detail of my time with Sean and Peter but no one clear path seemed right.

I did, however, see more distinctly how I had clung to Sean. After my parents' deaths, I was so tired of always having to be the responsible adult. The way Sean controlled everything around him had at first been a welcome relief to me. Having Melody in my life had given me the courage to stand again, but when Sean held my hand tonight I realized how much I'd missed having him to lean on. I missed the security I felt when he wrapped his arms around me. He blocked out the world for me in those moments.

Then there was Peter. We barely knew each other, but somehow I felt so comfortable with him. My best course of action, I concluded, would be to make the best home I could for Melody and me and hope that everything else would fall into place.

* * *

Monday night Suzette and I stood at the kitchen sink washing snapped beans from that morning's picking. Suzette had brought over her pressure cooker, some pint jars, and other canning equipment, and stayed to teach me how to bottle beans. Two sharp raps at the front door followed by a resonant, "Hello?" signaled Sean's trademark entry.

From the sink I called, "We're in the kitchen."

Suzette gave me a quizzical look.

She had seen me with him at church yesterday, but maybe she didn't expect him to visit again so soon. "Later," I whispered.

"All three girls in the kitchen I see." He walked to Melody's swing and wound it up again then peered over my shoulder into the sink. "What are you two up to tonight?"

I held up a handful of beans.

"Yes, I see them, but what are you planning to do with two dishpans full of beans?"

"Suzette is going to teach me how to pressure can them." I wondered uneasily what Suzette thought of Sean's presence.

"Why?" His face was a study of incredulity.

"Because I want to learn, and it will help out with my grocery bill in the coming year." I glanced at Suzette. She seemed unbothered by Sean's visit, but her tranquil face was hard to read.

"Enough to make all this work worth it?"

"I can use these for Melody's baby food." Seeing his blank look, I added, "It's quite expensive."

He started to say something but stopped himself.

"Want to help?"

"I'm here as the babysitter tonight. So far I only work on voice command, so you'll have to tell me what to do."

I chuckled. "She's fine for now. Just keep her swing going."

"Mind if I check out how the basement is coming?"

I shook my head. "You know the way."

When Sean returned a few minutes later, I was ladling boiling water into pint jars filled with beans. Suzette followed with a half teaspoon of canning salt for each filled jar.

"That really looks nice down there. Who's doing the work?" Sean asked, jerking his thumb toward the basement.

"My nephews and their sons," Suzette answered as she began placing lids and rings on the completed jars.

"You just need texture on the walls and you're ready to paint," Sean said.

"Hardly. The sheetrock is hung but I still have to mud, tape, and sand."

"It's done." Sean insisted. "Although it could use a going over with a good Shop-Vac down there."

"Done?"

"Yeah, it's taped, mudded, and sanded. Where do you think all this fine powder came from?" He pointed at his once-brown hiking boots now covered with white dust.

"That's from cutting the sheetrock. Nobody's been here since last Wednesday when Rick finished the sheetrock. He and David were here until one in the morning and then they all left for the family reunion Thursday morning."

"I'm pretty sure they got more done Wednesday than hanging sheetrock."

"Honestly, Sean. Have you ever seen a room under construction before? I saw what it looked like after they left. All nice and white with gaps between the pieces of sheetrock waiting to be filled."

"I know what mudding and taping is, and I'm telling you, it's done," he persisted. "Come and have a look."

"Did you turn the light on?"

"Please refrain from your sarcasm until you've seen for yourself."

"Let me finish these first," I said, wondering what Sean was talking about. Suzette and I placed the bottles in the pressure canner and secured the lid. She explained we had to let the steam exhaust for seven minutes before replacing the weight and building pressure. Wiping my hands on my apron, I turned toward the stairs.

I stepped off the last stair and turned to enter the family room area I planned to use for my preschool. I breathed in a sudden intake of air. My fingers jumped to my lips. Solid white walls met my eyes. "How?" I whirled to face Sean a few steps ahead to my left. "Did you do this?" I accused.

His eyes widened. "No. How would I?"

"Not you specifically. Did you hire a crew?"

"Eva, I didn't know you were remodeling the basement to house your preschool until you told me Saturday night."

He had a point. "But how?" I slowly twirled, leaning back on my heels. The entire room was done.

"You must not have noticed before."

"No. There was no mudding." Further investigation revealed the bathroom and two bedrooms were completed as well. Still perplexed, I climbed the stairs. As I emerged from the basement and saw Suzette smiling at Melody on her lap, it dawned on me. Last Friday night Suzette had insisted I bring Melody for an overnight visit with her to her brother's house in Nephi. She'd said she wanted to show off her only grandchild. Spending the night had seemed unnecessary, but Suzette never asked anything from me so I had agreed. Besides, it made it easier to leave for the reunion if we were both in the same town. Now I suspected that Peter had set the whole thing up and that's the reason he had shown up so late. He'd probably gotten home late Friday night and worked all night and most of Saturday. No wonder he looked rushed when Sean saw him in the grocery store. And Rick's excuse about driving home with Peter to finish up a project—the project was my basement, I suddenly realized. The final clue fell into place when I recalled Suzette asking me to bring the beans to her house to snap late this morning. I had ended up staying for lunch and well into the afternoon before returning home.

A loving fondness for Peter's considerate nature warmed my soul. A lump rose in my throat as I remembered his weary eyes at the reunion. He had spent his few hours home constantly caring for me.

"Elves must have visited Eva while you were gone Saturday," Sean directed his comment to Suzette.

She sat Melody on her knees and softly began bouncing her before looking up. "Oh?"

I crossed to Suzette and bent over under the guise of kissing Melody, but as I moved past Suzette's ear I whispered, "Elves named Peter, Rick, and Suzette."

Suzette winked at me then turned her head to Sean. "How does it look?"

"It's starting to look real," he said.

Suzette looked at me and then nodded toward the pressure cooker spewing a steady flow of steam. "Time to put the weight on and start building pressure." Then she handed Melody to Sean.

I made the necessary adjustments.

"According to our altitude, you should process at fourteen pounds' pressure. Since you're doing pints, time it for this long." She pointed to a number on the USU Extension paper we had printed off the Internet. "I think you can handle it from here." With one last kiss on the cheek for Melody, she opened the sliding door and left.

Sean moved beside me and put his arm around my shoulders while cradling Melody in his other. "What are you going to do with all of this when I convince you to marry me and go to Iceland?"

I looked up into his deep-blue eyes. "Sean, I appreciate all you are trying to do, but I have to look out for my future. Besides, even if we *did* decide that the wedding was back on—and that's a big if—I don't think we could pull off a wedding before you leave for Iceland. It would have to wait until you got back." I heard Peter's voice. *Please don't make any decisions to marry Sean and go to Iceland before I get back.*

"Is that a challenge?" He smiled broadly and squeezed my shoulder. "I thought you knew to never underestimate me."

CHAPTER 20

ONCE SEAN WAS GONE, I dialed Marie's number. It took a little coaxing, but she finally admitted that Peter had asked Rick to help him with the basement. She explained Peter's frustration at being gone so much and having to rely on his brothers to help me. He would much prefer to do it all himself.

"What if I had gone downstairs Saturday night or yesterday?"

"You would have been surprised then instead of now. By the way, Rick's coming back tomorrow night to spray the texture."

"This has gone far enough. I have money set aside to hire it done."

"Eva, we're family—"

"Not—"

"We're Melody's family, then, if you're going to be so picky about it. We have the expertise to help in this area, so we're helping."

"At least let me make you dinner tomorrow."

Marie chuckled. "Let's see, Rick does the work, and I get a night off of cooking for eight. Sounds great! What time?"

"Six?"

"Perfect."

"So Rick tells me he saw a black-cherry Escalade parked in front of your house tonight?"

I felt my stomach give a little flop. "Does that cancel out his help tomorrow night?"

"How serious is Sean?"

I chose my words carefully, not wanting to make more of this than it was. "He's determined to get to know Melody."

"And what do you think?"

I sighed. "Marie, I'd love to confide in you, but it's a bit awkward knowing Peter talks to you so much."

"We're friends regardless of who you choose to date."

"I could really use a friend."

"I'm listening."

I took a deep breath and plunged ahead. "I feel like I owe Sean at least the opportunity to show me he can change."

"And what about Peter?"

I raked a hand through my hair, considering how to answer. "That's where I'm conflicted. I really do care for Peter. And I know it bothers him that Sean still comes around. But at the same time, how long have I known Peter? Sean and I have dated for over a year now. It seems crazy to give up on a relationship with Sean when there's nothing certain with Peter—and it's far too soon for anything to be definite with Peter."

"May I make an observation?"

"Please."

"At this stage in your life do you date anyone you wouldn't consider marrying?"

"No."

"Neither does Peter . . . or Sean, for that matter."

Her words made my heart skip a beat. I hadn't dared let myself think of a future with Peter. However, Marie's remarks rang true. If I didn't believe Peter to be a suitable husband and father, I would never have agreed to date him in the first place.

"If you were honest with yourself, you'd realize that the real question for you is who you can spend eternity with."

The impact of her statement felt like jumping into a cold mountain lake. It awakened all my senses and left me gasping for air. I scrambled to say something coherent. "You don't dance around the point do you?"

"You're all three looking for the same thing whether you talk about it or not."

I took a deep breath. "I guess I haven't wanted to admit things are that serious with Peter."

"Your relationship may not be exclusive now, but you two aren't dating for fun. You're each looking for an eternal companion."

"Has Peter ever been close to getting married before?"

"Once that I know of. He was considering becoming engaged, but she couldn't handle his work. He was gun shy for a couple years after that, not even really trying to date seriously. I think he figured no girl could accept the time his work requires of him."

I considered this then said, "I'd think he'd be a little more careful about all the time he's away if he wanted to prevent that from happening again."

"He has to stay incredibly focused on any current projects. Peter's picked a strong woman this time. He knows it'll be tough for you, but your independence is quite attractive to him."

I sighed again. "Whatever happened to arranged marriages?"

Marie laughed. "Don't worry; you'll make the right decision, Eva. We'll see you tomorrow night."

"Bye." I hung up the phone, once again impressed with Peter's thoughtful care of me. I opened and closed my locket as I remembered his request: *Keep me close.*

I filled a cup with water and carried it to the basket of African violets I had moved to the kitchen table. While watering the flowers, the words from the Internet site ran through my mind: *watchfulness, faithfulness, I'll always be true, devotion.* Time and again Peter's actions demonstrated these characteristics. He used the little time he had home to be with me and to help my dreams become reality. There wasn't the subtle tug-of-war like there always was with Sean.

Sean. Was I leading him on with a second chance? My heart ached to know Peter more, to be with him. I was comfortable with Peter. He made it easier to be me. The more I was with him, the more awake and alive I felt. I was falling for him and, thanks to Melody, with my eyes wide open. But right now my focus had to be on building my preschool and a secure future for Melody.

* * *

The next day, I barbecued outside while Rick and Marie's children played squirt-gun freeze tag. Ruth cowered behind me for protection while her older brother Ben alternated between yelling at her to quit hiding behind big people and contemplating how to hit Ruth without hitting me. "Eva, don't move, and I promise I won't get you wet," Ben assured me.

"Ben! Go find someone else to squirt." Marie's voice of authority disrupted Ben's strategy.

A protest forming on his tortured face, Ben turned to negotiate with his mom.

Marie stretched out her arm and uttered a firm, "Go!"

Shoulders slumped, Ben kicked the lawn and said, "Aw, Mom," before slinking off toward the older boys.

Tim grabbed Craig in a headlock and proceeded to spray Craig's face at point blank range. Seeing his opportunity, Ben leaped into the air and streaked to Tim's aid.

"Anything I can help you with?" Marie, holding Melody in one arm, asked me as she looked over the picnic table.

"Craig's the one in need of help."

"Rick will fix that." Marie grinned. "I saw him sneaking around the other side of the house with a Super Soaker."

When all the boys were sufficiently drenched, Marie called them to eat. Dinner conversation was lively as the children related happenings from the morning's swimming lessons.

After dinner, Rick, helped by Tim and Craig, hauled equipment and supplies to the basement. Paper plates expedited meal cleanup, so before long, Marie and I were picking apricots off the tree in Peter's yard.

"How are plans for your preschool coming along?" Marie asked.

"I've contacted everyone on Lori's list. A few have registered with other preschools and didn't want to change. But as of right now I have enough for two full sessions. I need at least six more students for a third session."

"Have you done any advertising?"

I shook my head. "Got any suggestions?"

"Put some flyers up around town. The library's a good place to start."

"Hmm. I was planning to go to the library tomorrow anyway," I mused. Excitement filled me as it always did whenever I worked on plans for the preschool.

Later that night, after dark, I spied a flicker of light in the vacant house on the north. I double-checked my doors to make sure they were locked. I made a mental note to ask Suzette about who owned that house.

* * *

Sean popped in Wednesday night just as I started walking to the library. I needed to compile a list of picture books reinforcing my preschool units and hang the flyers I had made. Melody enjoyed the stroller ride but squirmed and fussed once inside the building. Sean dutifully paced the floor with her while I scrolled through computer screens and jotted notes. Then Melody began to wail, and a family of patrons turned to look at Sean. I thought for certain that he'd give the baby back to me, but he only smiled and took Melody outside to walk around.

Despite his confident expression, I wasn't sure how long Sean's patience would stretch with a crying baby, so I hurriedly scribbled a few last memos on my list and rushed outside with the stroller. As I flung open the heavy outside door and braced it with my hip, I hoisted the stroller across the threshold and then descended the steps.

Sean sat with one leg crossed on the cement planter surrounding an enormous shade tree. Melody lay diagonally across his lap with her head cradled in the bend of Sean's knee. Her fists punched the air excitedly.

As I approached, I remembered another July evening with Sean. Nearby pine trees evoked memories from a summer evening one year ago. We had water skied all day at Canyon Ferry Reservoir and then relaxed in the shade of an evergreen tree near the water's edge. I had sat comfortably at Sean's side while he regaled the others with tales of our water skiing adventures.

I felt the corners of my mouth pull up slightly as I pushed the stroller toward Sean and Melody.

Sean lifted his head when my flip-flops and the stroller sounded my approach. "I haven't seen you smile in a long while." His familiar bass voice sounded comforting.

My mouth pulled up into a real smile then. "I'd forgotten the good times we had together. We've done nothing but argue this summer."

He reached out his hand, searching for mine.

I grasped his hand and sank down beside him.

"For that, I'm really and truly sorry," his deep voice soothed.

I gazed into his eyes. "Me too." I looked at Melody happy in Sean's lap then back to Sean. "This is nice. It's how I had imagined life with the three of us as a family."

"So there's hope?" A smile played on his lips.

"We're making progress," I allowed. What did that mean for Peter? Someone would be hurt—and my choice would be the catalyst.

* * *

Saturday afternoon another plant was delivered to the house. Vibrant pink azalea blooms perched atop a stylish pink-white-and-orange striped square planter. It looked like it belonged on the round white wicker table flanked by two matching chairs on my front porch so I placed it there before reading the attached card: another white card with a single flower embossed across the front. Inside, Peter's neat script beckoned my eyes.

Dear Eva,

I hope you've enjoyed your surprises as much as I have enjoyed giving them to you. Know that I miss you and that if it were at all

possible, I would be there with you. My work is very demanding, but I hope I've showed you that I do my best to be there for those I care about. Hug Melody for me.
Thinking of you,
—Peter

The same website was written in the bottom left corner. I immediately accessed the Internet via my laptop on the kitchen table. When the site loaded, I scrolled down to Azalea and read, *Take care of yourself for me.* I stared at the message on the computer while my fingers traced the swirl design of my locket. I looked down at the card in my hand. "I wish you were here," I whispered.

At church, Sean continued to surprise me. He even asked to hold Melody after the sacrament and kept her until the meeting ended. Sean left for the airport immediately following church. Neil was flying in today.

Sean's absence allowed time for my thoughts to wander over my suddenly confusing love life. Peter's notes continued to bolster my growing attachment to him, yet Sean's recent behavior gave me hope that we might still have a future together. My thoughts ping-ponged between memories of Peter and Sean's change of heart.

By Sunday evening I paced the house straightening already tidy stacks of books, turning plants another degree this way or that only to turn them back again. Finally, I flopped down on the couch with the current month's *Ensign* and began reading. After scanning the same page three times, I commenced roaming the house again. Unable to tolerate walking from room to room for the umpteenth time, I strapped Melody into her stroller and set off up my front walk. As I neared the corner, Suzette rounded it. I waved.

She looked up and waved.

I smiled, waved again, then quickly closed the distance.

"I was coming to visit you," Suzette explained. "Mind if I walk with you?"

"Not at all. Which way do you want to go?"

She pointed back the way I had come. "Let's go that way. Then we won't cross paths with Jayne."

I hoped she didn't see the curious expression on my face. As I turned the stroller around, I wondered if she and Jayne had argued. I couldn't imagine anyone upsetting Suzette; nothing seemed to ruffle her. "Need some time away from family?" I asked casually.

"Jayne's so worried about Peter I can't listen to her anymore."

A pang of guilt rippled through me. "I'm the one causing the anxiety aren't I?"

She tapped my hand twice. "You're in the midst of it, yes. But don't let that bother you."

"It's because Sean keeps showing up."

"That's the crux of it." She inhaled deeply and slowly let her breath out before continuing. "I know this is just as difficult for you and probably very confusing. So many life-altering circumstances have presented themselves to you this summer."

I considered the range of emotions I had experienced since May. "I feel like I'm in a game of tug-of-war."

"You are."

I stopped walking.

Suzette's white hair framed her lined face. Her light-blue eyes met mine. "Eva, two men want to marry you."

I felt warmth flooding my cheeks. Hiding the color from Suzette, I bent over the stroller and adjusted Melody's straps. "Peter and I just met. We're not even close to talking marriage." With nothing else to tweak on the stroller, I reluctantly straightened and faced Suzette with burning cheeks.

"Perhaps not, but Peter is pursuing you with that goal." Her eyes moved back and forth across my face. "And I think you have considered it as well."

I started pushing the stroller again. Suzette kept pace beside me. "You and Marie certainly cut to the center of things."

"Jayne sees how happy you make Peter. Then she knows Sean is coming around, trying to change and trying to win your heart back. She knows it's your decision so she doesn't talk to you about it, but it doesn't stop her from talking to me about it. Day and night. You may have noticed her personality is a little more . . . high-strung than mine."

A soft giggle escaped my lips. "I do envy her energy."

"You've got more than enough yourself. It just manifests itself in a quieter manner. Look at all you're doing—picking and canning everything in sight, preparing to open a preschool while simultaneously adjusting to motherhood. It's exhausting to watch you. On top of all that, two men are earnestly seeking your hand in marriage. I didn't even mention the emotional trauma you've suffered this summer. You have an inner strength that shines through all your adversity. I can see why Rebecca chose you for Melody's mother. You are making sacrifices for her and me. You could have taken that job in New Mexico—"

"How did—"

"Peter told Jayne. The point is, you've put Melody first in all of your decisions even when it caused heartbreaking effects for you."

We paused at the corner, waiting for the street to clear before we crossed. "You mean Sean."

She nodded.

I tilted the stroller back, easing it down the curb and into the street. "I don't know what the outcome of all this will be, but I'm glad this happened before we got married. I'd deluded myself into thinking the chasm between our outlook on family wasn't a concern. We'd work it out."

"Sean seems to be rising to the challenge."

"He's certainly trying hard. I've been impressed with his progress." I paused, struggling with how best to verbalize my misgivings. "I want to believe he's changed, but I've dealt with his . . . persistence before. I keep waiting for it to rear again." Hearing my words, I suddenly understood why I couldn't let go of Peter. I leaned the stroller back, lifting its front wheels onto the curb.

"You're not convinced?" Suzette prodded.

I shrugged. "I guess not."

"He appears sincere."

"He's sincere in wanting to get back together."

"You don't think he's sincere about Melody?"

"He's certainly seems to have changed his attitude toward her. He's . . . more accepting. I'm still trying to discern his true feelings toward her."

"What about your feelings, Eva? Do you want to marry him?"

"I feel like I owe him a second chance. I said yes with all my heart when he asked me to marry him. I don't want to hurt him."

"Do you love him?"

We turned down a side street. "It never made sense that he wanted to be with me, that he chose to marry me. We have a rhythm together. I don't like to be the outgoing one at parties, but that's where he shines. I realized he didn't need someone just like him. I could hang back and let him take center stage, and we were both comfortable. He needs me behind the scenes working to make events come off smoothly." I wondered if Florence knew how much Sean needed a strong support system in the background.

"What do *you* need?"

"I hate making people unhappy. No matter what I choose, someone gets hurt."

She considered this then asked, "Do you think Heavenly Father loves you?"

"Of course."

"What about Sean and Peter? Does He love them?"

"Where's this leading?"

"You are so worried about not hurting one of them that you haven't considered our Father in Heaven's plan in all of this. It's called the plan of happiness. What will bring you joy, Eva? Will that decision bring joy to Sean or Peter? Heavenly Father loves each of you. He wants this most important of decisions to bring joy to *both* of you. You cannot be unequally yoked in marriage and experience joy. Resentment from either pulling too hard or being pushed too much upsets the balance of happiness. Marriage will offer many instances for you to help and support each other through difficult times. Knowing that you share the same convictions strengthens your ability to pull each other through trials. You can't bring happiness to another person if you're not truly happy. Consider carefully, because once you are sealed, you've committed yourself to do everything in your power to bring joy into your husband's life. It's much easier if you're on the same page to begin with."

We paused at another corner, and Suzette turned to face me. "It's better to endure the pain of a failed relationship now. Heavenly Father knows each of your hearts and what will bring you happiness. You have to search your soul for that answer. Take your time. I wouldn't tell anyone else this, Eva, but it may be the only way you'll understand me: be a little selfish. What will make *you* happy?" With that she pulled me into a brief hug, then turned down the street continuing her walk alone.

CHAPTER 21

LATER THAT NIGHT I SAT rocking Melody as I fed her a bottle. I'd never contemplated marrying someone after just knowing him for a month before, and I wasn't entirely comfortable doing so now, especially when there had been no proposal. I wished I could talk to my parents or Rebecca.

Marie and Suzette were right about intent. I wouldn't have agreed to date Peter if I hadn't seen him as a potential eternal companion. And Peter was worried about Pam! What would he think if he had heard Marie and Suzette? Just imagining Peter's horror helped me relax. I laughed out loud.

Melody spit her bottle out and fussed.

I soothed and rocked her as I contemplated Peter's and my budding relationship. Peter was not trying to rush into marriage with me. He was being careful to "keep it real," as he said. I reviewed the notes and flowers he had given me along with the help he had given me for my preschool. The biggest difference between him and Sean was the way they cared for me. Sean decided what was best for him or us and set about doing it. Peter waited to hear what I was doing and then set about helping me accomplish it.

When the phone rang at sunrise on Monday morning, I knew it would be Sean wanting to coordinate schedules.

I picked up the phone in my bedroom, grateful I had just rocked Melody back to sleep after her 5:00 a.m. bottle. "Hello?" I sat cross-legged on my unmade bed.

"Got a calendar in hand?"

He'd fallen back into the pattern of planning our week before breakfast on Mondays. "Hang on a sec." I should have grabbed it when my phone rang, but I knew in my heart that things weren't as back to normal as Sean considered them. I stretched to reach the calendar balanced on the corner of my overflowing white secretary desk. Half a dozen preschool units sprawled haphazardly across its surface.

"The big calendar item is Saturday. That's the barbeque you're catering."

"I've got it in ink already."

"Any chance you could cook outdoors in the middle of nowhere?"

I raised an eyebrow. "What's going on?"

"We've set up a base camp within our third set of search parameters. I thought it would be nice to hold the dinner there."

"Everything is Dutch oven, so as long as I don't have to pack it all in on my back I think it's doable."

Sean snickered. "We'll have four-wheelers for all of that. And bring Melody; I'll help out while you get the dinner going."

Even though I knew he was working hard to change, I was still a little stunned. Bring Melody to a business dinner? I couldn't think to formulate a response.

"Are you still there?"

I could visualize Sean pulling his phone away from his ear to check the connection strength. "Yeah, I'm just thinking it all through."

"Next on the agenda. I want to take you out this week. Can you get a sitter for Melody say on Thursday? I've got tickets for a dinner theater in Provo. We can shop for Saturday's dinner too. So I'll pick you up at four thirty."

I hesitated. Sean had definitely fallen back into our previous rhythm. And I didn't know if I was okay with that anymore.

He sighed. "Eva, you and I need time together as well."

I knew he thought my hesitation meant that I was worried about leaving Melody, but at the moment my mind's eye pictured Peter. How much would this hurt him if he knew? "Sure," I said finally, despite my misgivings. This was part of working things out, I reasoned. "I'll find a babysitter."

"Excellent. But I'm afraid that's it for this week. I'm moving to the base camp with the rest of the researchers, and it looks to be a pretty intense week of searching."

I finished the conversation with a few pleasantries and hoped Sean didn't sense my growing detachment. I picked up a stainless-steel dishpan and headed out to pick more beans while Melody still slept.

I zipped my jacket against the cool morning breeze. The sight of the green-mounded rows and sprawling vegetables loosened my tension. Admittedly, I was pleased with my garden. It required time and tending but it gave me a feeling of accomplishment, just as the growing number of bottles on the basement shelves lent an air of security to me. I could be a full-time mom for Melody until she reached kindergarten and perhaps even first grade. I planned to start applying for a teaching position when she turned five. It might take a couple of years to get on in Sanpete County, but if I were frugal, I could make the money last until then. *How does Sean fit into that picture?* I wondered.

I set the pan down next to the first fifty-foot row and searched the bushes for long beans no wider than my pinky finger. As the beans piled up I considered my coming date with Sean and my recent conversations with Marie and Suzette. Sean was determined to resolve our issues and continue with our planned marriage. But was that what I wanted? I remembered Suzette's admonition. Would I be happy as Sean's wife?

I forced myself to remember the night I gave the ring back. I still felt the echo of that painful act and the long night that followed. Many aspects of our relationship had come more sharply into focus in my conscience during those solitary hours. Facets I had previously refused to acknowledge that challenged my fundamental family values.

Although I could remember the agony, I felt another emotion now when I remembered that night . . . one that grew from the realization that I had faced an unspoken fear. Triumph. That was the other feeling. I dreaded admitting to myself that I might never marry; yet I had stood up to Sean rather than compromise my desire for a family. I gazed at Peter's empty home, wishing I could talk to him. I resolved to attend the temple. I needed spiritual direction.

When I was finished with the first row, I stood and stretched my cramped back. The sun warmed every surface it lighted and promising a scorching day. When my pan was full, I headed back to the house to rinse and prep the beans for canning—and to ask Suzette if she could tend Melody sometime so I could slip away to do a session at the temple.

Suzette was happy to watch her granddaughter for a few hours while I was gone, so before attending the temple I pondered what question I was seeking an answer to. Did I want to know if I should marry Sean, or—and I felt somewhat silly at even considering this question—if I should marry Peter? He and I had never discussed such things. I finally settled on asking for help in making the decisions that would bring happiness into my life and into Melody's.

At the end of the session, I chose a chair in a far corner of the celestial room. Silently, I bowed my head in prayer and explained my predicament to my Heavenly Father. I retraced the events of the summer, beginning with Rebecca's request that I raise Melody and the Spirit's witness to me that it was right. Then I poured out the anguish I felt at knowing I might fail to give Melody a home with a mother and father. I recounted both my worries about Sean as well as his apparent change of heart. Then I related my feelings about Peter. As I did, a calm settled over me, and I pleaded with my Father in Heaven to help me make decisions that would bring peace and joy to Melody and me. I remained eyes closed and unmoving, absorbing the tranquil atmosphere of the temple for a few minutes. Then the words *You will know* came into my heart and mind, and I knew I would.

The impatient part of me asked, "When? How?"

Only a feeling of peace answered my less reverent side. *Patience and trust.* The words from Peter's noted flitted across my mind. I could be patient and trust. Could Sean?

Then I remembered the words and the feeling of peace. *You will know.*

* * *

Thursday evening as Sean and I sat in our seats waiting for the play to start, I found myself enjoying our date. I hadn't realized I'd missed going out. I had kept myself preoccupied with caring for Melody, opening a preschool, and preserving food for the coming year. I'd given little thought to entertainment.

Sean put his arm around my shoulders. "You look more relaxed than I've seen you this entire summer."

I looked up into his blue eyes. "I was just thinking the same thing." I laid my head against him.

"Must be my influence on you." His fingertips traced the curve of my shoulder.

My skin tingled under his touch. "Could be."

"Ladies and gentleman, tonight's performance of . . . " The voice over the loud speaker called the audience's attention, but I was lost in thought. Maybe Sean and I weren't as different as I had imagined. Tonight, for instance, was typical of our relationship—we each worked intensely toward our goals but took time to relax and be together. Perhaps time *was* all we needed to adjust to our new set of circumstances.

* * *

"You look tired," I commented as Sean turned into my driveway.

"I am. Could I crash here tonight?" he asked casually. "I'll leave early before any neighbor is up." The car rolled to a stop and Sean cut the engine.

"Sean . . . " I hesitated.

"Yeah, yeah, I know. I hope I can stay awake all the way to the base camp though." He turned the ignition key. "The others shouldn't mind a four-wheeler waking them up in the dead of night."

I gritted my teeth as a wave of doubt swept through me. There he was blaming me. "You knew you'd be late when you asked me." I opened my car door.

"You're so fixated on the letter of the law you can't help someone in need?"

I jumped down and turned around. "I'll ask Suzette if you can stay there."

"No thanks."

"Suit yourself." I slammed the door on the all too familiar scene. Marriage was the only way to end this argument, I concluded. But was it an argument worth solving?

I started toward my car so I could pick up Melody from Suzette's, but a flicker of light drew my attention to the empty house to the north of mine. I waited a couple of minutes to see if the light would reappear. Suzette had said the owner was still in a retirement center and that the family hadn't sold or rented the house to anyone, but I knew someone was there.

CHAPTER 22

AROUND NOON ON SATURDAY, SEAN arrived to drive me to the base camp. A girl who looked to be about eighteen exited his front passenger seat. She wore jeans and a lemon-yellow T-shirt that contrasted with her straight dark hair cut in long layers to frame her almost perfectly round face.

"This is Michelle," Sean said as they climbed my porch steps.

"Hi." I gazed up at her from the white wicker chair where I sat with Melody.

"Pleased to meet you." She touched the baby's hand. "This must be Melody."

I nodded and looked at Sean.

"She's a sister of a friend—remember the photographer? I'm no baby expert, so Michelle is here to help me know what to do today."

"You can start by loading the boxes and coolers from my kitchen into your car." I frowned as I stood up. This was why he'd volunteered to watch Melody so easily: he'd recruited help.

Michelle followed Sean into the house.

I placed Melody in her carrier and adjusted the straps. Then I slung a red backpack over my shoulder that I was using as Melody's diaper bag for the day. I had probably overpacked—what, with bottled water to mix her formula, clothing for hot or cold weather, Melody's Snugi carrier, and two blankets besides the quilt draped over the back of my chair—but I hated being unprepared in the middle of nowhere.

With the car loaded, I buckled Melody into the backseat. Michelle took a seat next to her, and I sat in front with Sean. Michelle seemed nice enough. I learned she had just turned sixteen and frequently cared for her niece and two nephews.

The paved road gave way to dirt not far past an elk farm with signs announcing we were in Kane Valley. Deep, bone-dry ruts pocked the way, hinting that spring travel had been much more treacherous. I hoped Melody's car seat would keep her from being knocked around. All the same, I climbed in the back and tried to steady her head as we jostled over the road. After forty minutes of bouncing all around inside Sean's SUV, we arrived at a relatively flat grassy area. Several other vehicles were parked in clusters. Sean drove toward a group near a low flat trailer attached to an old brown pickup. Two four-wheelers waited next to it.

"How far is it to the camp on four-wheelers?" I asked.

"It's only about a mile. Real close." Sean said.

While Sean used bungee cords to secure the dinner supplies to the four-wheelers, I retrieved the Snugi and strapped it on before removing Melody from her car seat.

Melody and I rode with Sean on one four-wheeler and Michelle drove the other.

When we arrived at our destination, Sean passed Melody off to Michelle and helped me get the fire started and the camp kitchen arranged for my needs. Once the ribs were browned and simmering in barbeque sauce, Sean introduced me to the researchers and we joined them for a game of cards.

Michelle walked the camp with Melody. Sean noticed my eyes following her. "Melody's fine. Michelle knows what she's doing."

I bit back my response. I had thought Michelle was going to be a baby advisor for Sean, but I saw her role more clearly with every passing minute.

After two hours of chitchat and card games, Neil took center stage. Each joke he told was cruder than the last. I glanced up to check on Melody and Michelle, then excused myself to put the chicken in the Dutch oven. My mind raced as I made room for each chicken breast amid the ribs. I understood Sean wanting a little help caring for Melody—and this was his event after all, but why had he led me to believe he would be the one caring for her? It felt like a bait-and-switch. My thoughts were interrupted as I heard footsteps approaching as I replaced the Dutch oven lid.

"What's for dinner?" a familiar voice asked.

I turned and faced Neil with his trim muscular build and dark, closely cropped hair. "Barbeque ribs and chicken."

Sean emerged from his tent and started toward us with his laptop backpack slung over his left shoulder. "Have you finished breaking down the last quadrant?" Sean asked Neil.

"I think it'll be ready for Monday," Neil said, handing Sean a stack of relief maps. "I assigned smaller quadrants. You can see the names in the lower right corner." Neil pointed to a name written in red ink along the lower edge.

"Still no hot springs?" I asked, looking at both of them.

"Not yet." Sean gripped the strap of his backpack. "I have something to show you. Want to go for a walk?" he asked me.

"Sure," I said, curiosity momentarily outweighing my annoyance with him. I crossed to the camp kitchen and pumped some hand sanitizer on my hands before setting out.

Once out of sight behind the hill, Sean and I sat on a fallen log.

"Have you seen Peter lately?" Sean asked abruptly.

"Not for two weeks."

"Has he been camping?" Sean pulled his laptop from the backpack.

"Hardly. Unless you count some wilderness retreat a couple of weeks ago," I said, wondering where this was going. "He spends his time flying around the world on business."

"Not even earlier this week? It's been nice camping weather." He flipped open the computer and turned it on.

"Early Monday morning I grabbed my camera and went for a hike. I wanted to get a picture of the sun coming up through the mist in the mountain meadows."

I smiled briefly, remembering the countless photos stored on Sean's laptop. Photography was a hobby of his. Many of his photos ended up on the calendar his father put out for their hunting preserve clients.

"I headed into the territory Neil just finished mapping out for us. It's a place I hadn't been to before, since our efforts have been concentrated elsewhere. Anyway, I got some truly fantastic pictures and then observed a man come around the base of a hill. He started up the slope and I got out my telephoto lens to see if it was someone from camp." He looked at me and continued. "I recognized the man right away, and I'm sure you will too." Sean opened the file.

A man wearing olive cargo pants, a coffee-colored T-shirt, a baseball cap atop brown shoulder-length hair, and a full beard filled the screen. The hat brim blocked his face. I looked at Sean and shrugged.

He pointed at the screen and clicked to the next picture. The man held his hat in hand as his forearm wiped his brow.

I licked my lips. "How—"

"Wait." He clicked to the next photo, revealing a full face shot.

Stunned and confused, I felt my mouth drop open. "Peter? Wh-when was this taken?" I refused to look at Sean, to see the victory in his eyes.

He pointed to the time/date stamp in the left column of the screen. Three days ago.

On-screen, Peter's brown eyes stared back at me. I rummaged through my memories with Peter, seeking for a reason he would be *here*.

"He never told you he was camping." Sean closed the computer.

I stared at the dirt under my feet. "You've never liked him."

"I'm thinking of you and Melody."

I stood up and flung my arms wide. "Just because he shows up on your camera screen one day—"

"What kind of life can Peter give you if he lies about where he spends his time?" He stood and faced me.

What was with all the talk of me marrying Peter? "Who says I'm planning to have a life with Peter?"

"Your reaction to these pictures says it all. You told me I had to be honest with Florence. Don't you deserve honesty too?"

He'd taken the picture on Monday morning.

I suddenly felt nauseous. The nanny, the date on Thursday—he'd been building his case. "It's a little late to concern yourself with my future." I kept all emotion from my voice.

He took both my hands in his. "I'm still in love with you." He kissed my cheek.

I remained motionless.

"We are an ideal team, you and I." He squeezed my hands. "Today is just like so many other days we've worked together."

"Sean, I—"

"Let me finish before you say anything. I brought Michelle tonight to show you how a nanny could help us. I've tried your way; I thought it only fair you give my way a chance."

Anger bubbled inside of me. He had been purposefully misleading me into thinking he'd take care of Melody. Sean wasn't going to change, not for Melody, and not for our children. How had I ever thought he wanted to be an involved father? "I still—"

He dropped my right hand and put his finger over my lips. "I'm not finished." He pulled something out of his pocket and nimbly slid an engagement ring on my hand. "Back to its rightful owner."

I numbly stared at the ring. It embodied all I had once wanted in life. But now? Accepting this ring meant accepting Michelle and others like her in the years to come. It meant being on Sean's arm as his career no doubt climbed and soared. It meant being steamrolled whenever my opinion didn't match his. It meant giving up the hope of finding someone committed to family, someone like Peter.

Even more confusion swirled inside me when I thought of Peter.

Sean's cool hand cradled my face like so many times before. "Marry me, Eva. I love you." Then his lips were hard against mine, working, waiting for me to respond. His embrace held me tight against him, pressing Peter's compass into my heart.

Hot anger continued to flow through my veins. How dare he? Nothing had changed. I quickly turned my head.

He pulled back.

"We haven't resolved anything." I enunciated each word carefully. "We're still at the same impasse." I handed him the ring, "Not now, not ever." And then I marched back to camp.

At the camp kitchen, I grabbed an oversized bag of vegetables and a package of grated cheese.

Sean followed wordlessly a few paces behind.

At the campfire I dumped the contents of both bags in a new Dutch oven and used a shovel to arrange coals on its lid. Then I turned to the four-wheeler and my backpack. Once I had the Snugi carrier strapped on, I sought out Michelle and took Melody from her. "This way you'll have your hands free to eat," I explained.

"Aren't you eating too?" Her expression was puzzled.

"No, I need a break. I'm taking the four-wheeler for a ride." I said the words then looked behind Michelle at Sean hovering five feet away, obviously afraid, saying anything might cause a scene. I wouldn't tarnish his precious reputation, but I refused to pretend all through dinner with him. I stepped past Michelle and, in a too-nice voice, said, "The food will be ready in forty-five minutes." I slid Melody into the carrier. "It's self-serve style tonight. I'm taking the four-wheeler and I'll be back sometime after dinner." I gulped in an exaggerated breath of air. "I just can't get enough of this wide open space." I pushed my arms through the backpack straps and folded Melody's quilt over one arm.

In a voice so low only I could hear, Sean said, "Eva, you don't have to leave."

I set my jaw and in the most menacing whisper I could muster replied, "You built your case flawlessly, but I'm not a jury, Sean. I'm a real person." Even whispering, my voice broke on the last word. I spun around and headed for the four-wheeler.

I could feel Sean's eyes on my back, and after a few steps heard him start after me. At the four-wheeler, I swung my leg over and arranged Melody's blanket under me so it wouldn't blow away.

"How long are you going to be?"

"I'll be back by dark," I said curtly.

"That's five hours away."

I nodded my head and started the four-wheeler.

Sean's mouth moved, but the engine's roar drowned him out. I drove past him without looking at his face, made a wide turn, and gunned it. Let the camp think what they wanted. I needed time to process all of this before I was confined to a car with Sean again. The ride home wouldn't be pleasant. Maybe someone else was leaving tonight and I could catch a ride with them. I'd find out when I got back, but right now I wanted to be far away from Sean.

CHAPTER 23

MELODY SQUIRMED AND FUSSED. THE four-wheeler's noise and jostling distressed her, but I pressed on, thinking she would acclimate. After about three miles her protest had accelerated to a constant cry. I slowed down to cross a shallow ribbon of a stream then continued on toward a wooded area. I hoped Sean wouldn't come looking for me, but if he did, the trees would make it harder for him to spot me and the four-wheeler.

I parked near an incline with blue-green spruce trees and set out on foot, Melody snuggled closely against my chest. The quiet crunching of pine needles coupled with the cadence of my footfalls soon lulled her to sleep.

Anger and confusion warred inside my head. Peter had said it was his work keeping him away. Scenes from his family reunion flashed through my mind. His whole family believed that's where he was too! How could he be here? And then there was Sean. His way or no way. I could compromise when it came to things like china, but we were worlds apart when it came to how raise children.

I reached the hill's crest and descended a gentle slope into a relatively flat grove of aspen trees. Round leaves quivered in the breeze, creating the illusion of movement. The white trunks were surrounded by what appeared to be an ocean of seaweed. Upon closer observation, I realized the plants were in rows, not scattered about naturally as I had assumed from a distance. I waded into the undergrowth. Judging from the odor, a skunk must have been here recently. As I stepped between two rows of the yard-high weeds, my foot felt something that yielded. With one hand supporting Melody's head, I squatted down to see part of a black rubber hose protruding from the ground. It felt warm. I scanned the other rows and noted a mounded tunnel of dirt running between each column.

Warm water? Someone had already found the hot springs. What I didn't understand was why Sean didn't know about this. I thought he had coordinated with all of the GBEEC researchers. This had to be a GBEEC experimental plot to help control the watershed. It looked like all of the other GBEEC research trials that attempted to find the balance between allowing sheep to graze without creating flood situations for the town of Ephraim.

A gust of wind knocked at my back and the shadows deepened. Dark clouds that I hadn't noticed earlier slithered across the sky.

I had to get back before the storm hit. I climbed back up through the pine trees and scooted across the hilltop until I was sure the four-wheeler was below me. Then I walked down through aspens and spruce for another fifteen minutes. Finally, glimpsing the meadow ahead, I hurried through the last trees. I searched for the four-wheeler, only finding more grass. I strained my eyes to locate the meandering brook and saw only boulders and bluebells instead.

I cursed my lack of a sense of direction. If I hadn't been so angry with both Sean and Peter, I might have at least looked at the compass hanging around my neck when I'd dismounted the four-wheeler.

Melody whimpered. She'd spit out her pacifier. I searched the chest pack but couldn't find it. When I backtracked a few steps I still couldn't find it.

The breeze picked up strength as the temperature dropped.

I shivered. Shrugging off my backpack, I pulled out a blanket for Melody, draped it across the Snugi and tucked it in around her. How had I been so oblivious not to notice a storm moving in? I needed some sort of shelter, and quickly.

A cacophony of bleating sheep interrupted my thoughts. Masses of lumpy white shapes sprinkled with black flecks surged up and over the meadow's gentle swell. A splash of wet hit my cheek, and then another struck my hand. I scanned the meadow for protection from the coming storm. I saw nothing, however, and continued up the slope in hopes of finding a place to escape the weather. The stands of trees edging the meadow behind me might be my only option.

The rain came in tick-tock fashion, steady and even in its descent. Cresting the hill, I discerned a white, covered wagon-shaped trailer. Firewood lay neatly stacked along the side closest to me. A sheep camp. I hoped the herder would let Melody and me wait out the storm in his trailer.

When I had rapped on the sheep camp door for the third time, I slowly I turned the knob and opened the door a crack. "Hello?"

Nothing.

I pulled the door open wide and stood on the step. A skunky-sweet aroma assaulted my nose, along with the faint smell of bacon. My eyes slowly adjusted to the dim interior. Straight ahead, a table flanked by built-in benches gradually materialized. At about four feet up, a full-sized bed extended to the back wall. Blanket and pillow mounds gave misshapen bulk to the mattress. Green-and-brown plaid curtains framed a long narrow window above the bed as well as the windows above the dining benches. Cupboards ran the length of the wall at the foot of the bed.

"Hellooo," I called into the dark.

No one returned my greeting.

On my left I noticed a small sink and a two-burner stovetop with cupboards above and below. A diminutive dish drainer held dishes enough for two. I stepped inside and closed the door revealing an undersized wood-burning stove and a fridge adjacent to a closet. Slate-colored dirt scratched beneath my feet against the vinyl floor.

I jumped involuntarily as a crash of thunder sounded overhead. Melody shuddered and her alarmed cry sliced through the stillness.

"Shhh. It's all right," I soothed and peeked at her beneath the blanket I had stretched across the Snugi. A glance at my watch revealed it wasn't quite time to feed her. I removed my backpack and scooted myself to the back of the bench to my right. Then I sang a quiet lullaby and rocked Melody back to sleep. With my feet on the bench in front of me, I snuggled into the corner and drifted between sleep and wakefulness.

Voices signaled my sleepy eyes to open. I had no idea what time it was, but I was sure I had been asleep for at least a couple of hours. Men speaking Spanish were coming around the trailer. The door jerked open and I readied my explanation. Three backpacks sailed onto the bench opposite me. The trailer shook slightly as someone stepped inside. He hurled a string of Spanish over his shoulder as he stepped closer to me, telling the others to wait while he exchanged the backpacks for coats.

I held my breath as disbelief paralyzed me. I knew that voice. Peter? This was his consulting business, the reason he came and went at all hours of the night? A sheep camp?

Peter's hair brushed the tops of his shoulders as he strode toward me, still not looking in my direction. A full, bushy beard adorned his face, much like the one he'd had the night Rebecca's basement flooded.

My heart fluttered as a feeling of longing surged through me. Despite Sean's pictures, I had missed Peter. Instantly I chastised myself. He had outright lied to me. There was no hope for a relationship with him anymore.

Peter opened the creaky closet, blocking my view of the outside door. And then his eyes met mine. For a moment, he froze. A look of terror inscribed his features and a low hissing sound emanated from his lips. Simultaneously his arm swung the closet door wide. He placed a finger over his lips and with lightning speed retrieved an armload of jackets and raincoats, half of which he threw on top of me.

Instinctively, I raised my arm to shield Melody from the onslaught. She continued sleeping without interruption. I heard his quick steps exit the trailer and then the door slammed shut.

I almost threw the pile of coats off, but then I remembered Peter's panic-stricken face. I wondered why my presence here alarmed him to the point of concealing Melody and me beneath a pile of coats.

Outside Peter instructed his companions in Spanish to go on without him. He wanted a different coat, he explained.

Under the jackets, I waited for him to reenter the trailer, stinging at his furtive actions. Was he ashamed of me? Why didn't he want me to know he was a herder? Or maybe these were his sheep and he was a rancher. Why had he deflected my questions about his business? Was it so important to keep his livelihood a secret? Was he the ornery rancher chasing hunters and hikers off his grazing land? Was he the one using the hot springs? Then I thought about the look of fear on Peter's face. Something else was at stake here.

Finally the door opened and closed quickly. I felt the weight of coats being lifted off me.

I shivered. The opening and closing of the door had let in cooler air.

"Eva, we've got to get you out of here," Peter whispered.

Melody whimpered.

Peter's jaw fell open. "Not Melody too."

He must have been too distracted to have noticed her before. Maybe the blanket had hidden her from view. "What's going on here?" I asked accusingly.

"There's no time to waste." He grasped my elbow and pulled me up.

The whimpering turned to whining. "She's hungry. I need to make a bottle for her."

"How did you get here? We're miles from any road."

"Four-wheeler."

The color drained from Peter's face. "A red Polaris with camo saddlebags and a blanket across the seat?" He picked up my backpack.

"You know where it is?"

"Don't you?"

I shrugged, not wanting to explain.

"Those guys are out there looking for the rider right now." His arm pointed at the door.

Melody began crying.

"Peter, I need the backpack. She's hungry."

"Here." It clunked against the tabletop. "I have to think."

I mixed the bottle while I watched Peter massage his temples. I tested the formula's temperature on my wrist. Not warm enough. I hoped she was sufficiently hungry to drink it anyway. I spread her blanket on the table and lifted her out of the chest pack. I started to unstrap the Snugi, but Peter's hands blocked mine.

"Stop." His fingers refastened the straps. "You have to leave. Now."

I whirled on him. "Melody needs to eat. She's not going to settle down until she does." What was wrong with him? I undid the straps again. "Then I'll take one of those ponchos and with directions from you we'll be on our way." I said icily.

"You have no idea what you've stumbled into, do you?"

"How could I possibly know when you never answer my questions?" I hurled the words at him.

"Naiveté!" He stepped between the table and bench retrieving a pillowcase off the bed. Opening it he thrust it at me. "Look!'

If possible, the skunk smell intensified. Inside were more plant starts like those I'd seen in the aspens, nothing to warrant his overreaction. "And you also have an experimental garden in the aspens growing . . . high nutrient plants for sheep to graze?"

"Hardly, Eva. We keep the sheep out of the crop."

His rock-hard voice forced a lump in my throat. I swallowed hard, willing myself to feel anger, not the hurt creeping into my chest. "I'm really sorry I stumbled into your *secret* world." Was this the real Peter? A hermit living a hidden life in the mountains? "I needed to get Melody out of the rain. I think you could be a little more accepting of the situation." I turned back to Melody, hoping to distract myself from the overpowering awareness of his betrayal. I wrapped her up and nestled her in my arms with the bottle. Outside the purr of a motor grew closer.

Peter's hands grasped my shoulders and with sudden speed propelled me back into the bench. I was barely able to keep the bottle in Melody's mouth. She whimpered at the jarring disturbance to her meal.

Hot anger vaporized the last remnants of my hurt. I opened my mouth, but Peter clapped one hand over it and gathered coats with the other.

His eyes caught mine. There was a mournful pleading there and he whispered fiercely, "Please trust me. Don't move or make any sound!"

I felt a quiet voice whisper, *Do what he says.* Sensing his urgency, I nodded as the engine cut. My heart thudded wildly and I clutched Melody closer, patting her softly, soothing her complaints into silence. He removed his hand, cautioning me with his eyes. Carefully he spread a large black raincoat over the baby and me. Coats rained down on us as the door opened and the trailer dipped with a new arrival. A soft heap landed at my feet on the bench—the sack of plants, I supposed.

In rapid Spanish the newcomer informed Peter that the four-wheeler driver was nowhere to be seen. He suspected it was from a new camp he had seen two valleys over. He had sent one man to watch the vehicle and had posted the other two around the marijuana's perimeter. They were all armed and ready.

Marijuana! My pulse beat against my eardrums and I held my breath. It was so obvious. How had I missed it? I'd walked through the rows of marijuana plants warmed and watered by the hot springs. I silently prayed Melody would be still, that this new man would leave momentarily.

The man asked for a raincoat.

Footsteps approached me.

Let them be Peter's, I prayed, though I had no reason now to trust him any more than the others. Nausea threatened to overwhelm my stomach as the hot air under the coats pressed in against me. I felt a tugging and a careful rearranging within the mound, then Peter's Spanish explaining that this one kept the rain out best. I learned that the man's name was Hector.

"I found this in the trees on the edge of the crop. Given the baby blanket on the four-wheeler, I'd say we have a visitor," the Spanish-speaking man concluded.

"I'll search the trees behind the trailer and meet you back at the four-wheeler," Peter said.

Moments later the door opened and shut. Stillness echoed against the incessant tapping of rain. Neither Peter nor I moved. Seconds turned to a minute, then two. An engine roared to life and faded away.

Fabric rustled as my hiding place was peeled away.

Eyes wide, I stared at Peter. "Marijuana?" I whispered. "You're a drug dealer?" I kicked the pillowcase at my feet to the floor. It landed against the single table leg, green starts spilling onto the floor.

"No!" Peter bent to clean up the spilled profits. A clap of thunder echoed outside and a gust of wind blew the trailer door open.

I raised the blanket around Melody's head to shield her from the cold wind.

"All I want is to get out of here. But how am I going to leave with an armed man watching my four-wheeler?"

Peter's hand froze midway to the pillowcase. He stared up at me. "You speak Spanish."

"Mission in South America. Not that anything religious makes a difference to you."

"You know me better than that." He finished collecting the plants and threw the sack past me onto the bed.

"I thought I did."

He crossed to the door and pulled it shut, then sat down on the edge of the bench next to my feet. The wind sucked the door open again. "I'm an undercover cop, Eva."

A cold gust of air swept through the trailer, sucking my anger away and leaving surprise and relief in its place. I looked in his eyes and knew he was telling me the truth. "Thank you," I whispered.

An extended bout of rumbling sounded, and the trailer trembled slightly as he studied me, eyebrows furrowed into a question. "I don't usually get that response from women I'm dating."

"I was afraid I'd made you into what I wanted, just like I did with Sean." It poured out of my mouth before I realized I had revealed too much, made myself vulnerable.

"You want me?"

I stared down at Melody, grateful my wet hair fell in front of my face. She finished the bottle. I brought her up to my shoulder to burp her and glanced around Peter toward the open door.

An electric shock of terror shot across my chest and through my shoulders. Thunder had concealed the four-wheeler's return. It wasn't the wind that had sucked the door open a second time; I shuddered as I stared into the black eyes of the man I presumed to be Hector.

CHAPTER 24

READING MY EXPRESSION, PETER WHIRLED around.

Hector waved the handgun at him, motioning him to sit across from me.

Peter complied.

"My English good enough know the word *cop*." He spat the word like a wad of chew. Then he backhanded Peter with his pistol.

Peter's head snapped back against the trailer then limply swung forward. I heard a scream and realized it was mine.

Abruptly, Melody began to cry.

Peter regained his composure, despite the pain he must be in as evidenced by the red mark along the entire right side of his face.

"Hands on table," Hector ordered Peter.

Without a word, Peter slowly stretched his fingers out, palms down, and rested them on the table.

My pounding heart thudded in my ears as I struggled to soothe Melody with wooden arms.

Pointing the gun at me, Hector said, "Wife."

"No," Peter and I said at the same time. In Spanish, Peter explained, "She waited out the storm in the empty trailer. I found her when we came back."

"This," Hector held up Melody's pacifier and continued in Spanish, "is all the proof I need to get rid of her. She knows too much." The incessant rain continued its tapping.

Peter hesitated then said, "It's her four-wheeler you're watching. If she doesn't get back soon her friends will have search and rescue combing these mountains." He met Hector's menacing stare.

Then queasiness claimed my stomach again as I realized that Sean and the others would come looking for me soon and that they would find me with armed men protecting an underground operation.

Hector considered the information. "Either way, we have to leave this field."

"You don't have to add murder to your list of crimes."

Murder. The word leached all warmth from me. I shuddered and bit down on my tongue until I tasted blood.

"They'll never know it's me," Hector said.

"There's a way you can get her to promise not to say anything for forty-eight hours, maybe longer. That's more time than you'll have if search and rescue is called."

"The baby." His eyes gleamed, and he stepped toward me.

I turned into the corner, clutching Melody tighter in my arms.

"No. A baby will only slow you down," Peter nearly yelled.

"Enough!" Hector waved the gun at him.

Peter veered to the left, narrowly missing a second encounter with Hector's gun. "She won't say anything until I contact her. Even if it means waiting four or five days." He spoke fluent Spanish to Hector, but his eyes never left mine.

He must have known that Hector didn't plan on letting him live, since he didn't include himself in the bargain. How could I make such a promise? I looked down at Melody's light-brown eyes. She was my priority and Peter knew it. He knew I would protect her at all costs.

Peter looped his finger under my locket. "Keep me close."

I curled my hand around his. "I can't leave you here." I looked up to see Hector smirking at me.

"She means something to you." Hector sneered at Peter.

"I gave her this locket to remind her of me when I was gone." He said the words to Hector, but I knew he meant them for me. "We take them both back to the four-wheeler and let them go. I stay here with you."

"There's got to be another way," I whispered.

Peter shook his head quietly, pleading with me.

Peter's life for Melody's and mine. I couldn't have accepted the terms if it were just for me.

I closed my eyes and took a deep breath. "Okay," I said.

Across the table, Peter turned back to Hector. "She'll keep quiet. Take them back to the four-wheeler and let them go. You won't have the mountain crawling with search and rescue, and you'll have me."

"Let's go," Hector's gruff voice commanded as he gestured with the gun for me to stand up.

In Spanish I explained, "I need a blanket for the baby."

Hector only uttered one word. "Hurry."

I began unzipping the backpack when Hector grabbed it with his free hand and dumped the contents onto the table. Satisfied that baby wipes, diapers, formula, bottled water, a blanket and granola bars were harmless, he swiped three oat-and-honey bars and took a step back. I gathered everything back into my pack, strapped on the chest pack, and nestled Melody inside. Finally, I carefully tucked Melody's blanket around me to screen her from the falling drops.

"She needs a poncho. There's one on the floor under the table I can get," Peter said.

Hector bobbed his head once. "Slow."

I stepped to my right and placed my back against the closet door while I watched.

Peter slid out of his bench and dropped to his knees all while keeping his hands up. As if pushing against an unseen force, his arm lowered to the floor and retrieved a black cowboy-style raincoat with a slit up the back for straddling a horse. He held it out to me.

"What will you wear?"

"Just put it on."

Grateful to have something more to shield Melody with, I pulled my arms through, zipped it up, then pulled one arm back in so I could maintain contact with the baby. Peter put on a pair of sunglasses that partially concealed the swelling bruise now forming across his right cheek. As we exited the trailer, Peter whispered, "Hector agreed to this plan a little too easily. Stay alert."

Hector led the three of us behind the trailer, and we moved down a gently sloping hill toward the line of trees. After a half hour of climbing we reached the summit. Twenty minutes later we emerged into a long meadow with a familiar brook ambling through its center. The last drops of rain danced through the sun-kissed clouds as I scanned the field for my four-wheeler.

"Company," Peter said and stopped.

I followed his gaze and observed Sean and Neil standing by my four-wheeler accompanied by two men wearing long black coats matching mine. Up until this point, Peter had been leading with me following and Hector bringing up the rear. Now Peter shifted to walk alongside me. Hector remained behind, the gun ever present beneath his poncho.

About thirty yards from our rendezvous point, Peter stopped and held his hands out to his sides. I halted with him. Slowly he turned to face Hector. I rotated a quarter turn toward Peter, my heart thudding wildly.

Melody complained now that we weren't moving.

I swayed to calm her.

"Let me do the talking, and we'll get out of here faster," Peter instructed in Spanish. He looked at me. "Eva, just follow my lead."

I nodded and then we continued to close the gap. With ten yards to go, Sean shouted, "Eva, is that you?" and began jogging toward us.

The raincoat and hood must have obscured my identity before now. I'd probably looked like another one of Hector's men at a distance.

Sean pulled up short and eyed Peter. "So what brings your consulting expertise to the mountains?"

"Sean, let it go," I said.

"Eva, honesty is fundamental to a relationship, remember?"

Neil caught up to us then. The sun gleamed off his black hair. "Looks like you found some protection from the storm." His gaze focused behind me to where Hector waited.

I began unzipping the coat. "Thanks, Peter," I handed it to him and peeked at Melody beneath her blanket.

"You two more than neighbors?" Neil asked me.

"He thought he could impress Eva with his consulting business. He's nothing but a sheep herder," Sean said.

"Time to go, Hector," Peter said.

I stepped toward Sean.

"Had your quota of lies today?" Sean spoke to me, but his eyes never left Peter.

I pursed my lips tightly, worry for Peter making it difficult to focus on what Sean was saying. "I don't want to talk about it."

Hector moved alongside Peter and stretched a clenched hand toward Neil, who extended his palm to catch the object Hector released. A pink pacifier.

"Let's go." I tugged on Sean's sleeve.

"Is this yours?" Neil held up the pink pacifier.

I nodded my head.

Neil looked at Hector and began conversing in Spanish. "Where did you find it?"

"In the crop."

My stomach heaved. This was a new low—even for Neil. Hector wasn't returning the binky, only updating Neil on the situation. Hector had never planned on letting me go.

I looked at Peter. His sunglasses blocked any emotion I might have read there. Did he know Neil?

"My orders were specific: protect at all costs." Neil's Spanish continued.

"If she disappeared, search and rescue would be all over this mountain," Peter said. "She won't say anything for at least forty-eight hours. It's only a matter of time with them here now, anyway," Peter replied in Spanish and then nodded his head at Sean.

"I'm managing that intrusion quite well." Neil's eyes narrowed.

"Eva, what are they saying?" Sean asked at the same instant Hector punched Peter in the stomach and said, "Cop," to Neil in English.

Peter doubled over, and a whimper escaped my lips.

"Hey. Cool off there, buddy," Sean said. "Leave him alone to count his losses." He turned to me. "What's he all fired up about?"

I couldn't answer Sean. Instead I watched Peter press his hands into his thighs. Would Hector even let Peter live another forty-eight hours? I had to find help for him, no matter what I had promised.

Neil glanced from Peter to me. "Figures you'd take up with a cop," he said in Spanish while his cold, dark eyes focused on me. Then he turned to Hector. "Take all three of them back to our base camp," he ordered. "I'll take care of the four-wheeler and explain that Sean found Eva and drove her home. I'll have to move his car." Neil looked toward the two figures standing next to the Polaris. "One of them can pick me up."

My heart beat faster and I gulped in air. Frantically, I began a silent prayer.

"What are they saying?" Sean asked again, more urgently.

There had to be some way to get back to Sean's camp alive. And then it hit me. "If Michelle doesn't get back tonight—"

"I already sent her home with Victor and his wife," Sean said. Relieved I was speaking in English, he continued. "Without Melody there was nothing for her to do."

Disappointment flooded me, and I wracked my brain for another out.

Up until now, Hector had kept his gun concealed beneath his raincoat. With a nod from Neil, he now pushed his arm through the sleeve of the poncho.

"What's this, Peter? You convinced Eva your shrine to murderers was nothing to worry about." Sean focused his anger on the wrong individual.

"This guy is a piece of work, Neil. You should see what's on his living room wall."

"I'm going to guess newspaper articles and red spray paint?" Neil replied.

"You've seen it?" Sean asked.

That's when I knew I'd missed something big. My mind raced back to the day I'd found Neil coming out of Peter's house. He'd let me believe that Sean had sent him to check up on Peter. But it was Neil checking up on Peter—leaving him an ominous message. That's what Peter had meant about scare tactics. The board was meant to keep him in line. That's why there were no newspapers in Peter's house, and how an article printed three days before he got home had appeared on the bulletin board. Neil had visited Peter's house to add another article, another warning.

"I put it there," Neil said, then he let out a piercing whistle and Hector motioned for the two men by the four-wheeler to join us.

"You did what?" Sean asked, looking confused.

Sean's head swiveled from Hector and Peter to Neil and back again. "What did he do, Eva?" he asked angrily.

I knew he was referring to Peter.

"Your *friend* has all the answers," I said.

Neil pulled some coiled rope from the front pocket of his coat.

"Arms out front, wrists crossed," Neil ordered Peter.

Hector stood just out of reach, brandishing the handgun.

"Guns and now rope? If it's that serious just turn Shaggy over to the cops like Pistol Man said earlier. I'll help you bring him in."

Neil expertly wove the rope around Peter's wrists, completely ignoring Sean. Once Peter's hands were bound, Neil cut the excess rope with his pocketknife and turned to Sean. "Same thing, Sean."

"I don't know what you have against Peter, but this is me, Neil." Sean tapped his own chest indignantly. "We go way back."

"Hector can persuade you to be more cooperative if you'd like."

"You can't be serious, Neil."

"Cross your wrists."

Hector stepped forward.

"We're outnumbered, Sean," Peter coaxed.

"*We* aren't anything," Sean's menacing tone sneered. "Don't include me in your parcel of lies."

Consumed with blaming Peter for our predicament, Sean failed to see Neil's upraised arm. A muffled thud sounded as Neil's fist connected with Sean's lower back.

As I watched Sean slump to the ground, Peter's explanation of the bulletin board sounded in my mind, *They have a kill-or-be-killed mentality.* Suddenly the gravity of the situation overwhelmed me, and my knees buckled. I swayed, arms flailing for balance, before I crumpled sideways and landed on my hip, straining to hold my torso above ground with one arm cradling Melody. Lights sputtered before my eyes as Melody's cry stung my ears. How would I get her out of here unharmed? A lump formed in my throat as I contemplated the impossibility of escape. The men outnumbered us even without weapons.

Nausea surged up, and I twisted away from Melody as my stomach emptied itself. Another convulsion and I dry heaved into the meadow.

"Eva, stand up." I heard Peter's voice and realized he'd repeated this instruction at least three times. Hector's top-heavy frame lumbered toward me.

The urgency of Peter's command now registered. I clawed a handful of grass from the soft ground and wiped my mouth, then gulped more rain-cleansed air, and pushed my hands against the wet sod to regain a standing position. Hector halted his approach.

Sean knelt in front of Neil, wrists bound with rope. Neil once again cut the extra rope and turned to me. Sean seized his opportunity. From his knees he jumped to his feet, wrapped his legs around Neil, and brought him crashing to the ground. The two men Hector had motioned over were instantly on top of Sean prying him off Neil. Hector stood ready, gun trained on the mass of struggling men. Sean repeatedly shouted amid the struggle, "We were friends, Neil! Like brothers."

When Neil's henchman had peeled Sean off of Neil, I got my first good look at the two men who had joined the group. "Felix?" He wouldn't make eye contact with me, but I knew it was my ESL student. This was the new job he'd found. This was why he'd stopped coming to my afterschool English classes last spring.

Neil punched Sean in the stomach. "We were never like brothers, Sean. You, with all your money and privilege. You don't know what it's like when your kid gets real sick and you don't have insurance. You don't know how fast you go under like that. You don't know what it's like to live in a country where you can't read the language. You don't know what it's like to work sixty hours a week to survive. No, we're not brothers."

Between the punch and Neil's words, Sean was too stunned to reply.

Neil came over to me. "Your turn. Take off your backpack."

"It's just got water and formula in it. Hector already searched it." My voice trembled.

Neil verified my claim with Hector, then said, "Hold out your wrists."

"Please, I have to take care of the baby." I stroked Melody's back with shaking hands. "I won't cause any problems." I finished in a whisper.

Neil's eyes flashed from me to the two men who now joined Hector. "Felix, you stay close and watch her. Quin, you're with me." His Spanish held no foreign accent. In English, he added, "Let's rock and roll." Then Neil lowered his voice and I couldn't hear what else he said before starting back to the four-wheeler with Quin.

Hector waved his gun and spoke one English word. "Go."

Peter started off, and Sean and I followed behind. Felix fell into step beside me, looking straight ahead, and Hector brought up the rear.

"Where are we going?" Sean asked, and I detected the slightest shakiness in his voice.

"Back to their camp. I waited out the storm in their trailer."

"No talking!" Hector barked.

Sunlight glistened off the damp grass and leaves; the bright evening sun glowed in stark contrast to our somber march back up the wooded hill and down through spruce into the remote camp. I emerged from the trees and swept my eyes across the rolling valley surrounded by steeply forested inclines. It must have been quite a feat for them to maneuver a trailer through the rough terrain into this secluded hideaway.

Hector halted at the back of the trailer. "Sit," he pointed to the wet dirt. With the point of his gun, he directed us into a line with three-foot gaps between us, watching until we all sat down.

"Felix," Hector called then said in Spanish, "Watch them. I'll check the perimeter." He held out the gun.

Felix licked his lips a couple of times then removed his raincoat and tossed it over a tree branch before grasping his weapon. His trim form and fluid movements projected a gentler demeanor than his current job required. He focused on me then moved down the line to Sean and finally to Peter. I read the bewilderment in his expression before he began pacing in front of us.

"Eva, what's going on?" Sean whispered.

"Marijuana's growing not far from here," I whispered back and watched Felix for a reaction. He showed no concern over us talking so I continued. "I hid in the trailer during the storm. Peter found me and told me he's an undercover cop, but Hector overheard him. That's why they hate him. He had arranged with Hector to get Melody and me out, but—"

"I didn't know Neil would be with you," Peter explained. "We suspected someone on your team was involved in this op. Every time you hold a big gathering, supplies from Mexico arrive in my garage." He jerked his head toward the trailer.

Both Sean and I turned to see bottles labeled *Raticida*—"Rat Poison"— standing in rows under the sheep camp tailer along with bags of fertilizer also with Spanish labels. "It seemed more than coincidence; especially when I learned that Neil lived in Las Cruces." Peter's eyes never left Felix.

"They delivered supplies to your garage with Eva next door?"

"My partner, Javier, has been watching her. That house wasn't my idea. The agency seized it a few years ago, and it worked to use it for this op."

"Javier has been watching from the house on the north side of mine!" I said with sudden realization.

Peter nodded.

"How do you know so much about Neil?" Sean asked suspiciously.

"Remember the interview you set up for Eva? It started to click then. That's when I realized Neil was in Boise, Ephraim, and Las Cruces, New Mexico. He connected all the dots. He had to be the alpha." Peter studied Felix, who tugged at his thick black hair while he changed directions. Then he quickly changed topics. "We need something for a bribe."

My mind categorized the contents of my backpack. Nothing of value there, and I doubted the pack itself was of any worth. My watch was a five-dollar special from Walmart, and the only jewelry I was wearing today was my compass locket. Not exactly the kind of jewelry we could use as a bribe. Not that any jewelry I did wear could be considered valuable . . . except . . . "Sean, what'd you do with the ring?" I hissed.

"You want it now?" His voice, though a hoarse whisper, was incredulous.

"It's the perfect bribe."

Peter recognized the import of my statement. His eyes broke away from Felix. "Have you got it on you?"

"It's in my pocket, but . . ."

"Follow my lead, or you're not getting out of here alive." Then to prove his point, he called to Felix.

Felix stopped in front of Peter.

"What are they doing with them?" Peter asked in Spanish then bobbed his head toward Sean and me.

"They're going to die in a car accident later tonight," Felix's Spanish explained, then to me, he added, "*Lo siento, señorita.*"

The horrific reality sucked the air from my lungs. I hugged Melody to me and buried my face against her soft hair. Hot tears coursed down my cheeks. I supposed it would be a fitting end for me; all those times I felt I should have died in the Memorial Day accident.

"What did he say?" Sean asked.

"You'll meet your end in a car accident after dark tonight." Peter said.

"Is that true, Eva?"

I lifted my head and turned toward Sean. I nodded.

"This is just the situation you dreaded." Peter spoke to Felix, who stood just in front of him.

Felix stared back at Peter. I saw the hesitation written on Felix's face. He opened and closed his mouth, then settled for licking his lips and nodding.

"There's another way," Peter's calm Spanish continued.

Felix's eyes widened. "I can't, Peter. My family needs the money."

"I know that's the only reason you took this job. You hate what they ask you to do."

"Your words don't change anything." Felix dug at the moist ground with the toe of his boot.

"We can get out of here alive. All of us . . . with your help," Peter continued.

"I have to stay until I get paid."

"We can pay you."

"If I let you go, I won't get paid."

"We can pay you tonight." Peter looked at Sean and continued in English. "We can pay him tonight, right?"

Sean looked at me.

"It's the only way," I said.

He turned back to Peter with a stony expression. "All right. But how do you know he won't double-cross us?" he muttered under his breath.

CHAPTER 25

PETER, SEAN, AND I STILL sat spaced a yard apart behind the sheep camp when I fed Melody her nine o'clock bottle. Quin now stood guard while Felix took a turn in the aspens. Felix was still wavering on whether to accept the ring as a bribe before he went off guard shift. I suspected he feared for his family. If Neil had placed threatening reminders in Peter's home to keep him in line, what threats had he made to Felix? I heard murmurings of conversation from Neil and Hector inside the trailer but couldn't pick out any words. We had another hour of waiting before darkness descended. An evening breeze stirred the meadow grass.

I shivered in jeans wet from sitting on the damp ground. The wind came again and I inhaled deeply. Its scent was clean and fresh—no hint of campfire smoke. There was no one camped near here. Peter's previous description of working in a remote place few people knew about echoed in my mind. If Felix didn't decide to help us and accept the ring as payment, there would be no rescue. Melody finished her bottle and I began to burp her as I mentally reviewed Peter's instructions for what would happen if the escape plan was set in motion. It all hinged on Felix being able to overpower Quin. I fingered the compass around my neck while quietly repeating the coordinates and landmarks I needed to find.

The sun slipped behind the western mountains. Felix joined Quin on guard duty and directed us to stand up and move down toward the trees. Peter and Sean hesitated, but I hurried to stand and started ahead of them. With only my ears to guide me, I padded down the slope—my every muscle tensed for the signal. Then I heard it—the crack of contact.

I whipped my head around in time to see Quin slump to the ground. Felix yanked out his pocketknife and slashed first Peter's rope and then Sean's. Peter and Sean each collected their ropes and a fist-sized rock then crept down opposite sides of the trailer. Felix, gun in hand, approached the door and disappeared from sight.

Peter was the only person within view. He motioned for me to continue west up the next hillside. I hid behind a spruce and peered through its prickly branches, one arm patting Melody in the Snugi. "It's going to be okay, Melody," I said more to convince myself than reassure her. She lay snug and warm nestled against me in the chest pack with a blanket tucked securely around her. While I had been fidgety and uneasy sitting under constant guard on the wet ground, she'd sprawled on my lap enjoying the new scenery and demonstrating her latest cooing sounds. That stimulation combined with her recent bottle made for a sleepy baby. Now she gazed dreamy-eyed at the pine needles screening us from view.

I held my breath. No sound carried through the still night. This was the part of the plan I feared most. I had wanted all of us to make a run for it without confronting Neil and Hector, but Peter felt duty-bound to bring in Neil. Could they overpower Neil and Hector, or would it all go awry? Should I wait or get away and go for help while I still had a chance? I could find Peter's hidden car with my compass and his directions. It might be my only chance if Sean and Peter were caught. But how could I leave them? How could I risk not getting Melody out of here? My mind reeled with the possibilities. Then reason surfaced, and I knew I had to follow the plan; I had to make my break. If I got out, I could bring help back. It was the only way.

Uttering yet another silent prayer, I turned my back on the trailer and quickly but gingerly picked my way through the trees. About twenty yards up the slope, I paused to open my compass, and then I heard it. Twigs snapped, leaves rustled, and quick footfalls approached.

My heart pounded as anxiety coursed through tightened muscles. Someone was rapidly drawing near. It couldn't be Peter or Sean—surely they would call out to me. I checked my heading, visualized the first landmark, and then scurried diagonally up through the trees with one arm around Melody's Snugi.

A baby on my front and backpack behind created a running-through-molasses sensation. Branches scraped my face and arms. I ran. My legs burned. Still I ran. My breath came in gasps. But I ran. When every breath stung my lungs, I stopped and concealed myself behind a large boulder with a spruce tree growing from beneath it—the first of Peter's landmarks. Slowly I peeked my head around the rock's edge.

Nearly all light was gone now. I could only make out a man's silhouette darting around an outstretched branch then leaping over a fallen log—a feat eliminating portly Hector as my pursuer. The figure jerked his head to the right and left, never slowing his pace. He was too small to be Sean . . . or Peter . . . or even Quin's lanky, beanpole figure. Was it Felix? Or Neil?

I concentrated on breathing quietly, but my heart raced and my breath came faster still. I had to defend myself. I searched the dark ground for a stick. Only a couple of rocks rested near the boulder's base. It was impossible though—I couldn't hit a moving target in the dark! My aching legs reminded me I couldn't outrun him either. As I reached down to pick up the stones, my backpack shifted and I felt the formula can slide toward my head. *That's it!* At least it would buy me some time. I shrugged off the pack, pulled out the formula, and ripped off the lid.

Melody whimpered as I crouched uncomfortably behind the boulder. I bounced on the balls of my feet to calm her. The crunching of pine needles grew ever closer. When I heard my pursuer's labored breathing, I seized a fistful of formula with one hand and a rock with the other. I stood and cocked my left arm just as Neil rounded the boulder. I flung the formula into his face.

His arms flailed wildly. He must have inhaled just as the powder hit him because he coughed and spluttered. I raised my right arm and focused all my energy into hitting my target. "Here's your rock," I said under my breath then launched the rock into the air. A sickening crack sounded just before Neil fell to the ground. "Now go roll."

My knees wobbled, and I reached for the boulder to steady myself as adrenaline raced through my veins, making me feel dizzy. Regaining my composure, I slung the pack over my back and found north on the compass. I gave Neil's sprawling body and bloodied face a wide berth but noted the steady rise and fall of his chest with some degree of relief. His breathing, although reassuring, was worrisome enough to hasten my speed. I curled one arm around Melody, hoping to insulate her from too much jostling. The three-quarter moon lit up the now darkened sky.

I walked through the moonlit forest for what felt like hours, jumping at the tiniest sounds and constantly checking my course by compass. A quick look at my watch revealed it had only been thirty minutes. Melody had drifted off to sleep as we moved along, her head now tilted to one side. Presently, I heard the quiet trickle of the next landmark—a small triangular-shaped clearing about ten feet across at its widest point with a brook running through it. I paused to gaze at the numerous stars twinkling overhead. No city lights dulled their winking gleam. A quick look at my fingernails confirmed that I'd chewed three nails to the quick wondering if Peter and Sean had been able to subdue Hector and tie him up.

Grateful for the moon's light, I once again took my bearings from the compass then gingerly made my way across the rock-littered creek bed. Melody stirred a little at my uneven movements but thankfully remained asleep. I headed west, down through an aspen forest tinged silver in the moonlight. Abundant trees combined with an increasingly steep terrain meant a circuitous descent. I picked my way slowly down the slope, one hand carefully wrapped around Melody. Several times I grasped at tree trunks to keep from sliding down the mountain. All the while, worry for Peter and Sean gnawed at me.

Finally the incline lessened. Another compass consultation aimed my path laterally across the gentle slope. I commenced in that direction until a rustling sound halted my steps.

My stomach tightened with a sense of dread. I stood rooted to the spot, unable to force my stiffened muscles to relax enough to turn and face the danger. Melody sensed my tension and began to stir uneasily. The night breeze swept over my bare arms, raising goose bumps.

I shuddered and slowly turned around. The breeze swished the aspens' spherical leaves into a gentle murmur. The noise was only the breeze, I reasoned, but my eyes refused to relax; they scoured the hillside anyway. In the shadows between the trees, I thought I saw a movement. Motionless myself, I peered harder into the woods. Another movement.

I stopped breathing and stroked Melody's back, praying she'd stay silent. My mind raced. Hector? Felix? Or was it Sean or Peter? I quickly dismissed the latter two; they would be coming from an entirely different direction. Peter had insisted on that so as not to lead anyone directly to me. That is, if I had followed Peter's directions correctly. My infamous sense of direction could have easily landed me deeper in the middle of nowhere by now.

I squinted into the dark, trying to make sense of the rhythmic movement of the figure as he drew ever closer. And then I understood. He was at a full-out run. I could now make out the definite crunching of leaves in time with the movements. A second flutter of motion behind the first caught my attention. Two of them.

My heart raced; I knew I couldn't outrun anyone, especially not while carrying the baby. A quick inspection of my immediate surroundings revealed that even the more mature aspen trees couldn't hide me completely. A surge of despair rushed through me. Sobs threatened to erupt and disclose my position. I had tried so hard to get Melody out safely. Turning, I bolted through the trees. Maybe I couldn't outrun my pursuers, but I had to be close to Peter's hidden car by now. It would afford at least some protection. Frantically my eyes scanned the shadowy landscape. Twenty feet ahead a large fuzzy shape rested at the base of the hill.

Hope energized my weary legs. I wrapped my arms around Melody as she began to cry, her sleep disrupted by the jouncing. I ran harder. It must be the chokecherry bush that was the last landmark. The distance closed quickly. When I was only ten feet away from it, a figure stepped around the bramble.

An electric-like current radiated across my shoulders. My stomach heaved against its emptiness. I grabbed a tree trunk with one hand and skidded to a stop. Dirt, pebbles, and leaves tumbled down the slope. Melody's wails intensified.

"Eva."

My throat ached and a sob flew out. Peter.

He reached me in two quick but uneven steps and put one arm around me. With his other hand, Peter rubbed gentle, reassuring circles on Melody's back, quieting her cries.

I jerked my head back the way we had come. "People are—"

"It's only Sean and Felix. I sent them to help you." His hand traced the side of my face. "I couldn't stand the thought that I might lose you," he whispered, kissing the top of my head, and then guided me around the chokecherry bush with a halting gait. "I *will* get both you and Melody out safely." He wiped away the tears on my cheeks.

I put my arm around his waist, pulling him closer and melting into his embrace. "I was so afraid for you."

He shuffled clumsily.

"What's wrong?" I studied his feet then continued up his legs, resting my gaze on his thigh. A knotted flannel shirt encircled his left leg, mostly concealing a dark blotch on his cargo pants.

I inhaled sharply. "What happened?" I reached for his leg, but he grabbed my hand and placed it back at my side.

"Never mind that now. How's Melody?" Peter lifted the blanket.

Wide-eyed, Melody gazed up at him. She had stopped crying, but two little tear trails on her cheeks glistened in the moonlight. "Hey, girl, you're safe now." He kissed the top of her head then lifted his eyes to mine. "You're both safe now." His palm brushed my cheek as Sean and Felix rounded the chokecherry bush.

"Sean?" I asked.

"Right here, Eva," Sean said and bent over to catch his breath.

Felix pulled up a few feet in front of me, breathing hard. "You're a pretty good aim with a rock, Miss Black."

My mind processed Felix's Spanish, but my eyes never left the gun in Sean's hand.

Sean noted my focus. "We traded."

Moonlight glinted off the diamond ring on Felix's little finger.

"I thought you were coming by a different route." I spoke to Sean.

"After we took care of Hector and tied up Quin, Sean and Felix went after Neil . . . and you," Peter explained. His eyes darted to his leg. "I didn't want to slow them down."

Peter and the others removed the branches of scrub oak obscuring the car nearby then opened the door and I ducked inside.

The moment I sat down, Melody began squirming. I peeled back the blanket just in time to see frustration wrinkling her tiny features. "Shh, shh." I smoothed her forehead with my fingertips then kissed the top of her soft head. "Mommy's here," I whispered and breathed in her scent. She quieted, but I wished for her pacifier during what was sure to be a long and bumpy ride home.

Both back doors opened simultaneously as Sean and Felix scrambled inside. Peter looked around before climbing into the driver's seat. While turning the key in the ignition, he used his free arm to retrieve a prepaid cell phone from under his seat. He quickly punched the keypad before holding the phone out to me. "As soon as you get a strong enough signal, hit redial."

When Peter flipped on the headlights, I glimpsed two barely visible tire tracks in the tall grass. We drove down the little-used road and my eyes repeatedly drifted to Peter's blood-soaked pant leg. Once he grimaced as we bumped over a particularly bad stretch of road.

I rested my hand on his shoulder, wishing I could help him.

He reached up and took my hand. "I'm fine, really."

I raised his hands to my lips and kissed his fingertips.

He winked at me.

A movement in the backseat caught my attention. Sean, sitting directly behind Peter, with a clear view of my affectionate display, had turned his head and was staring out the window into the black night, the tendon along his neck popping in and out.

A pang of remorse tugged at my heart. I hated for anyone to be hurting. Scenes from earlier today flitted across my mind's stage, and then I thought of the diamond ring on Felix's pinky. Sean had lost a lot tonight.

After thirty minutes of bouncing around in silence, we turned onto a more traveled dirt road, and the cell phone's signal strengthened. I hit redial and handed the phone to Peter.

"Javier, my cover's blown. Send a team to pick up two at the sheep camp." Peter paused and looked in the rearview mirror. "Where's Neil?"

Sean and Felix answered at once, each in his native tongue. "Unconscious and secured to a tree." Felix's reply clarified, "Tied to a tree by the spruce and four-foot boulder."

Peter relayed compass coordinates for Javier to find Neil, then said, "Yeah, he's the one we've been waiting for . . . three states and eighteen months of work, but we got him." Triumph colored his tone. "Make the calls. It's take-down time." He listened and then said, "I'm sending three witnesses to the police station, so get someone to take their statements. I'll hike back to Neil and wait for you there." He snapped the phone shut, placed it in the console cubby, and reclaimed my hand with a squeeze.

"You're going back?" I asked, unable to conceal my worry.

"I can't take a chance on Neil escaping. All our work . . ." He slowly made a U-turn.

"Your leg—"

"—is fine. I hiked out on it once." Peter focused on Sean in his rearview mirror. "Sean, do you know where we are?"

Still staring out the window, Sean said, "If we'd kept going, we would have connected with a dirt road that forks. We need to take the left one to get down the mountain."

"With all your mapping and searching this summer you know this area as well as I do now."

"I never came across your camp."

"Neil prevented that."

Sean let out a long, low sigh. "I never saw that one coming."

"The DEA's been after him for eighteen months. Tonight's the first time I've seen him or known his name for sure. He's got marijuana operations in the mountains of New Mexico, Idaho, and Utah."

"Eighteen months."

"Take Eva and Felix to the police station. They'll want to interview all of you."

We traveled in silence for a time. The darkness prohibited me from determining how badly Peter was injured. My worry had increased even more knowing that he would hike back on that leg. I didn't want him to take the risk but knew any argument was futile.

"So what happened back at the trailer?" I broke the silence.

"We should have tied Quin up before we invited Hector and Neil out to play," Peter replied.

CHAPTER 26

"I WAS WRONG ABOUT PETER." It was the first Sean had spoken since we'd dropped Peter off forty-five minutes earlier.

"You're not the only one."

"Do you love him?" Sean hazarded a glance in my direction.

I studied his profile in the dusky car while I searched my heart. "Yes," I whispered.

The tendon along his neck flexed.

I absently rubbed Melody's back. We didn't speak again.

Once we were all separated at the police station, it took most of the night to process our statements. Sean only gazed at me without speaking in the moments we passed each other in the hall. Melody held up surprisingly well until four when nothing consoled her screams. She wanted her bed and wanted it now. I'm sure the officer assigned to drive me home yearned for soundproof glass.

When we were home at last, I laid Melody in her crib. She stretched her tiny frame then squirmed into her favorite sleeping position on her tummy—fists tucked under her hips.

I softly closed her door and moved toward the stairs. All at once my legs felt incapable of carrying me farther. I paused at Rebecca's closed door. One day I would have to enter that room. Why not tonight?

I turned the knob and pushed the door open. Moonlight streamed through the window, gently illuminating the quilt and an array of decorative pillows Rebecca had arranged on her bed the morning we'd left to visit our parents' graves in Logan. The excruciating loss I expected to feel in her room was strangely absent.

Instead, a quiet peace filled my soul. I was home. Melody was home. We were a family. I peeled off my grimy clothes and reached under Rebecca's pillow for her pajamas. Then I rinsed my face in the master bathroom before slipping between the cool sheets and losing myself to sleep.

I awoke to a light-filled room just before ten. Melody had slept through her usual nine o'clock feeding, proof of her fatigue. If I got up now, I could make it to church in time for sacrament meeting. Perhaps Peter would be there. The thought propelled me out of bed. I made it two steps before my body protested the rude awakening. My shoulders throbbed from cushioning Melody's and my wild ride through the trees, and every muscle from the waist down shouted its complaint. I sincerely hoped the shower's warm pressure would soothe my aches.

After my shower, I scurried downstairs to my room and slipped into a skirt and blouse just before Melody began to cry. I went back upstairs and opened Melody's door. Instantly, I grabbed the doorframe for support. Standing in front of the crib holding Melody and a gun was Neil. An agonizing despair ripped through me. If Neil was here, what had happened to Peter?

"That was quite the headache you gave me last night," he said, raising his eyebrows toward the large blood-encrusted bump on his forehead.

I could only stare at Melody and the gun while my mind spun out of control. Had he killed Peter?

"Where's your boyfriend?"

Confusion delayed my response. He didn't know where Peter was? "I don't know where Sean went last night," I said, stalling as I surveyed the room for a possible weapon.

"Not Sean!" he yelled. Melody's face crumpled and she began to wail. "Peter. The one you were too messed up to be dating. Isn't that what you told me?"

Relief flooded me. Peter was alive. "We left him on the mountain. He went back to find you." Rocking chair, crib, changing table, lamp, humidifier. My mind began cataloging everything in Melody's room, trying to find something I could use against Neil.

"And now you will help me find him."

"I have no way to contact him. I never have. He just shows up." How could I get Melody away from him, down the stairs, and to somewhere safe? I forced myself to think harder.

"Then we'll wait." Using the gun, Neil motioned for me to sit in the rocking chair as Melody's crying intensified. "Does she ever shut up? No wonder Sean dumped you."

"She's hungry." *And you're scaring her*, I thought. "She wants her bottle."

"Let's go, then," he waved his gun toward the open door.

I stood on trembling legs and began descending the stairs with a tight grip on the handrail. Neil followed with a crying Melody. When we entered the kitchen, Neil said, "This is how it's gonna work. Hold your hands up slowly over your head. You have to keep one hand above your head at all times. When you move your other arm, it's in slow motion. Got it?"

"I'm just getting the formula out," I explained as I slowly opened the cupboard and set the can on the counter. "Now I'm getting a bottle," I said as I reached back inside the cabinet. At least there were knives in the kitchen. But I didn't think they would be any help against a gun. I had to get the gun away from him to have any chance of escaping with Melody. What else could I use? "I need some water."

Neil waved the gun toward the sink.

I inched my way to the faucet, carefully filled the bottle, and added formula. Getting Melody away from Neil was my first priority, I decided. Maybe I could convince Neil to let me feed her. I tried to screw on the bottle nipple with one hand but couldn't. "Neil, I need two hands for this."

He shook his head and shifted the gun into his other hand with Melody. Then he stepped toward me, and grasped the bottle with his free hand. "Now tighten it."

When I reached out to tighten the ring, Melody lunged for me, startling Neil enough that he pulled the trigger. The bottle of milk exploded, Neil screamed, and I pulled Melody free all in the same instant. White milk mingled with Neil's red blood as it ran over the counter and dripped onto the floor. I realized that Neil had shot his hand through the bottle of formula. Without hesitating, I yanked the toaster from the counter and swung it at Neil. I made contact with the side of his head just as someone flew at him from behind. Neil's body smacked the tile floor as a man landed on top of him and then yanked Neil's arms behind him. He snapped handcuffs onto Neil as he said, "You're under arrest. You have the right to remain silent."

I dropped the toaster and tried to console Melody.

The man finished and then looked up at me. "It's nice to finally meet you, Eva. I'm Javier."

"What happened? Where's Peter?"

"He's at the hospital getting that stab wound taken care of. When Peter hiked back in last night, Neil was gone. He sent me back here to watch you just in case Neil had gotten off the mountain. Good thing he did."

* * *

Looking out my front window after I laid Melody down for an afternoon nap, I glimpsed Peter hobbling toward his house on one crutch while Sean walked up my sidewalk. I yearned to run to Peter's house, but first I had to deal with Sean. He'd been given a lot to think about last night. I opened the door as Sean stepped onto the front porch. Dark circles rimmed his eyes—evidence he'd slept little, if at all, yet. I moved through the door. "Hi."

Sean squared his shoulders. "I'm not giving up on you, Eva." I swallowed. I should have known he wouldn't walk away, even after last night.

"Sean, I—"

"Peter's not such a bad guy, but that doesn't mean he's right for you."

"I meant what I said on the mountain." I didn't want to repeat my refusal, to reject him again. Surely he could see I'd chosen Peter.

"Please, hear me out." He grasped my hands in his. "Peter can't give you the life you want. He's never home."

"How often are you gone flying around the world on business, Sean?"

"But I'm not off the grid. You can still contact me by phone and e-mail."

"This whole special agent thing is not reason enough for me to give up on him." My stomach felt surprisingly steady, as if it didn't know an argument was developing.

"You didn't even know he worked for the DEA until last night."

"You think that changes the way I feel?"

"You're rushing into a relationship. I don't want to see you get hurt."

"It's not like that." I pulled my hands away, folding them around myself.

"Think about the money." Now he was grasping. Sean knew I wasn't swayed by money. "Cops don't make anything. You'll always be scraping by."

"You know me better than that."

"A little money isn't so bad. I can give you—and Melody—so much more."

He'd saved mentioning Melody until his third argument. "You're skirting around the key issue."

His Adam's apple bobbed as he swallowed. "I know you're worried about Melody. I'm trying, Eva. You must know that. I make a lot of mistakes, but I'm progressing. You'll see . . . we can work this out."

"I know you're trying, and you've come a long way. But that's just the thing, Sean, you said it yourself—it will be a struggle every step of the way. And it will cause a lot of friction. Is that really the life you want?"

"I want you."

I fingered my locket and took a deep breath. "You want what you thought I was, what I thought I could be." Hearing myself speak those words released a calm in me.

"I've known you for almost two years. I know who you are."

"You know who I've let you see."

Sean shook his head. "You're not a good liar. If someone else was hiding in there, I'd have seen her by now."

"Like the mom I turned into when Rebecca died? You thought I was going to put Melody up for adoption!"

"I misunderstood you."

"Yes. You misunderstood me—who I am. I'm sorry I deceived you. I didn't understand that's what I was doing. I was so flattered that you—that highly successful, incredibly striking Sean Langley—liked me, wanted *me*. I let myself believe I wanted your lifestyle. When Melody came into my life, I couldn't deny my true self any longer. Can you honestly say you'd be happy living in this little house, growing a garden, going for walks with Melody, being absorbed into the Finch family? Because this is what I crave. It's what I need. And it's not what you need."

"We can be a family." The words came out quietly, almost like he was trying to convince himself.

I took his hand. "I don't want to hold you back, and I don't want to run alongside you as your career soars. This quieter, stay-back-and-hold-things-together life suits me. You know it's true."

"Eva . . ." He looked down at me, conflict in his eyes.

I hugged him as tears collected. "I'm so sorry, Sean."

His arms encircled me. "I know." It came out as a choked whisper. He released me, turned abruptly, and briskly walked to his Escalade.

I watched him drive away, then stepped into the house, closed the door, and leaned back against it as the tears fell. I thought I finally understood what my dad meant by falling into faith. It was scary to let go, to take that first step and feel as if I were falling, but that feeling of falling when I had given Sean the ring back had awakened all of my senses. I had felt as if I were falling awake. I grasped my locket then and pressed it to my lips.

"I'd like to do that . . . if you don't mind."

My eyelids flew open. There standing by the stone hearth was Peter, one arm resting on a crutch. His full beard was trimmed into a neat goatee and his caramel hair was secured at the nape of his neck.

My heart raced the butterflies in my stomach. "Peter!" I crossed the room in an instant.

Then his arms were around me and mine around him. My fingertips traced his lips. He clasped my hand and brushed his lips past mine.

I groaned. "No teasing!"

He bent his head, placed his lips on mine, and gave me a tiny peck.

"Is this how you're going to greet me after every undercover job?" I asked.

"Are you proposing?"

"That depends."

"On?"

"If you ever really kiss me."

"Seems like a lot of pressure for one kiss."

"If that's the way you want it." I unwrapped my arms and pushed my palms against his chest.

He tightened his embrace, leaned down, and tenderly placed his lips on mine. A warm sensation radiated through me as my lips responded to his touch.

"Eva," he murmured after we moved apart.

I gazed into his eyes. "How are you?" I whispered.

"Glad to be home." He rested his forehead against mine and drew a deep breath. "With family."

ABOUT THE AUTHOR

KATE BEGAN HER CAREER AS an elementary school teacher but was soon promoted to full-time mom. She is the mother of six, and she and her family live in the country, where her husband is trying to teach her to be a farm girl. She can't saddle a horse, but she knows how to butcher a chicken. After a day of chasing children, cooking meals, and doing laundry, she likes to escape into a good book.